"This is the right kind of introduction to Joseph Campbell's work—TOUGH-MINDED, CLEAR, AND STEEPED IN A REAL KNOWLEDGE OF THE SACRED FIELD. It should be a valuable guide for anyone who wishes authentically to integrate the mythic perspective into the living of life."
>—John Beebe M. D., editor of
>*The San Francisco Jung Institute Library Journal*

"Segal's book is an important step toward an adequate assessment of Campbell's oeuvre: his precise reading of Campbell's texts and his careful analysis of the theoretical superstructure will be indispensable to future studies."
>—*Religion*

"HIGHLY RECOMMENDED . . . Segal is this country's authority on Campbell's theory of myths."
>—Alan Dundes,
>Professor of Anthropology and Folklore
>University of California, Berkeley

"The first systematic exposition and assessment of Campbell's achievement. This book should accompany any serious reading of Campbell."
>—Gregory Nagy,
>Francis Jones Professor of Classical Greek Literature and Professor of Comparative Literature,
>Harvard University

"Despite the volume of [Campbell's] work and the fame he has achieved, however, no major analysis of Campbell has been undertaken. Robert Segal's JOSEPH CAMPBELL now corrects that deficiency."
>—*Annals of Scholarship*

ROBERT SEGAL is a professor of religious studies at Louisiana State University, Baton Rouge, and specializes in theories of myth and in Biblical and classical mythology. He is the author of *The Poimandres as Myth* and *Religion and the Social Sciences*.

Joseph Campbell

An Introduction

by

Robert A. Segal

A MENTOR BOOK

MENTOR
Published by the Penguin Group
Penguin Books USA Inc., 375 Hudson Street,
New York, New York, 10014, U.S.A.
Penguin Books Ltd, 27 Wrights Lane,
London W8 5TZ, England
Penguin Books Australia Ltd, Ringwood,
Victoria, Australia
Penguin Books Canada, Ltd, 2801 John Street,
Markham, Ontario, Canada L3R 1B4
Penguin Books (N.Z.) Ltd, 182–190 Wairau Road,
Auckland 10, New Zealand

Penguin Books Ltd, Registered Offices:
Harmondsworth, Middlesex, England

First Mentor Printing, April, 1990
10 9 8 7 6 5 4 3

This is a revised edition of a hardcover book published by
Garland Publishing, Inc.

 REGISTERED TRADEMARK—MARCA REGISTRADA

Library of Congress Catalog Card Number: 89-63804

Printed in the United States of America

CONTENTS

PREFACE

No one in this generation did more to revive popular interest in myth than Joseph Campbell. He preached myth the way others preach religion. Indeed, he came to *contrast* myth to religion. Only myth has saving power. Everybody needs myth, and anyone bereft of myth is forlorn. Campbell devoted himself to beseeching humanity to "live by" myth. Because living by myth requires understanding myth, Campbell not only amassed myths but, even more, analyzed them. His explanation of the origin and the function of myth kept changing, but his interpretation of the meaning of myth never fluctuated.

This book is both a presentation and an assessment of Campbell as a theorist of myth. The book was originally published in hardcover before Campbell's death in 1987. Still in print, the hardcover is directed to a more academic audience. For the paperback I have pared down the footnotes, added a biographical chapter, and updated the book to take into account Campbell's final works. Those works include *The Power of Myth*, the edited transcript of the spring 1988 Public Television series of interviews with Bill Moyers.

Campbell had been popular ever since his first book, *The Hero with a Thousand Faces* (1949), but the Moyers series made him legendary. Not only *The Power of*

Myth but also Campbell's earlier books have become best-sellers. The television interviews are now available on video. An authorized biography is being written. Thousands of followers testify that Campbell's words have transformed their lives. In death, the man has become a phenomenon.

Yet even now surprisingly little has been written about him. Doubtless many scholars of myth view Campbell as a mere popularizer, though his posthumous fame is spurring reconsideration of his worth. Still, there remains no other book about him and few articles. Most writing about him remains in the form of book reviews and interviews, some published only after his death. There also continue to be applications to fictional and nonfictional works alike of the heroic pattern in *Hero*.

After a short biographical chapter I summarize Campbell's views of myth book by book. I concentrate on Campbell's interpretation of the *meaning* of myth: what the real subject matter of myth is and what myth is saying about that subject matter. I focus on *Hero*, *The Masks of God*, *The Mythic Image*, the *Atlas*, *The Inner Reaches of Outer Space*, and *An Open Life*. While I often cite Campbell's essays, including those collected in *The Flight of the Wild Gander* and *Myths to Live By*, I devote no separate chapters to them. Nor do I consider the works of Heinrich Zimmer edited by Campbell after Zimmer's death in 1943.

After seven chapters on Campbell's individual books I turn to topics that span the books. In chapter nine I consider Campbell as a consummate comparativist: as someone preoccupied with the similarities rather than the differences among myths. In chapters ten and eleven I discuss Campbell's explanation of the origin and function of myth. In chapter twelve I evaluate

Campbell as a Jungian—an epithet that, rightly or wrongly, is continually used of him. In the last chapter I try to account for Campbell's appeal.

Throughout the book I use Campbell's own, exceedingly broad definition of myth, which includes rituals and beliefs as well as stories of all kinds. I also use his term ''primitive.'' References to Campbell's *Myths to Live By* are to the paperback edition. References to Campbell's other books are to the hardcover editions, which usually, but not always, have the same pagination as the paperbacks.

For their many suggestions for this edition I want to thank David Madden, Adriana Berger, Bainard Cowan, and especially Daniel Noel, John Beebe, Timothy Hatcher, and my editor at New American Library, Susan Rogers.

CHAPTER ONE

CAMPBELL'S LIFE

Joseph Campbell was born in New York City in 1904, the son of a hosiery importer and wholesaler. He traced his "career as a mythologist" all the way back to childhood trips to "Buffalo Bill's Wild West Show at Madison Square Garden."[1] Visits to the American Museum of Natural History deepened his interest in American Indians:

> On Sundays, Dad would ask us what we wanted to do. We'd choose from the aquarium down in the Battery, the Bronx Zoo and the Museum of Natural History. And *there*—they have it to this day—in a magnificent room, with really grandiose totem poles, was an enormous Kwakiutl canoe from the northwest coast, and in it were these dummies of Indians paddling and another [Indian], in a bearskin, standing up. So I started reading Indian stories, legends. . . .[2]

When, at age nine, Campbell moved with his family to New Rochelle, New York, he started reading all the children's books on Indians in the library next door: "Within a year I'd read all the American Indian books and was admitted to the stacks of the main library, where I began reading the annual reports of the Bureau of Ethnology."[3] "Meanwhile, I was being educated by the nuns in the Roman Catholic religion and it didn't take me very long to realize that there were virgin births, deaths and resurrections in both mythological systems."[4] Nor did it take him long to conclude that events so similar, not to mention so miraculous, were unlikely to be historical: the coincidence was too great. Campbell continued to read and compare myths while a student at Canterbury Preparatory School in New Milford, Connecticut.

Entering Dartmouth, Campbell found himself "light-years ahead of his classmates"[5] and transferred to Columbia, where his focus shifted "from biology and mathematics to the history of literature, history of art, of music, and so on."[6] Here, too, he found his courses easy but preferred the city and stayed four years. Outside of class he was a star half-miler and played the saxophone in a band.

The summer before his graduation Campbell's family took a trip to Europe. On the steamer he met the Indian spiritual leader Jiddu Krishnamurti. The woman who introduced the two of them "gave me a copy of Edwin Arnold's *The Light of Asia* and that was my introduction to Buddhism and Hinduism."[7] Again, he detected similarities—here between East and West.

Campbell graduated from Columbia in 1925 and remained another year for a master's degree in order to be able to continue competing in track:

> As a result of having transferred from Dartmouth, I couldn't compete in inter-collegiate athletics until my junior year. Since one was allowed three years of competition, I had another year of athletic competition before me, so I went back to graduate work in order to have a third year.[8]

Enrolling in English, he concentrated on medieval and Romantic literature. Once again, he spotted cross-cultural similarities: "Well, when I started reading the medieval material I became *so* excited. There were the old myth motifs again which I remembered from my Indian days, particularly in the Arthurian stuff."[9]

Campbell's master's thesis on *Le Morte d'Arthur* won him a traveling fellowship from Columbia, and he spent the next two years, 1927–1929, at the Universities of Paris and Munich. While mastering Romance philology in Paris and Sanskrit in Munich, he discovered modernism:

> Well, it opened up first in Paris. Something! Everybody was there—Picasso, Joyce, Matisse; I'll never forget the exhibit of the Intransigents out in the Bois de Boulogne. I knew nothing about art; New York knew nothing. And the whole thing opened up like crazy when I found *Ulysses*, which was forbidden in the States. The first drafts of *Finnegans Wake* were being published in the magazine *transition*, edited by Eugene Jolas. Sylvia Beach at the Shakespeare Book Shop introduced me into how to read these things. . . . Suddenly *the whole modern world* opened up! With a bang! . . . I went into Sanskrit for the philological side but got caught up in the philosophy, the mythology, literature, and that was *far, far away* from where I was supposed to be in medieval French.[10]

In Germany Campbell discovered Mann, Freud, and Jung. Freud and Jung provided him the keys to interpreting the by now universal themes he had found in myths.

Upon returning home, Campbell realized that academic life was not for him and abandoned his pursuit of a Ph.D.: "The world had blown open. I'm no longer in the Ph.D. bottle. I don't want to go on with my little Arthurian pieces. I had *much* more exciting things to do—and I didn't know what they were."[11]

Because Campbell had returned just at the time of the 1929 stock market crash, there were few jobs. For the next five years he survived on the money he had earned in the band. He lived frugally in Woodstock, New York, and in Carmel, California, where he met John Steinbeck. He spent his time writing short stories and, even more, reading. At the Carmel library he discovered Spengler, Goethe, Schopenhauer, and Nietzsche.

In 1932–1933 Campbell got a job teaching French, German, and ancient history at Canterbury, his preparatory alma mater. The next year he began teaching at the recently founded Sarah Lawrence College, where he stayed until retirement thirty-eight years later. Still a stalwart nonacademic, he found the school ideal:

I could write my own ticket there. I never had to fit into anybody's slot. I did not give a damn about teaching in a large university, or about whether I was an instructor or a full professor, or about the specialist attitude, which I never could tolerate. I was much too interested in these comparative reaches.

Sarah Lawrence had no demand for publish or perish. I didn't have to publish a lot of junk in those official scrap baskets, *Publications of the Modern Language Association* and *Journal of the American Oriental Society*. Who the hell reads 'em?[12]

Campbell and his students proved a perfect fit:

I was teaching young women who weren't the least
bit interested in academic affairs. They wanted to
know what a myth might mean to *them.* . . . I was
held to the *life* of my subject, and this is the thing
that built whatever it is I have had as a career, which
I think has been a pretty good one.[13]

As a teacher, Campbell was, by all accounts, extraordinary.

In 1938 he married Jean Erdman, who had been his
student at Sarah Lawrence. A member of Martha Gra-
ham's dance troupe, she became a distinguished cho-
reographer and founded a dance company and school
of her own.

Campbell's writings on myth date from *A Skeleton
Key to Finnegans Wake,* which he wrote with Henry
Morton Robinson, later the author of the best-seller
The Cardinal: "In 1939 'Finnegans Wake' appeared.
One day Robinson said, 'Somebody has to write a key
to it and it might as well be us.' "[14] The *Key* remains
a standard introduction to the work.

While Campbell was working on the *Key,* Heinrich
Zimmer, renowned scholar of Indian thought, came to
the United States as a refugee from Nazi Germany.
Campbell went to hear him lecture at Columbia and
was dazzled:

What an ebullient man! Wonderful! The first person I ever met who was way down the road that I
found, interpreting symbols positively, deep in Oriental material; and if anybody should ask me who
my guru was, it was Zimmer, who really just kicked
it: I was just ready for the signal of that man. I was
thirty-six, thirty-seven.[15]

In the second year of his lectures Zimmer contracted
pneumonia and died suddenly at fifty-two. His widow

asked Campbell, with whom he had become very close, to edit his lectures. Campbell agreed. What he had expected to take three years took twelve. But he called them "the best years, while I was in my forties. I have never regretted one minute of it."[16] Campbell turned "a chaotic mass of lecture notes and fragmentary manuscripts"[17] into four volumes on the religion, philosophy, and psychology of India: *Myths and Symbols in Indian Art and Civilization, The King and the Corpse, Philosophies of India,* and *The Art of Indian Asia.* Although Campbell was officially just the editor,

> he actually deciphered and developed Zimmer's rough notes, translated many pages, drew on scholarship that he knew Zimmer had used, and employed a type of research that he described as follows: "I would write down the questions requiring answers . . . and I'd close my eyes and ask Zimmer those questions, and I'd take down his answers. His voice was still very much alive to me."[18]

In conjuring up Zimmer's image and conversing with it, Campbell was practicing what Jungians call the "active imagination."

Zimmer even more than Jung was Campbell's hero: "If I do have a guru, . . . it would be Zimmer—the one who really gave me the courage to interpret myths out of what I knew of their common symbol."[19] Zimmer pioneered the heroic journey to the symbolic depths of myth and returned to guide Campbell and others:

> Hearing Zimmer's lectures and the way in which these myths came out, not as curiosities over there somewhere, but as *models* for understanding your own life—this is what I had felt myths to be all this

time. Of course, Jung had it, but not the way Zimmer did. Zimmer was much more in [sic] myth than
Jung was. Jung tends to put forms on the myths
with those archetypes; the Jungians kind of cookie-
molded the thing. None of that with Zimmer. I
never knew anyone who had such a gift for interpreting a symbolic image. You'd sit down at the
table with him and bring up something—he'd talk
about the symbolism of onion soup.[20]

Whether Jung more than Campbell or even as much
as Campbell "cookie-molds" myths is a question that
will be considered.

From Zimmer Campbell likely took the extrovertive
brand of mysticism that he was to decipher in all myths
and religions. Divinity, or ultimate reality, is here
found *in* the secular, everyday world rather than beyond it:

"Just as in true love," wrote Zimmer, in a brilliant
exposition of Indian philosophy, *Ewiges Indien*,
published in 1930, "or just as in a true marriage,
the two no longer live 'for one another' but are
within each other, so is the eternally living Divine
Principle ever within the world as its animating
power."[21]

The Zimmer works edited by Campbell were published in the Bollingen Series, for which Zimmer himself had been the impetus. Zimmer had proposed
Campbell for the commentary to *Where the Two Came
to Their Father*, the Navaho war ceremony that was
recorded as the first volume in the Series. Zimmer had
even recommended that the *Skeleton Key* be the initial
entry in the Series and, more, that Campbell be named

editor of the Series, but these recommendations "didn't come to pass."[22]

In 1954 Campbell did what Zimmer himself had never gotten the chance to do: visit India. Far from entranced, Campbell was revolted, and in his later writings he reversed his prior praise of the East and scorn for the West. Campbell was "appalled" not only by the poverty but also "by the caste system and by the lack of respect for the individual." He "returned a confirmed Westerner, celebrating the uniqueness of the person."[23] Jung, too, was disgusted by the sordidness of India, but, unlike Campbell, he never lost his respect for the wisdom of the East—perhaps because *his* respect had always been tempered.

Even before turning to editing Zimmer's writings, Campbell had begun work on his *Hero with a Thousand Faces:*

> I started writing simply what I used to say in my course at Sarah Lawrence. But it got longer and longer—this was the introduction—and my wife said, "Joe, isn't that a long introduction?" So I chopped it up and had the first half of "The Hero with a Thousand Faces."[24]

Two publishers rejected the book as uncommercial, but Bollingen eventually accepted it. Campbell considered *Hero* his "most important work."[25] It remains his best-known one and has sold a quarter of a million copies—second only to the *I Ching* among Bollingen titles.[26]

While working on the Zimmer volumes, Campbell began editing selections from the Eranos Yearbooks. The Eranos Conferences, held annually since 1933 in Ascona, Switzerland, consist of lectures by scholars of a quasi-Jungian bent. Campbell himself attended the 1953 conference and gave lectures in 1957 and 1959. He eventually edited a six-volume selection.

Campbell had long planned to write a complementary work to his *Hero:* one that would treat the differences among myths rather than, as in *Hero,* the similarities. That work, originally entitled "The Basic Mythologies of Mankind," became the four-volume *Masks of God,* published by Viking Press.

Campbell's popularity grew not only with *Masks* but also with the 1960s, when *Hero* became the Bible of a generation:

> That was the era of inward discovery in its LSD phase. Suddenly, *The Hero with a Thousand Faces* became a kind of triptych for the inward journey, and people were finding something in that book that could help them interpret their own experience. . . . Anybody going on a journey, inward or outward, to find values, will be on a journey that has been described many times in the myths of mankind, and I simply put them all together in that book.[27]

Ironically, Campbell himself was politically conservative; was not the least religious; never practiced meditation, let alone took drugs; and above all grasped the unconscious meaning of myths through sheer reading rather than through any encounter with the unconscious:

> I never wanted to [meditate]. I don't know why. I guess the main reason is if I sit down to meditate, I'm not getting my reading done. That's been my main career—reading. I remember Alan Watts once

asked me, "Joe, how do you meditate?" I said, "I meditate by underlining sentences."

I prefer the gradual path—the way of study. My feeling is that mythic forms reveal themselves gradually in the course of your life if you know what they are and how to pay attention to their emergence. My own initiation into the mythical depths of the unconscious has been through the mind, through the books that surround me in this library.[28]

Campbell's intellectual approach to the unconscious would satisfy few Jungians, who insist on a direct, if channeled, encounter with it. Campbell's detachment likely accounts for what will prove to be his confidence in dealing with the unconscious: where a Jungian hero is chastened by his confrontation with the unconscious, Campbell's is emboldened.

Upon his retirement from Sarah Lawrence in 1972 Campbell and his wife moved to Honolulu, where she was born. In the 1970s and 1980s he became even more popular. Not only did his *Mythic Image* and *Historical Atlas of World Mythology* appear; he now went on the lecture circuit. In 1985–1986 he was interviewed in California by TV journalist Bill Moyers at the Skywalker Ranch of George Lucas, who credited Campbell with inspiring the "Star Wars" trilogy. From those interviews, together with ones at the Museum of Modern History in New York, came the six-hour Public Television series shown nationally in the spring of 1988. Campbell did not live to see the series or to witness the explosion of popularity that followed and that has yet to abate. He died of cancer in Honolulu in October 1987.

Like Zimmer, Campbell embodied as well as es-

poused the extrovertive, life-affirming outlook that he
found in all myths. That outlook embraces the everyday, physical world as the medium rather than the bar-
rier to highest reality. As Alan Watts, the popularizer
of Eastern lore, said of his friend:

> Joe is simultaneously an athlete and a *jñana* yogi—
> a man of wonderful physique who, however, has a
> wisdom that does not seem to have been attained
> by formal meditation under any guru, or by being
> psychoanalyzed, or anything of that kind.[29]

Campbell himself put his extrovertive and upbeat outlook more concretely:

> In spite of all this interest in the Orient, I have a
> very strong, what the Jungians call "extroverted,"
> side; and athletics, that's a kind of meditation.
> When I swim, I guess you could call that some kind
> of meditation.
>
> One of the finest students I have taught in recent
> years asked me the other day, "Have you ever hated
> life?" I thought back and tried to recall some time
> that I could possibly have hated life. And I said,
> "No, I don't honestly think I ever have, and I don't
> see how I ever could."[30]

This brief biography is meant as a chronology, not
an analysis, of Campbell's life. Yet it may not be in-
appropriate to note a few darker features of Campbell's
personality: a contempt for academia that, in light of
the mixed reception Campbell secured from scholars,
cannot but seem defensive;[31] an embittered hostility
toward his boyhood Roman Catholicism, which he
damns for stymying what he considers the true, indi-

vidualistic rather than institutionalized nature of spirituality;[32] an even more unsettling hostility toward Judaism, which in almost antisemitic fashion he caricatures as chauvinistic and literalistic;[33] and, as noted, a later disdain for the East, which he similarly caricatures as totalitarian and barbaric. These convictions, evinced again and again not only in interviews but also in Campbell's books[34] and in remarks to friends, partly shaped the views about to be presented.

NOTES

[1]Campbell, interview with Donald Newlove, *Esquire*, 88 (September 1977), p. 102.

[2]*Ibid.*

[3]*Ibid.*

[4]Campbell, *Open Life*, p. 119.

[5]Campbell, interview with Newlove, p. 102.

[6]*Ibid*, p. 103.

[7]*Ibid*, p. 132.

[8]Campbell, interview with Susan Hecht and Louise Foltz, *Stonecloud*, 6 (1976), p. 46.

[9]Campbell, interview with Newlove, p. 103.

[10]*Ibid*, p. 132.

[11]*Ibid.*

[12]*Campbell, interview with Joseph Barbato, Chronicle of Higher Education*, 28 (March 21, 1984), p. 7; interview with Newlove, p. 136.

[13]Campbell, interview with Michael McKnight, *Parabola*, 5 (February 1980), pp. 63–64.

[14]Campbell, interview with D.J.R. Bruckner, *New York Times Book Review* (December 18, 1983), p. 25.

[15]Campbell, interview with Newlove, p. 136.

[16]Campbell, interview with Hecht and Foltz, p. 48.

[17]William McGuire, *Bollingen* (Princeton, NJ: Princeton University Press, 1982), p. 66.

[18]William McGuire, "Joseph Campbell (1904–1987)," *Quadrant,* 21 (Spring 1988), p. 6.

[19]Campbell, *Open Life,* p. 123.

[20]Campbell, interview with McKnight, pp. 59–60.

[21]Joseph Campbell, "Heinrich Zimmer (1890–1943)," *Partisan Review,* 20 (July 1953), p. 450.

[22]McGuire, "Joseph Campbell (1904–1987)," p. 6.

[23]Sam Keen, interview with Campbell, in Keen, *Voices and Visions* (New York: Harper & Row, 1974), p. 71.

[24]Campbell, interview with Bruckner, p. 26.

[25]Campbell, interview with Hecht and Foltz, p. 53.

[26]See McGuire, *Bollingen,* p. 142; "Joseph Campbell (1904–1987)," p. 7.

[27]Campbell, interview with Lorraine Kisly, *Parabola,* 1 (Spring 1976), p. 79.

[28]Campbell, interview with Hecth and Foltz, p. 51; interview with Keen, pp. 74–75. See also Campbell, interview with Hecht and Foltz, pp. 53–55, 57–58.

[29]Alan Watts, *In My Own Way* (New York: Vintage, 1973), pp. 264–265.

[30]Campbell, interview with Hecht and Foltz, p. 51; interview with Keen, pp. 82–83.

[31]See Campbell, interview with Newlove, p. 136.

[32]See Campbell, interview with Kisly, pp. 75–76.

[33]See Campbell, interview with Keen, pp. 75–77.

[34]On Catholicism see, for example, Campbell, *Masks: Creative,* pp. 260–261, 366–373, 637; on Judaism, *Inner Reaches,* pp. 32–34, 43–44; *Power of Myth,* pp. 18, 22, 141, 171; on the East, *Masks: Oriental,* ch. 9.

CHAPTER TWO

THE HERO WITH A THOUSAND FACES—I

There are many kinds of myths: myths of the origin of the world, myths of the origin of human beings, myths of paradise, flood myths, and myths of the end of the world. In later books Joseph Campbell discusses myths of all kinds, but in *The Hero with a Thousand Faces,* his first full-fledged book and still his best-known one, he concentrates on hero myths alone.

Many questions can be asked of hero myths and of myths generally:

(1) how similar are they?
(2) what do they mean?
(3) how and why do they originate?
(4) how and why do they function?
(5) who creates them?
(6) who tells them?
(7) do all cultures have them?

In *Hero,* Campbell focuses on the first and the second of these questions. He seeks first to show that all hero myths have the same plot and therefore the same meaning. For Campbell, there is really only a single hero, who merely displays a thousand faces, just as in his later four-volume tome a single god wears many "masks."

Campbell seeks next to show that the uniform meaning of all hero myths is at once psychological and metaphysical: rightly understood, hero myths describe not the outward, physical adventures of legendary or historical figures but the inward, mental adventures of adherents to the myths. Rather than the discovery of a lost continent by some famous figure, a hero myth actually describes the rediscovery of a lost part both of the human personality and of the cosmos.

Campbell takes for granted that all cultures and indeed all individuals possess hero myths. He does not try to prove this point. Similarly, he takes for granted that hero myths are told, if not created, by individual "sages" within each culture. While he does not directly discuss the origin and function of hero myths, his stress on the uniformity of the meaning of hero myths surely implies that for him all have the same origin and function. Hero myths originate in encounters with the lost dimensions of the mind and the world. They function to enable others to encounter those dimensions themselves.

Establishing the Hero Pattern

Campbell says modestly that his aim in *Hero* is merely to *establish* the common plot of hero myths, not to explain the origin and function of the myths or to interpret their meaning: "The present volume is a comparative, not genetic, study. Its purpose is to show that essential parallels exist in the myths themselves . . ." (*Hero*, p. 39, note 43). Here Campbell is laying the groundwork for future volumes, in which he can proceed to explain and interpret the similarities he has established.

In *Hero* Campbell is seeking to justify a "comparativist" rather than "particularistic" approach to hero myths and to myths generally. Particularists analyze *individual* hero or other myths. Comparativists analyze hero or other myths *as a group*. Particularists assume that the differences among hero myths outweigh the similarities, which they dismiss as vague and sketchy. Comparativists assume the reverse: that the similarities among hero myths count more than the differences, which they spurn as trivial and incidental.

Campbell is an arch-comparativist. By demonstrating the similarities among hero myths, he seeks to justify a comparativist approach. If he can show that hero myths follow the same plot, he can claim that their meaning, origin, and function must be the same as well.

Campbell is by no means the first person to compare hero myths. Some of his predecessors have also sought merely to prove that all hero myths fit a single pattern, not what the meaning, origin, or function of that pattern is. For example, back in 1876 there appeared a table by Johann Georg von Hahn,[1] who used fourteen cases to argue that all "Aryan" hero tales follow the same biographical scheme. In each case the hero is born illegitimately, out of the fear of the prophecy of his future greatness is abandoned by his father, is saved by animals and raised by a lowly couple, fights wars, returns home triumphant, defeats his persecutors, frees his mother, becomes king, founds cities, and dies young.

Writing in 1871, the anthropologist Edward Tylor[2] argued that hero myths follow a similar but less elaborate pattern. The hero is exposed at birth, is then saved by other humans or animals, and grows up to become a national hero—the pattern ending here. Tylor, too, sought only to establish, not to analyze, the pattern.

Similarly, the folklorist Vladimir Propp,[3] writing in the 1920s, sought to demonstrate that Russian fairy tales follow a common pattern, in which the hero goes off on a successful adventure and upon his return marries and gains the throne. Propp's pattern skirts both the birth and the death of the hero. Like Hahn and Tylor, Propp sought not to analyze but only to establish the pattern.

Campbell's openness to all kinds of explanations and interpretations of hero myths suggests that he, too, is trying only to establish a pattern:

> Mythology has been interpreted by the modern intellect as a primitive, fumbling effort to explain the world of nature (Frazer); as a production of poetical fantasy from prehistoric times, misunderstood by succeeding ages (Müller); as a repository of allegorical instruction, to shape the individual to his group (Durkheim); as a group dream, symptomatic of archetypal urges within the depths of the human psyche (Jung). . . . Mythology is all of these. (*Hero,* p. 382)

Indeed, Campbell, writing after World War II, argues that the establishment of the sheer similarities among myths can abet world peace. If all peoples realize that their myths are the same, they may realize that they themselves are at heart the same:

> There are of course differences between the numerous mythologies and religions of mankind, but this is a book about the similarities. . . . My hope

is that a comparative elucidation may contribute to the perhaps not-quite-desperate cause of those forces that are working in the present world for unification, not in the name of some ecclesiastical or political empire, but in the sense of human mutual understanding. (*Hero*, p. viii)

Interpreting the Hero Pattern

Yet Campbell in fact ventures beyond demonstrating the similarities among hero myths to explaining their origin and function and, even more, to interpreting their meaning. He asks not just whether hero myths are similar but why, and what their uniformity means: "Why is mythology everywhere the same, beneath its varieties of costume? And what does it teach?"(*Hero*, p. 4)

Just as Campbell is not the first person to suggest similarities among hero myths, so he is not the first to explain or interpret those similarities. His most prominent predecessors are Otto Rank, the psychologist[4] who in 1909 gave a Freudian analysis, and the folklorist Lord Raglan,[5] who in 1934 and 1936 gave what is called a "myth-ritualist" one. Their analyses will be compared with Campbell's.

Because one of the meanings of hero myths is psychological, Campbell proposes using psychoanalysis to decipher it:

The old teachers knew what they were saying. Once we have learned to read again their symbolic language, it requires no more than the talent of an anthologist to let their teaching be heard. But first we must learn the grammar of the symbols, and as a key to this mystery I know of no better tool than psychoanalysis. (*Hero*, p. vii)

Campbell uses the term "psychoanalysis" broadly to include the psychology of Carl Jung as well as that of Sigmund Freud. All those who deem the subject of myth the human mind rather than the outer, physical world are for Campbell "psychoanalysts."

To read myth psychologically is to read it symbolically. While *any* comparativist approach to myth necessarily stresses the similarities among myths, those similarities need not be taken symbolically. Raglan, for example, takes individual heroes not as symbols of something else but only as instances of the category hero. He interprets literally, not symbolically, the deeds of each hero. Campbell's interpretation is symbolic not because it is comparative but because it is psychological: heroes are not whole persons but the minds of persons, and their deeds are treks not to unknown lands but to unknown parts of their minds.

For both Freud and Jung, the meaning of myth had always been unknown. Psychoanalysis reveals it for the first time. For Campbell, the meaning was originally known, somehow became lost, and must be rediscovered. Hence the "old teachers," who interpreted, if not invented, myths, were fully aware of their psychological meaning (*Hero*, p. 178, note 150), which Campbell is thereby merely restoring. Campbell has a far more romantic view of "ancients" than either Freud or even Jung. "Moderns" for Campbell have nothing to teach ancients, whom they can at most only equal. Psychoanalysis, then, is either a modern technique that ancients, directly in touch with myths, never needed or, less likely, a universal technique that ancients themselves employed.

Comparativism

Campbell's dual aims in *Hero* are truly distinct, and he must argue for both. On the one hand his argument for a comparativist rather than particularistic approach needs to be supplemented by an argument for a psychological one. On the other hand his argument for a psychological approach needs to be preceded by an argument for a comparativist one.

Campbell's argument for comparativism is his presentation of the similarities themselves among hero myths. He argues first that all hero myths conform to a pattern, which, adopting a term from James Joyce, he calls the "monomyth":

> The standard path of the mythological adventure of the hero is a magnification of the formula represented in the rites of passage: separation-initiation-return: . . . A hero ventures forth from the world of common day into a region of supernatural wonder: fabulous forces are there encountered and a decisive victory is won: the hero comes back from this mysterious adventure with the power to bestow boons on his fellow man. (*Hero,* p. 30)[6]

Campbell argues second that the universality of the pattern proves that the meaning of a myth must lie in it. The similarities are for Campbell too numerous to be coincidental. Campbell acknowledges the differences among myths but, in light of the similarities, dismisses them as secondary:

The same objection might be brought, however, against any textbook or chart of anatomy, where the physiological variations of race are disregarded in the interest of a basic general understanding of the human physique. There are of course differences between the numerous mythologies and religions of mankind, but this is a book about the similarities; and once these are understood the differences will be found to be much less great than is popularly (and politically) supposed. (*Hero,* p. viii)

Campbell deems the meaning of all hero myths not just similar but identical: "As we are told in the Vedas: 'Truth is one, the sages speak of it by many names'." (*Hero,* p. viii)

The Psychological Meaning of Heroism

For Campbell, the hero of a myth is heroic for two reasons. He does what no one else either will or can do, and he does it on behalf of everyone else as well as himself. No one else either dares or manages to venture forth to a strange, supernatural world, confront yet usually befriend its inhabitants, and return home to share their bounty with his countrymen:

Prometheus ascended to the heavens, stole fire from the gods, and descended. Jason sailed through the Clashing Rocks into a sea of marvels, circumvented the dragon that guarded the Golden Fleece, and returned with the fleece and the power to wrest his rightful throne from a usurper. Aeneas went down into the underworld, crossed the dreadful river of the dead, threw a sop to the three-headed

watchdog Cerberus, and conversed, at last, with
the shade of his dead father. All things were un-
folded to him: the destiny of souls, the destiny of
Rome, which he was about to found. . . . He returned through the ivory gate to his work in the
world. (*Hero,* pp. 30–31)

The hero may be a prince, a warrior, a saint, or a
god. He can be a local hero or a universal one. The
treasure he seeks can be wealth, a bride, or wisdom.
He can be seeking it for only his people or for all
humanity. At the same time Campbell's hero is always
male. Like Hahn, Tylor, Propp, Rank, and Raglan,
Campbell ignores heroines.[7]

If literally a hero discovers a strange external world,
symbolically, or psychologically, he discovers a strange
internal one. Literally, the hero discovers that there is
more to the world than the physical world. Symbolically, he discovers that there is more to him than his
consciousness. Literally, the hero discovers the ultimate nature of the world. Symbolically, he discovers
his own ultimate nature. He discovers his true identity. He discovers who he really is.

For Erik Erikson,[8] the contemporary psychoanalyst,
the quest for identity is a quest for a place in society,
a place expressed most concretely in a career. A hero
is one who, in a changing society, forges a new place
for others as well as himself. For Campbell as well, a
hero finds a place for others as well as for himself. But that place is one that he and they have
always had, just not recognized. Campbell's hero discovers, not creates, a deeper side to his, and others',
personality. He discovers the unconscious. The quest
for identity is therefore a quest for a place less in society than within oneself. The distinction that Camp-

bell draws between the modern hero, who somehow alone undertakes an inner journey, and earlier heroes, who somehow undertook an outer one, is therefore hard to understand:

> The center of gravity, that is to say, of the realm of mystery and danger has definitely shifted. For the primitive hunting peoples of those remotest human millenniums when the sabertooth tiger, the mammoth, and the lesser presences of the animal kingdom were the primary manifestations of what was alien . . . the great human problem was to become linked psychologically to the task of sharing the wilderness with these beings. . . . Not the animal world, not the plant world . . . but man himself is now the crucial mystery. Man is that alien presence with whom the forces of egoism must come to terms. . . . (*Hero*, pp. 390–391)

If literally Campbell's hero, like Erikson's, proceeds to serve others, symbolically he proceeds to serve himself. For symbolically he is returning not to society but to consciousness, even if the focus of that consciousness, the external world, includes society. If symbolically the hero somehow still serves others, he does so by revealing to them the existence of the unconscious: theirs as well as his. If literally the "boon" he confers on them can be anything, symbolically it is knowledge.

If literally the hero is a historical or legendary figure, symbolically he is either the creator of the myth or else someone moved by it. Whoever invents or uses the myth to deal with the unconscious is the true hero. Yet the true hero is also every human being. For the quest Campbell's hero undertakes is one which all human beings, female as well as male, must undertake:

"The whole sense of the ubiquitous myth of the hero's passage is that it shall serve as a general pattern for men and women . . ." (*Hero,* p. 121). Even if Campbell's heroes are exclusively male, they somehow symbolize all humanity. The idiosyncrasies of each hero simply reflect the particular brand of heroism of each society.

To say that every hero symbolizes all human beings is to say that he symbolizes what all humans ought to be, not what they are. For in practice few are heroic. All may harbor a deeper side of themselves awaiting discovery, but only a few possess the courage and perseverance to discover it. The hero is heroic exactly because he does what everyone else either will not or cannot do. Indeed, by no means does everyone else even want to emulate him: "The usual person is more than content, he is even proud, to remain within the indicated bounds . . ." (*Hero,* p.78). The hero is heroic to those who create, tell, or hear his tale, not to his countrymen within it. He is typically without honor in his own country.

Campbell says that the meaning of hero myths is the rediscovery of the unconscious, of which not just the hero but his countrymen are otherwise unaware. Indeed, the meaning is the rediscovery of the unconscious in the mythmaker, teller, and hearer as well: they are the true heroes of the myth.

On the other hand Campbell claims, as noted, that the meaning of hero myths has until recent times been conscious—psychoanalysis being necessary to tell "moderns" what their forebears always knew.[9] Is Campbell thereby inconsistent? No. Surely he can consistently contend that hero myths are really about the unconscious in everyone and that all but moderns have known this fact. If he were claiming that all humanity once knew of the unconscious without myth, myth would be superfluous. But he is likely claiming that myth served "ancients" the same way that it does moderns: to reveal to them the existence of the unconscious. The difference between ancients and moderns is that ancients had teachers, or "sages," to interpret myth psychologically. Until psychoanalysis moderns have had either no teachers or ignorant ones, ones who obtusely interpreted myth literally.

Heroism in the First Half of Life

Heroism can take place in what Campbell, following Jung, calls either the first or the second half of life. Where Freud deals wholly with problems of the first half of life, Jung deals mainly with problems of the second.

For Freud and Jung alike, the first half of life—birth, childhood, adolescence, and young adulthood—involves the establishment of oneself as an independent person, one with a firm place in society. The attainment of independence expresses itself concretely in the securing of a job and a mate. The attainment of independence requires separation from one's parents and mastery of one's instincts. Independence of one's parents means independence of the invariably possessive, smothering aspect of all parents, who to some degree always want their children to remain dependent on them. Independence of one's parents means not the rejection of them but self-sufficiency.

Independence of one's instincts means not the rejection of them either but rather control over them. It means not the denial of instincts but the re-routing of them into socially acceptable outlets. For example, sexual desire may get displaced from one's mother or father onto other women or men. Alternatively, it may get redirected, or sublimated, into nonerotic love or into art. Similarly, aggression may get sublimated into competition. Indeed, the attainment of a mate and a job constitutes the harnessing of instincts that otherwise might vent themselves in incest and violence. When Freud says that the test of happiness is the ability to work and love, he is clearly referring to the goals of the first half of life, which for him, to be sure, continue through the rest of life.

Because the Freudian aim is social adjustment, Freudian problems are those of external maladjustment. They involve a lingering attachment to either parents or instincts. Either to depend on one's parents for the satisfaction of instincts or to satisfy instincts in antisocial ways is to be stuck, or fixated, at childhood.

At the same time the domestication of one's instincts, if not also the break with one's parents, can never be complete. Because sexual and aggressive instincts invariably remain partly unsocialized, the Freudian goal is as much a mere truce as outright harmony between the individual and society: in return for denying antisocial instincts, the individual gains the satisfaction of other, tamer instincts or desires—for example, for food, clothing, and shelter.[10] Indeed, a Freudian hero is one who, unlike ordinary members of society, defiantly refuses to deny his antisocial instincts.

By contrast, the hero for Erikson, who has a far rosier view of human nature than Freud, seeks outright harmony with society. For the satisfaction he seeks is exactly that of acceptance into society. The need for identity is the need for social identity. Where for Freud the nonheroic individual seeks to adjust to society only in order to secure other satisfactions from it, for Erikson the individual, heroic or not, seeks to adjust to society as an end in itself.

Nevertheless, heroism for both Freud and Erikson falls within the first half of life: it involves relations with parents and instincts. For Jung, heroism in even the first, not to mention the second, half of life involves, in addition, relations with the unconscious. In the first half of life a Jungian hero seeks to separate himself from not only his parents and his antisocial instincts but also his unconscious.

For both Freud and Erikson, the unconscious is the product of the containment, or repression, of instincts. For Jung, the unconscious is inherited rather than created and includes more than bottled-up instincts. Independence of the Jungian unconscious therefore means more than independence of the instincts. It means the formation of consciousness. The initial focus of consciousness is the external world, so that for Jung as well as for Freud and Erikson the goal of the first half of life is adjustment to the external world. For Jung, however, adjustment means not just, as for them, socialization but also consciousness. One is adjusted to the external world not only when one has secured a job and a mate but, more fundamentally, when one is at least partly conscious of the world in itself, even if one's contact with it remains filtered through the projections of the Jungian unconscious.

Heroism in the Second Half of Life

The goal of the second half of life is likewise consciousness, but now consciousness of the Jungian unconscious rather than of the external world. One must return to the unconscious, from which one has invariably become severed. But the aim is not to sever one's ties to the external world. The aim is not return to the state at birth. On the contrary, the aim is return in turn to the external world. The ideal is a balance between the external and the internal worlds, between consciousness of the external world and consciousness of the unconscious. Indeed, one returns to the unconscious in order to raise it to consciousness. The aim is literally "consciousness raising": the enlargement, not the rejection, of consciousness. The aim is to supplement, not abandon, the achievements of the first half of life.

Jung assumes that in establishing themselves in the external world humans have typically not wholly severed their ties to either their parents or their instincts. At the same time the pull of both has begun to fade. In establishing their independence most humans *have,* by contrast, considerably severed their umbilical ties to their unconscious, with which they must therefore be reconnected.

The attainment of the goal of the second half of life can begin whenever one reaches adulthood. It begins any time after the establishment of oneself in the external world. It begins any time after one has become both socialized and conscious. Socialization as much abets consciousness as presupposes it: if adaptation to society presupposes consciousness of it, adaptation to society also weans one away from the unconscious.

Just as classic Freudian problems involved the failure to establish oneself externally, so distinctively Jungian problems involve the failure to establish oneself internally. Freudian problems stem from excessive attachment to the world of childhood; Jungian ones, from excessive attachment to the world that one enters upon breaking free of the childhood world: the external world, social and physical alike. Either one is so fully severed from the internal world that, like the countrymen the hero leaves behind, one is no longer even aware of it, or else one feels empty, lost, cut off—external rewards no longer providing the satisfaction they once did. One may not be aware of the source of this feeling, but feel it one does. Most moderns for Jung are oblivious to the internal world. From the elite few who feel empty and therefore long for it come many, though certainly not most, Jungian patients.

In psychological lingo the goal of the first half of life is for both Freud and Jung the establishment of a strong ego. For both, a strong ego means one able to resist parents and instincts alike. Neurotics are those with egos too weak to resist either. For Jung, a strong ego is, in addition, one conscious of the external world, something that resistance to both parents and instincts at once presupposes and promotes.

The goal of the second half of life is not the weakening but the refocusing of the ego. Till now the sole focus of consciousness by the ego has been the external world. Now what is misleadingly called ''ego,'' or ordinary, consciousness—misleading because the ego remains the agent of consciousness—gets supplemented, not replaced, by consciousness of the internal world of the unconscious. That unconscious is not,

again, the repressed Freudian one but the naturally
unconscious Jungian one, which for various reasons
Jung calls the collective unconscious.

Were the ego, in shifting its focus, to abandon rather
than merely supplement ordinary consciousness, the
result would not be mere regression but outright psychosis: one would have literally lost touch with everyday reality. One would be crazy. The ego does abandon
ordinary consciousness, but only temporarily. It does
so only to reconnect itself to the unconscious. The real
aim is to become as fully conscious as possible of both
worlds. The aim is to forge a balanced relationship to
both worlds.

Campbell's Hero: Freudian or Jungian?

Campbell implies that his psychological interpretation
of hero myths is Freudian as well as Jungian. In de-
claring at the outset that to unravel the "mystery" of
myth he will use "psychoanalysis" (*Hero*, p. vii), he
can scarcely be excluding Freud. Indeed, he cites
Freud and the Freudian anthropologist Géza Róheim
nearly as often as Jung.

Yet Campbell's interpretation of hero myths is in
fact far more Jungian than Freudian,[11] and in no small
part because of the stage of life of the hero. A Freudian hero would be a young adult and would be dealing
with the typical problems of young adulthood: trying
to find both a job and a mate. The quintessential
Freudian hero is Oedipus, who indeed lands both a
job and a mate. A Jungian hero would be already settled and would instead be trying to find a purpose in
life beyond professional and even marital fulfillment.

A typical Jungian hero is Odysseus, whose story begins with his departure from his kingship and family in Ithaca and centers on his adventures en route back from the Trojan War to Ithaca.

Though Campbell never specifies the age, occupation, or marital state of his hero, the hero is always, like Odysseus, an adult ensconced in society. The hero is heroic precisely because he is willing to leave the security and comfort of society for an unknown world. Campbell's hero must, then, be in the second half of life.

The hero's goal, moreover, is likewise that of the second half of life: not separation from one's roots—parental, instinctual, and unconscious—but reconnection with at least the unconscious ones, which Odysseus encounters upon leaving Troy for home. The unconscious, from which the hero is above all severed, is also alone capable of giving the meaning he now seeks. Campbell thus says that the hero's

> first step, detachment or withdrawal, consists in a radical transfer of emphasis from the external to the internal world, . . . a retreat from the desperations of the [external] waste land to the peace of the everlasting realm that is within. (*Hero,* p. 17)

Rank's Freudian Hero

The best way to distinguish Campbell's Jungian hero from a Freudian one is to contrast Campbell's hero pattern to the Freudian one of Otto Rank. Though Rank later broke with Freud, at the time he wrote *The Myth of the Birth of the Hero* he was a disciple. Freudian theory itself has changed significantly since 1909, the date of Rank's essay, and present-day Freudians are considerably closer to Jungians in their analyses of myths than earlier ones were. Like Jungians from the start, contemporary Freudians view myth much more positively than Rank and Freud do. Myths *solve* problems rather than, as for Rank and Freud, *perpetuate* them.[12] Still, even contemporary Freudians are not Jungians, and Rank's Freudian approach to hero myths provides a useful foil to Campbell's largely Jungian approach.

Rank's scheme covers the first half of life: from the hero's birth to his attainment of both a career and, if usually only unconsciously, a mate. The scheme begins with the hero's parents, who are nobility and typically royalty. Because of continence, barrenness, or other impediments conception proves difficult. Either before or during pregnancy a prophecy warns the parents against the birth. If born, it usually declares, the child, who is always male, will kill his father. To circumvent the prophecy the parents abandon the child at birth. But the child is saved and raised by either animals or a lowly couple. Once grown, he knowingly or unknowingly returns to his birthplace, kills his father, and succeeds him as, usually, king.

Literally, or consciously, the hero is a historical or legendary figure like Oedipus. The hero is heroic because he rises from obscurity to the throne. Literally, the hero is an innocent victim of either his parents or, ultimately, fate. True, his parents have yearned for a child and abandon him only to save the father, but they nevertheless do choose to abandon him. The child's revenge, if the parricide is even done knowingly, is therefore understandable: who would not consider killing someone who had sought to kill one?

Symbolically, or unconsciously, the hero is either the creator of the myth or anyone stirred by it. In identifying himself with the literal hero, which he can do consciously, the creator or reader of the myth actually replaces him: the creator or reader becomes the true subject of the myth. Symbolically, the hero is heroic not because he dares to win a throne but because he dares to kill his father. Furthermore, the killing is definitely intentional, and the cause is not revenge but frustration: the father has refused to surrender his wife, who is the real object of the son's efforts.

Too horrendous to face, the true meaning of the hero myth gets covered up by the literal one. Rather than the culprit, the hero becomes an innocent victim or at worst a justified avenger. What he seeks becomes power, not incest. Who is seeking it becomes not the mythmaker or reader but some third party, a historical or legendary figure.

Why the hero must usually be the son of royalty Rank never explains. Perhaps the filial clash thereby becomes even more titanic: it is over power as well as revenge. Indeed, when literally the hero kills his father unknowingly, the motive can hardly be revenge, so that power provides a motive.

Literally, the myth culminates in the hero's attainment of a throne. Symbolically, the hero gains a mate as well. One might, then, conclude that the myth fittingly expresses the Freudian goal of the first half of life.

In actuality, it expresses the opposite. The wish it fulfills is not for detachment from one's parents and from one's antisocial instincts but, on the contrary, the most intense possible relationship to one's parents and the most antisocial of urges: incest and parricide. Independence of one's parents means not domination over them but autonomy, which indeed allows for a loving relationship to them. Seizing one's father's job and one's mother as one's spouse does not quite spell independence.

The mythmaker or reader is an adult, but the wish vented by the myth is that of a child of three to five: it is the Oedipal wish to kill one's father in order to be able to have sex with one's mother. The myth fulfills a wish never outgrown by the adult, who either invents or uses the myth. That adult is neurotic: he has never mastered his Oedipal drives. He is psychologically an eternal child. Since no mere child can overpower his father, the mythmaker fantasizes being old enough to do so. In short, the myth expresses not the Freudian goal of the first half of life but the childhood goal that keeps one from fulfilling it.

Campbell's Jungian Hero

In contrast to Rank's Freudian hero stands Campbell's Jungian one.[13] Rank's hero must be the son of royal or at least distinguished parents. Campbell's need not be, though often he is. Rank's scheme begins with the hero's birth; Campbell's, with his adventure. Where Rank's scheme ends, Campbell's begins: with the adult hero settled at home. Rank's hero must be young enough for his father and in some cases even his grandfather still to be alive and reigning. Campbell does not specify the age of his hero, but he must be no younger than the age at which Rank's hero myth therefore ends: young adulthood. He must, again, be in the second half of life.[14]

The hero's adventure begins not with any initiative

of his own but with a call. While Campbell stresses that the hero is heroic exactly because he is willing as well as able to undertake the adventure, he also says that the hero may initially undertake it either unknowingly or even involuntarily, in which case there is hardly a call:

> The hero can go forth of his own volition to accomplish the adventure, as did Theseus when he arrived in his father's city, Athens, and heard the horrible story of the Minotaur; or he may be carried or sent abroad by some benign or malignant agent, as was Odysseus, driven about the Mediterranean by the winds of the angered god, Poseidon. The adventure may begin as a mere blunder. . . . (*Hero*, p. 58)

Where Rank's hero returns to his birthplace, Campbell's ventures forth to a strange, new world, a world that he has not only never visited but never even known existed:

> . . . destiny has summoned the hero and transferred his spiritual center of gravity from within the pale of his society to a zone unknown. This fateful region . . . may be variously represented: as a distant land, a forest, a kingdom underground, beneath the waves, or above the sky, a secret island, lofty mountaintop, or profound dream state; but it is always a place of strangely fluid and polymorphous beings, unimaginable torments, superhuman deeds, and impossible delight. (*Hero*, p. 58)

In this strange, supernatural world the hero encounters first the supreme female god and then the supreme male god. The maternal goddess is loving and caring:

> She is the paragon of all paragons of beauty, the
> reply to all desire, the bliss-bestowing goal of every
> hero's earthly and unearthly quest. She is mother,
> sister, mistress, bride. . . . For she is the incarna-
> tion of the promise of perfection; the soul's assur-
> ance that, at the conclusion of its exile in a world
> of organized inadequacies, the bliss that once was
> known will be known again: the comforting, the
> nourishing, the "good" mother. . . . (*Hero,* pp.
> 110–111)

By contrast, the male god is tyrannical and merciless.
He is an "ogre" (*Hero,* p. 126).

The hero has sex with the goddess and marries her.
He then kills and eats the god. Yet with both, not just
the goddess, he thereby becomes mystically one.

Where Rank's hero *returns* home to encounter his
father and mother, Campbell's hero *leaves* home to
encounter a male and female god, who are neither his
parents nor mates. Yet the two heroes' encounters are
remarkably akin: just as Rank's hero kills his father
and, if often only latently, marries his mother, so
Campbell's hero, in reverse order, first marries the
goddess and then kills the god.

The differences, however, are even more significant.
Because the goddess is not the hero's mother, sex with
her does not constitute incest. Moreover, the two not
only marry but become mystically one.

Despite appearances, the hero's relationship to the
male god is for Campbell no less positive. The relationship *seems* blatantly Oedipal: the son fears castration by the father, who in turn fears death at the
hands of the son. Campbell thus cites Róheim's
Freudian analysis of Australian myths and rituals of
initiation:

The native Australian mythologies teach that the first initiation rites were carried out in such a way that all the young men were killed. The ritual is thus shown to be, among other things, a dramatized expression of the Oedipal [counter] aggression [on the part] of the elder generation; and the circumcision, a mitigated castration. But the rites provide also for the cannibal, patricidal impulse of the younger, rising group of males. . . . (*Hero*, p. 139)

Róheim himself, however, departs from a strictly Freudian interpretation. To be sure, the ritual still acts out a long-simmering clash between sons and fathers over the sons' mothers, the sons still seek to kill their fathers, and in defense the fathers still seek to castrate their sons. What the sons seek is not, however, *intercourse* with their mothers but *reunion* with them. They seek to fulfill not their Oedipal desires but their even earlier, infantile ones. Their fathers oppose those desires not because, in Oedipal fashion, they want to keep their wives for themselves but because they want to break their sons of their infantile ties to their mothers. If the fathers try to sever those ties by threatening their sons with castration, they also try to sever the ties by offering themselves as substitutes for their wives. The fathers thus selflessly nourish their sons with their own blood, occasionally dying in the process:

. . . at the same time [the rites] reveal the benign self-giving aspect of the archetypal father; for during the long period of symbolical instruction, there is a time when the initiates are forced to live only on the fresh-drawn blood of the older men. . . . Frequently the men who give their blood faint and remain in a state of coma for an hour or more because of exhaustion. (*Hero*, pp. 139–141)

Campbell adopts Róheim's more harmonious, non-Freudian interpretation of the clash between sons and fathers. But he carries it even further. Since Campbell's hero is in the second half of life, he is not, like Róheim's young initiates, seeking a separation from his mother. He is seeking reintegration with her. Furthermore, he is seeking reintegration with his father as well. Indeed, he is not really fighting with his father over his mother. For, again, the two gods are neither his parents nor a couple. He is seeking from the god the same love that he has just won from the goddess. To secure it he need not give up the goddess but only trust in the god and thereby surrender himself to him: "One must have a faith that the father is merciful, and then a reliance on that mercy" (*Hero,* p. 130). The father stands for the god, who during the initiation rite thereby lets himself be killed by the son—much as, Campbell says later in *Masks: Primitive,* the hunted does in primitive hunting rites.

For Freud, the killing of a god during a ritual, initiatory or otherwise, would only seemingly be an act of self-sacrifice. It would really, if unconsciously, be an act of revenge: the god would stand for one's father, whom one would be killing for barring sex with one's mother.[15] For Campbell, however, the unconscious as well as the conscious meaning of the act is one of self-sacrifice. The conscious meaning thus masks no unacceptable unconscious one, in which case the unconscious meaning is not, as for Rank and Freud, being repressed. It is simply, as for Jung, unknown. Even for Róheim the latent level is repressed: the infantile yearning for which "male bonding" is a substitute is repressed because it is unacceptable.

Having killed the god, the hero or initiate proceeds

to eat him. By ingestion he becomes mystically one with him:

> The traditional idea of initiation combines an introduction of the candidate into the techniques, duties, and prerogatives of his vocation with a radical readjustment of his emotional relationship to the parental images. . . . He is the twice-born: he has become himself the father. (*Hero*, pp. 136–137)

Rank's hero merely kills, not eats, his father—the eating being part not of the hero myth but of the communion ritual interpreted by Freud. The eating for Freud is done out of greed and hatred: participants eat their fathers both to acquire their power and, in revenge for their sexual tyranny, to tear them apart. For Campbell, the eating is done out of love: participants eat their fathers in order to become one with them and thereby with god.

Having become mystically one with the supreme two gods, Campbell's hero proceeds to become one with the whole cosmos.

In *Hero*, Campbell concentrates on the meaning rather than the origin of hero myths. But should he be saying that the meaning is unconscious because it is naturally so rather than because it has been repressed, his explanation would be close to Jung's.

When Campbell says that the contents of the unconscious represent "all the life-potentialities that we never managed to bring to adult realization, those other portions of ourself [sic]" (*Hero*, p. 17), he may be saying that those "life-potentialities" are innately unconscious. If so, his explanation would, again, be like Jung's. He would be saying that those heretofore unconscious sides of ourselves are unconscious not because they have first been conscious and have been made unconscious but because they have never been conscious.

When Campbell says that rituals "reveal the benign self-giving aspect of the *archetypal* father" (*Hero*, pp. 139–140), he may be using the term "archetypal" as loosely as he does the term "psychoanalysis." Just as he uses "psychoanalysis" to include Jung, so he may be using "archetypal," a word usually associated with Jung, to include Freud. If he is following Freud, as he does in part in his later *Masks of God*, god and goddess "archetypes" stand for the hero's, or initiate's, parents. If he is following Jung, whom he actually names (*Hero*, p. 17), the god and goddess stand for father and mother archetypes, components of the hero's personality. The hero's relationship to these gods thereby symbolizes not, as for Freud, Rank, and Roheim, his relationship to other persons—his parents—but the relationship between one side of himself—his ego—and another—his unconscious. That Jungian unconscious is composed of various archetypes, of which the father and the mother are but two.

By identifying himself with the hero of a myth, Rank's mythmaker or reader vicariously lives out in his mind an adventure that, if ever directly fulfilled, would take place in the real world. The creator or user of the myth would act out his Oedipal desires on his parents themselves. While similarly identifying himself with the hero of a myth, Campbell's Jungian mythmaker or reader vicariously lives out in his mind an adventure that even when directly fulfilled would still take place within his mind. For parts of his mind are what he is really encountering.

On his journey Campbell's hero is seemingly discovering a new world. In fact, he is rediscovering an old one. The ego is returning to the unconscious, out of which it emerged but from which it has gradually become severed. It must rediscover its roots:

> . . . now it appears that the perilous journey was a labor not of attainment but of reattainment, not discovery but rediscovery. The godly powers sought and dangerously won are revealed to have been within the heart of the hero all the time. (*Hero*, p. 39)

NOTES

¹See Johann Georg von Hahn, *Sagwissenschaftliche Studien* (Jena: Mauke, 1876), p. 340. Han's chart on p. 340 is translated by Henry Wilson in John C. Dunlop, *History of Prose Fiction*, rev. Wilson (London: Bell, 1888), in an unnumbered attachment to the last page of volume one.

²See Edward B. Tylor, *Primitive Culture*, fifth ed. (New York: Harper Torchbooks, 1958), I (retitled *The Origins of Culture*), pp. 281–282.

³See Vladimir Propp, *Morphology of the Folktale*, tr. Laurence Scott, second ed. rev. and ed. Louis A. Wagner (Austin: University of Texas Press, 1968).

⁴See Otto Rank, *The Myth of the Birth of the Hero*, trs. F. Robbins and Smith Ely Jelliffe (New York: Journal of Nervous and Mental Disease, 1914). The German original appeared in 1909. All citations are from the reprint: *The Myth of the Birth of the Hero and Other Writings*, ed. Philip Freund (New York: Vintage, 1959), pp. 3–96.

⁵See Lord Raglan, "The Hero of Tradition," *Folk-lore*, 45 (September 1934), pp. 212–231; *The Hero* (London: Methuen, 1936). All citations from the book are from the reprint: *The Hero* (New York: Vintage, 1956).

⁶Campbell (*Hero*, p. 10, note 10) takes his three-part scheme of separation, initiation, and return from French anthropologist Arnold Van Gennep's *The Rites of Passage*

(trs. Monika B. Vizedom and Gabrielle L. Caffee [Chicago: University of Chicago Press, 1960]). But Campbell uses that scheme very differently from Van Gennep.

[7]Elsewhere (*Power of Myth*, p. 125) Campbell recognizes heroines. While Campbell actually cites female heroes in *Hero*, his pattern presupposes exclusively male heroes—for example, in the relationship between the hero and the two supreme gods.

[8]See Erik H. Erikson, *Young Man Luther* (New York: Norton, 1958).

[9]Yet elsewhere (*Myths to Live By*, pp. 8–9) Campbell says that past as well as present ''multitudes'' have been oblivious to the true meaning of myth.

[10]See Sigmund Freud, *Civilization and its Discontents*, tr. and ed. James Strachey (New York: Norton, 1962), passim.

[11]Campbell's interpretation is predominantly Jungian even though, on the basis of his reliance on Róheim, he says elsewhere that at the time he wrote *Hero*, Freud and Jung ''were equal in my thinking'' (*Open Life*, p. 121).

[12]See, for example, Jacob A. Arlow, ''Ego Psychology and the Study of Mythology,'' *Journal of the American Psychoanalytic Association*, 9 (July 1961), pp. 371–393. Ironically, Bruno Bettelheim says roughly the same as Arlow of fairy tales *rather than* myths, where he is more like Rank: see his *The Uses of Enchantment* (New York: Vintage, 1970), pp. 35–41, 194–199.

[13]For Jung's interpretation of heroism in the first as well as the distinctively Jungian second half of life see his ''The Psychology of the Child Archetype,'' in his *The Archetypes and the Collective Unconscious*, The Collected Works of C.G. Jung, eds. Sir Herbert Read and others, trs. R.F.C. Hull and others, IX, part 1, first ed. (New York: Pantheon, 1959), pp. 151–181; *Symbols of Transformation*, The Collected Works, V, first ed. (New York: Pantheon, 1956), pp. 171–444; *Psychology and Alchemy*, The Collected Works, XII, first ed. (New York: Pantheon, 1953), pp. 333–339;

Analytical Psychology (New York: Vintage, 1970), pp. 117–123.

[14]Campbell does briefly discuss the first half of the hero's life (*Hero*, pp. 318–334), but it falls outside his monomyth.

[15]See Freud, *Totem and Taboo*, tr. James Strachey (New York: Norton, 1950), ch. 4.

CHAPTER THREE

THE HERO WITH
A THOUSAND FACES—II

The Hero's Return

Having initially managed to break free of the secure, everyday world and go off to a dangerous new one, the hero, to complete his journey, must in turn break free of the new world, in which he has by now become settled, and return to the everyday one. So enticing is the new world that leaving *it* is harder than leaving home was. Circe, Calypso, the Sirens, and the Lotus Eaters all offer Odysseus not just a comfortable, long life but a carefree, immortal one. Not surprisingly, "numerous indeed are the heroes fabled to have taken up residence forever in the blessed isle of the unaging Goddess of Immortal Being" (*Hero*, p. 193).

The strongest temptation is the prospect of *reabsorption* in the new world. For the "new" world is really the oldest world. It is the one out of which the hero emerged at birth. The temptation is to surrender oneself to it and thereby be spared the responsibility entailed by individuality.

In psychological terms, the ego is tempted to surrender itself to the rediscovered unconscious, out of which it once emerged. More precisely, the temptation is to abandon not the ego itself but ego, or ordinary, consciousness: consciousness of the external, every-day world. The ego itself remains, for it is what does the abandoning.

Even if the hero manages to break free of the new world and return to the everyday one, he must still win acceptance back home, where his countrymen are skeptical, suspicious, and resentful:

> . . . he has yet to re-enter with his boon the long-forgotten atmosphere where men who are fractions imagine themselves to be complete. He has yet to confront society with his ego-shattering, life-redeeming elixir, and take the return blow of reasonable queries, hard resentment, and good people at a loss to comprehend. (*Hero*, p. 216)

In interpreting the hero's return, Campbell seems to be abandoning his otherwise relentlessly symbolic, psychological analysis and instead taking the myth literally. For he interprets the hero's return not as the ego's reacclimation to everyday consciousness but as the wanderer's readjustment to society. Indeed, even if the "boon" the hero bestows on others is the revelation of the unconscious within them, he is still revealing it to other persons. He is not talking to himself.

Campbell as Mystic

Yet Campbell does "psychologize" the hero's return to society as the reintegration of the now enlightened ego with the everyday world of ego consciousness to form what Jung calls the "self." As Campbell says of the hero's return, "Having died to his personal ego, he arose again established in the Self" (*Hero,* p. 243).

For Jung himself, however, the ego remains the center of consciousness: it alone is in touch with both the inner and the outer world. It is ego consciousness itself that gets replaced, and even it gets supplemented rather than replaced by consciousness of the unconsciousness. Insofar as Campbell means to be a Jungian, it is, then, misleading for him to speak of the "death" of the ego.

Yet in speaking of the death of the ego, Campbell reveals that he is not a Jungian after all. He is a mystic. His interpretation remains psychological, and his brand of psychology is far more Jungian than Freudian, but it is finally not Jungian.

Though often misconstrued, Jung no less than Freud opposes a state of sheer unconsciousness. Both seek to make the unconscious conscious. While they differ over the origin of the unconscious and over its capacity to be made conscious, the ideal for both remains consciousness. Jung opposes the rejection of consciousness for unconsciousness as relentlessly as he opposes the rejection of unconsciousness for consciousness. He seeks a balance between ego consciousness and consciousness of the unconscious. For Jung, the loss of ego consciousness, let alone of the ego itself, would mean the hero's failure, not his success: it would mean his failure to break free of the unconscious. It would mean his failure to return home.

Campbell himself recognizes that neither Jung nor Freud espouses a return to sheer unconsciousness. He *contrasts* the typical Eastern goal, the dissolution of the ego itself, to the conventional Western one, represented by Jung as well as by Freud. He says that even if Jung does not, like Freud, seek the dissolution

of the unconscious, he does not seek the dissolution of
the ego either. Rather, Jung seeks a balance between
the ego and the unconscious:

> A psychological approach to the mystery of the uni-
> verse . . . underlies not only Hinduism, but also
> Jainism and Buddhism; and the fundamental insight
> is, firstly, that the notion of ego (*aham*) is the initial
> error from which all fears and desires pro-
> ceed. . . . [E]go *(aham)* is the nuclear point of the
> world delusion and egolessness the first end to be
> attained. . . . Freud's view is epitomized in his cel-
> ebrated phrase: ''Where there is *id* there shall be
> *ego.* '' The meaning is, that the rational, conscious
> ego must become the ultimate director of each in-
> dividual life—and such a view, surely, is as repul-
> sive to the psychology of the Orient as the negative
> way of *neti neti* to the West. Carl G. Jung, on the
> other hand, represents the ideal of a running dia-
> logue between the rational, self-defensive and ag-
> gressive ego, and the deeper, apparently irrational
> but actually superrational, superindividual forces of
> the inner force. . . . [1]

Insofar as Campbell in *Hero* is a Jungian, he cannot
be advocating the extinction of the ego. But he can be
describing the heroic goal as extinction of the ego. He
can be saying that the hero's goal *is* a return to sheer
unconsciousness without saying that it *should be.* Jung
himself hardly approves of all the psychological states
evinced in the myths he interprets.

Since, furthermore, Campbell himself stresses the
indispensability of the hero's return from the unconscious, he, least of all, seems to be interpreting the
goal as the dissolution of even ego consciousness,
much less of the ego itself. Indeed, he contrasts the

hero as "saint," who alone does not return, to all other kinds of heroes, who do (*Hero*, p. 354-356). In the saintly hero alone "the ego is burnt out" (*Hero*, p. 354).

Yet Campbell himself not only interprets the goal of *all* heroes as the dissolution of the ego but also endorses it. First, contrasting psychoanalysis to Buddhism, Campbell dismisses the psychoanalytic goal exactly because it merely returns the patient to the troublesome everyday world of ego consciousness rather than, like the Buddhist goal, detaching him from it and even the ego altogether:

Psychoanalysis is a technique to cure excessively suffering individuals of the unconsciously misdirected desires and hostilities that weave around them their private webs of unreal terrors and ambivalent attractions; the patient released from these finds himself able to participate with comparative satisfaction in the more realistic fears, hostilities, erotic and religious practices, business enterprises, wars, pastimes, and household tasks offered to him by his particular culture. But for the one who has deliberately undertaken the difficult and dangerous journey beyond the village compound, these [worldly] interests, too, are to be regarded as based on error. Therefore the aim of the religious teaching is not to cure the individual back again to the general delusion, but to detach him from delusion altogether. . . . Having surpassed the delusions of his formerly self-assertive, self-defensive, self-concerned ego, he knows without and within the same repose. . . . And he is filled with compassion for the self-terrorized beings who live in fright of their own nightmare. He rises, returns to them, and dwells with them as an egoless center, through whom the principle of emptiness is made manifest in its own simplicity. (*Hero,* pp. 164–166)

He who "has deliberately undertaken the difficult and dangerous journey" toward "an egoless center" (*Hero,* p. 166) is, of course, the hero. Surely, then, Campbell is not only saying that the hero rejects the ego but also praising him for doing so.

But since Campbell himself insists on the hero's return to the everyday world, can the hero really be spurning it? Yes, for the world to which Campbell's hero returns is not really the everyday world. It is still the strange new world, which turns out to pervade the everyday one. The hero "does not abandon life. Turning his regard from the inner sphere of thought-transcending truth . . . outward again to the phenomenal world, he perceives without the same ocean of being that he found within" (*Hero,* p. 165). The hero discovers that he need never have left the everyday world after all: "Hence separateness, withdrawal, is no longer necessary. Wherever the hero may wander, whatever he may do, he is ever in the presence of his own essence—for he has the perfected eye to see. There is no separateness" (*Hero,* p. 386).

No separate everyday world exists. It and the new world are really one:

The two worlds, the divine [i.e., new] and the human [i.e., everyday] can be pictured only as distinct from each other—different as life and death, as day and night. The hero adventures out of the land we know into darkness; there he accomplishes his adventure, or again is simply lost to us, imprisoned, or in danger; and his return is described as a coming back out of that yonder zone. Nevertheless—and here is a great key to the understanding of myth and symbol—the two kingdoms are actually one. The realm of the gods is a forgotten dimension of the world we know. . . . The values and distinctions that in normal life seem important disappear with the terrifying assimilation of [what is now] the self into what formerly was [to the ego] only otherness. (*Hero,* p. 217)

To say that the everyday world and the new world are one is to say that the everyday world is an illusion. Campbell thus dismisses the "values and distinctions" of the everyday world. If no everyday world exists, the hero's would-be return to it is a sham.

To dismiss the everyday world as illusory is to dismiss as illusory any would-be consciousness of it. Since the everyday world does not exist, ego consciousness, which purports to be consciousness of that world, does not exist either. As the purported link between ego consciousness and the unconscious, the ego itself proves illusory as well.

By contrast to Campbell, Jung never denies the existence of the everyday world and so of ego consciousness. He rejects the object of ego consciousness as the *sole* reality, not as *a* reality. He retains the ego exactly as the indispensable nexus between the everyday world and the new one. While he seeks to integrate the two worlds, he denies that it is possible to fuse them, at least without thereby dissolving the everyday world. Similarly, he denies that it is possible to fuse the ego with the unconscious without dissolving the ego. Like Jung, Campbell may speak of the higher state the returning hero achieves as a "self" (*Hero,* p. 243), but insofar as that state transcends rather than supplements the everyday world, it is very different from what Jung means by the self.

Campbell's hero returns home for two reasons, both of which presuppose a devaluation of the everyday world. First, the hero returns because he finds the new world back home. He would not return if he did not. Second, the hero returns selflessly to save others:

> When the hero-quest has been accomplished, . . . the adventurer still must return with his life-transmuting trophy. The full round, the norm of the monomyth, requires that the hero shall now begin the labor of bringing the runes of wisdom, the Golden Fleece, or his sleeping princess, back into the kingdom of humanity, where the boon may redound to the renewing of the community, the nation, the planet, or the ten thousand worlds. (*Hero*, p. 193)

If the hero's return is selfless, the everyday world to which he is returning is worthless. Indeed, he is returning only to apprise others of the fact. Here the everyday world *is* distinct from the new one, but for exactly that reason it is no less worthless now than it is when the two worlds are one. Not coincidentally, then, Campbell's heroes include the selfless Buddha, Aeneas, Moses, and Jesus.

So obsessed is Campbell with the hero's bestowal of a "boon" (*Hero*, pp. 30, 246) on his community that he distinguishes a myth from a fairy tale on precisely the grounds that the triumph of a mythic hero is more than personal (*Hero*, pp. 37–38). For Campbell, the mythic hero is a true savior, offering his people the knowledge that gives them salvation:

The effect of the successful adventure of the hero is the unlocking and release again of the flow of life into the body of the world. The miracle of this flow may be represented in physical terms as a circulation of food substance, dynamically as a streaming of energy, or spiritually as a manifestation of grace. (*Hero*, p. 40)

Campbell's characterization of the hero as triumphant reveals another fundamental break with Jung: Campbell's hero remains bound to the first half of life. Even though Campbell's hero has already achieved the goals of the first half of life, truly re-encounters the unconscious, must even guard against succumbing to it, and returns home transformed, he also returns *triumphant*. He thinks he has tamed the unconscious. He is confident enough to proceed to save others.

Jung would say that Campbell's hero has in fact missed the depth and power of the unconscious. A Jungian hero would return humbled rather than elevated, wary rather than brash, the saved rather than the savior. A Jungian hero would abandon any effort at control of the unconscious and instead would seek a modus vivendi with it. Where Campbell's hero is, in Jungian terms, simply an "inflated" ego, Jung's is a full-fledged self. If on the one hand Campbell, venturing beyond Jung, interprets heroism as the transcendence of the ego in mystical union with the unconscious, on the other hand he, stopping far short of Jung, simultaneously interprets heroism as the ego's mastery over the unconscious. Only because Campbell assumes that the ego remains in control can he, without trepidation, envision the fusion of the ego with the unconscious. Jung would deny that in a deeper encounter with the unconscious the ego either could or should stay in control.[2]

Raglan's Frazerian Hero

One way to elucidate the "boon" provided by Campbell's hero is to contrast it to that provided by the hero of Lord Raglan's pattern.[3] Where Campbell's hero need not die, Raglan's must. Where Campbell's hero undertakes a dangerous journey to aid his community, Raglan's hero is, in the myth, driven *from* his community and, in the accompanying ritual, is sacrificed *by* the community. Campbell's hero can be anyone. Raglan's must be a king.

In a scheme that ultimately goes back to James Frazer's famous *Golden Bough,*[4] the king, according to Raglan, is killed by the community in order to ensure its welfare. The ritual in which the king is killed enacts the myth of the life of the god of vegetation above all: his death, rebirth, victory, marriage, and enthronement. The god resides in the king, so that the literal or, later, symbolic death of the king *is* the death of that god and therefore of what that god controls. Similarly, the rebirth of the king or, if he is killed, the accession of a successor *is* the rebirth of the god and of what the god controls. The function of the ritual, performed either after a fixed term of office or upon the weakening of the king, is to provide the community with food and other benefits.

Going beyond Frazer, Raglan equates the king with a hero. For Frazer, the king may in effect be a hero to the community, but Frazer does not, like Raglan, label him one.

For both Raglan and Campbell, heroes are heroic because they serve their communities. For Raglan, heroes in myth defeat those who threaten the people's physical welfare: Oedipus, for example, topples the Sphinx, which is starving Thebes. Heroes in ritual, which Raglan fails to connect to hero myths, sacrifice themselves to their communities. For Campbell, heroes in myth, under which he includes ritual, serve their communities by their return home with the "boon" they have secured, often secured only by defeating or at least taming monsters. The "boon" bestowed by Raglan's hero is tangible. That bestowed by Campbell's is intangible: it is not food but knowledge. Without Raglan's hero the community would die. Without Campbell's it would be unenlightened.

The Metaphysical Meaning of Heroism

Having interpreted hero myths psychologically, Campbell proceeds to interpret them philosophically, or metaphysically, as well. The hero's journey, he says, takes him to not just a deeper human world but also a deeper cosmic one. He discovers an unknown part of not just himself but the cosmos itself as well. Just as psychologically the hero discovers not only that he has an unconscious but also that his ego originated out of it, so metaphysically he discovers not only that there is an invisible immaterial world but also that the everyday, visible, material one originated out of it:

> And so, to grasp the full value of the mythological figures that have come down to us, we must understand that they are not only symptoms of the unconscious (as indeed are all human thoughts and acts) but also controlled and intended statements of

certain spiritual principles, which have remained as constant throughout the course of human history as the form and nervous structure of the human physique itself. Briefly formulated, the universal doctrine teaches that all the visible structures of the world—all things and beings—are the effects of a ubiquitous power out of which they rise, which supports and fills them during the period of their manifestations, and back into which they must ultimately dissolve. (*Hero*, p. 257)

So insistent is Campbell on a metaphysical as well as psychological interpretation of hero myths that he spurns those who allow for only a psychological interpretation. Thus he distinguishes between the still psychological *source* of the symbols used and their metaphysical *meaning:*

In the published psychoanalytical literature, the dream sources of the symbols are analyzed, as well as their latent meanings for the unconscious, and the effects of their operation upon the psyche; but the further fact that great teachers have employed them consciously as [mere] metaphors remains unregarded. . . . (*Hero*, p. 178, note 150)

The ultimate meaning of hero myths is that all is one. Psychologically, not only is there an unconscious realm beyond the conscious one, but the two realms are really one, and consciousness will eventually return to its unconscious origins. Metaphysically, not only is there an immaterial realm beyond the material one, but again the two are really one, and the material realm will one day return to its immaterial roots:

> The constriction of consciousness, to which we owe
> the fact that we see not the source of the universal
> power but only the phenomenal forms reflected
> from that power, turns superconsciousness [i.e., the
> primordial unconscious] into unconsciousness [i.e.,
> the ego's obliviousness to the primordial uncon-
> scious] and, at the same instant and by the same
> token, creates the world. Redemption consists in
> the return to superconsciousness and therewith the
> dissolution of the world. This is the great theme
> and formula of the cosmogonic cycle, the mythical
> image of the world's coming to [material] manifes-
> tation and subsequent return into the [immaterial]
> nonmanifest condition. Equally, the birth, life, and
> death of the individual may be regarded as a de-
> scent into unconsciousness [i.e., the ego's oblivi-
> ousness to the primordial unconscious] and return.
> The hero is the one who, while still alive, knows
> and represents the claims of the superconsciousness
> which throughout creation is more or less uncon-
> scious [i.e., unknown to the ego back home].
> (*Hero,* p. 259)

Furthermore, the psychological and metaphysical
realms are themselves really one:

> The key to the modern systems of psychological
> interpretation therefore is this: the metaphysical
> realm = the unconscious. Correspondingly, the key
> to open the door the other way is the same equation
> in reverse: the unconscious = the metaphysical
> realm. "For," as Jesus states it, "behold, the king-
> dom of God is within you." (*Hero,* p. 259)

Indeed, *all* distinctions prove illusory: between one
individual and another, one nation and another, one
race and another, one class and another, one religion
and another, one generation and another, male and

female, father and mother, human and god, outer and inner, material and immaterial, and life and death. Moderns most of all cling to the false or at least superficial distinctions of nation, race, religion, sex, class, and age: "The differentiations of sex, age, and occupation are not essential to our character, but mere costumes [masks?'] which we wear for a time on the stage of the world. The image of man within is not to be confounded with the garments. We think of ourselves as Americans, children of the twentieth century, Occidentals, civilized Christians. . . . Yet such designations do not tell what it is to be a man, they denote only the accidents of geography, birth-date, and income" (*Hero*, p. 385). Where both in *Hero* and in the earlier volumes of *The Masks of God* Campbell condemns the modern Western obsession with individuality and therefore with distinctions, in volume four of *Masks* he applauds it.

Again, Campbell is far more mystical than Jungian. Where Jung seeks only to balance opposites, which he deems real and so incapable of being fused, Campbell deems all opposites illusory and so seeks their fusion.

Yet the identity of at least the psychological and metaphysical realms seems akin to Jung's notion of synchronicity: the belief that there is a "meaningful coincidence" between what is occurring internally, within a person's mind, and what is occurring externally, in the outside world.[5] But in fact Campbell goes far beyond Jung, who deems synchronicity an entirely empirical phenomenon: by the outside world Jung means physical, not metaphysical, reality, and by synchronicity he means parallel, not identical, events.

In saying that the meaning of hero myths, not to say of all myths, is both metaphysical and psychological and that the metaphysical and psychological meaning alike is the oneness of all things, Campbell may be merely presenting the meaning of hero myths for those who believe in them. But in saying that the true meaning of hero myths is psychological and metaphysical rather than, as he assumes moderns take it, literal and historical, he is clearly presenting not just the meaning of the myths for believers but the meaning of them in fact. Yet he may be going further still. He may be saying not just what the true meaning of hero myths is but also that that meaning is true. He may be saying not just that hero myths really preach the oneness of all things but also that all things are really one. Certainly Campbell's relentless enthusiasm for the true meaning of hero myths suggests strongly that he endorses that meaning as itself true. How he himself knows that all things are really one he never says.

NOTES

[1]Campbell, "Oriental Philosophy and Occidental Psychoanalysis," in *Proceedings of the IXth International Congress for the History of Religions* (Tokyo: Maruzen, 1960), pp. 492–495. See Jung's own criticism of the East for lopsidedly seeking to dissolve the ego and return to sheer unconsciousness: see his *Psychology and Religion: West and East,* The Collected Works, XI, first ed. (New York: Pantheon, 1958), part II, esp. p. 493.

[2]The difference between Campbell's brand of heroism and Jung's Jungian analyst Joseph Henderson calls that between heroism per se and initiation: see his *Thresholds of Initiation* (Middletown, CT: Wesleyan University Press, 1967), esp. pp. 101–102, 134–135, 151–152, 159, 178–180; "Ancient Myths and Modern Man," in Jung and others, *Man and His Symbols* (New York: Dell, 1968), esp. pp. 101–125. See also John Beebe, introduction to *Aspects of the Mas-*

culine, ed. Beebe (Princeton, NJ: Princeton University Press, 1989), esp. pp. xi–xiii.

³See Lord Raglan, *The Hero* (New York: Vintage, 1956).

⁴See James G. Frazer, *The Golden Bough,* one-vol. abridgment (London: Macmillan, 1922), chs. 24–26, 29.

⁵On synchronicity see Jung, "Synchronicity: An Acausal Connecting Principle," and "On Synchronicity" in his *The Structure and Dynamics of the Psyche,* The Collected Words, VIII, first ed. (New York: Pantheon, 1960), pp. 417–519 and 520–531.

CHAPTER FOUR

THE MASKS OF GOD:
PRIMITIVE MYTHOLOGY

In *The Hero with a Thousand Faces* Campbell focuses on hero myths exclusively. In *The Masks of God* he discusses myths of all kinds. In *Hero* Campbell stresses the similarities among hero myths. In *Masks* he emphasizes the differences among all myths: differences not between one category of myth and another but between the myths of one category of *people* and another. Each of the four volumes of *Masks* is devoted to the mythology of a different category of people: primitive, Oriental, Occidental, and creative. Primitive mythology means that of nonliterate peoples. Oriental, or Eastern, mythology is that of the peoples of India, Southeast Asia, China, Japan, Mesopotamia, Egypt, pre-Columbian Middle America, and Peru. Occidental, or Western, mythology refers to that of both the Near East—Jews, Christians, Muslims, and Zoroastrians—and native Europe—Greeks, Romans, Celts, and Germans. Iran is for him the border between East and West, although he considers Zoroastrianism Western. By creative mythology Campbell means the mythology of the *modern* West, which he dates from the middle of the twelfth century on.

In *Masks: Primitive* Campbell follows the explorer and ethnologist Leo Frobenius in grouping all primitive peoples into hunters and planters.[1] This economic difference results from geographical and climatic ones, and yields social and metaphysical ones, which myths express.

The Differences Between Hunters and Planters

The difference between those who eat by killing and those who eat by growing is for Campbell the difference between those who disrupt the cycle of nature and those who abide by it. For hunters, life ends not simply in death, itself natural, but in violent death. One either kills or gets killed. For planters, life ends naturally. Plants get picked rather than killed and die on their own at the end of their period of fertility:

> Among the hunting tribes, whose life style is based on the art of killing, who live in a world of animals that kill and are killed and hardly know the organic experience of a natural death, all death is a consequence of violence and is generally ascribed not to the natural destiny of temporal beings but to magic. . . . For the planting folk of the fertile steppes and tropical jungles, on the other hand, death is a natural phase of life, comparable to the moment of the planting of the seed, for rebirth. (*Masks: Primitive,* pp. 125–27)

Because plants are reborn the next season, there is really immortality rather than death.

If Campbell were to stop here, he would be like James Frazer. Frazer does see all mythology as agricultural and so makes no separate category for hunting, which he somehow subsumes under planting. But

he as well as Campbell stresses above all the cycle of
the death and rebirth of crops. Campbell, however,
ventures beyond Frazer, for whom people hunt and
plant simply to eat. For Campbell, people who hunt
harbor a wholly different outlook from those who plant.

Socially, hunters for Campbell are individualists.
They may hunt for the community, but they hunt on
their own and the community is often small. Planting,
by contrast, is a communal activity, to which participants cede their individuality. Hunters hunt when and
where they please. Planters are bound by time and
place:

> This, then, is to be our first distinction between the
> mythologies of the hunters and those of the plant-
> ers. The accent of the planting rites is on the group;
> that of the hunters, rather, on the individual—though
> even here, of course, the group does not disap-
> pear. . . . In such a [planting] society there is little
> room for individual play. There is a rigid relation-
> ship not only of the individual to his fellows, but
> also of village life to the calendric cycle; for the
> planters are intensely aware of their dependency
> upon the gods of the elements. One short period of
> too much or too little rain at the critical moment,
> and a whole year of labor results in famine. Whereas
> for the hunter—hunter's luck is a very different thing.
> (*Masks: Primitive*, pp. 241, 230)

The Similarities Between
Hunters and Planters

Metaphysically, hunters believe that whatever they kill
does not die. Its body dies, but its immortal essence

gets reincarnated. Hunters also believe that their victims voluntarily sacrifice themselves—their bodies—to their killers: "The buffalo dance, properly performed, insures that the creatures slaughtered shall be giving only their bodies, not their essence, not their lives. . . . The hunt itself, therefore, is a rite of sacrifice . . ." (*Masks: Primitive,* p. 293).

Yet Campbell also says that hunters consider themselves mystically united with their prey: "And where the animal rites are properly celebrated by the people, there is a magical, wonderful accord between the beasts and those who have to hunt them" (*Masks: Primitive,* p. 293). Only unity explains the willingness of the victims to be killed—exactly the way Campbell explains altruism.[2]

These three beliefs—in immortality, self-sacrifice, and mystical unity—seemingly efface the very distinctions between hunters and planters. Hunters no more than planters disrupt the cycle of nature for their own selfish ends. Hunters do not really extinguish their prey, and their prey are not really victims. Rather, both hunters and hunted form a communal and mystical bond. Hunters may still work individually rather than, like planters, collectively, but otherwise they prove to be agrarian at heart: they are at peace with the world rather than in conflict with it.

At the same time planters are really like hunters. Plants, argues Campbell, do not at death retain an immortal essence that gets reincarnated the next season. Instead, they get absorbed by nature as a whole. Campbell even contrasts the fate of a dead hunter, a particle of whose bone remains, to that of a dead planter, whose body, by contrast, somehow dissolves altogether. The fates of hunter and planter symbolize those of hunted and planted:

> The bone [of the hunter] does not [like the seed] disintegrate and germinate into something else, but is the undestroyed base from which the same individual that was there before becomes magically reconstructed, to pick up life where he left it. The same man comes back; that is the point. Immortality is not thought of as a function of the group, the race, the species, but of the individual. The planter's view is [by contrast] based on a sense of group participation; the hunter's, on that sense of an immortal inhabitant within the individual. . . . (*Masks: Primitive,* p. 291)

The dissolution of the planter must be reconciled with the purported immortality and rebirth of the plant.

Campbell contends, furthermore, that even if the death of plants occurs naturally, their rebirth does not. Planting, like hunting, requires sacrifices: of virgins, kings, and gods. In both planting and hunting others must die so that the community may live. The sacrifices in planting are no less voluntary than those in hunting. Campbell elsewhere sums up the similarity of hunters and planters:

> Essentially, then, the informing observation supporting these two widely flung mythologies is the same. It is that life lives on life, and that without this continuing sacrifice there would be no life whatsoever on this earth. The other part of the realization is that there is a renewing principle everywhere operative that is of the nature of the earth and of the mystery of the womb, which receives seed and returns it as renewed life. . . . The individual is thereby united with the way of nature, centered not in self-preservation but in accord with the wonder of the whole. ("Myths from West to East," p. 35)

Just as Campbell in *Masks* pits hunters against planters yet actually sees hunters as planters in disguise and vice versa, so in volumes two and three of *Masks* he seemingly pits the West against the East yet actually sees the West as the East in disguise, though not here vice versa. Indeed, in *Masks: Primitive* he really means only to be making hunters into planters, not vice versa: as akin to hunting as planting becomes, it retains the communal and mystical bond that is the heart of planting and that Campbell applauds above all.

In later volumes of *Masks* Campbell goes further: he parallels the beliefs of the West to those of hunters and the beliefs of the East to those of planters. To the extent that Western myths are like hunting ones, Eastern myths like planting ones, hunting and planting myths like each other, and Western and Eastern myths like each other, all myths are one. The differences among groups of myths would therefore be mere "masks." There would not be a single plot to myths, as there is in *Hero*, but there would be a single meaning: the mystical oneness of all things.

Patriarchy and Matriarchy

Campbell associates hunting with males and planting with females:

> And the role of women [in planting] has perhaps already been greatly enhanced, both socially and symbolically; for whereas in the hunting period the chief contributors to the sustenance of the tribes had been the men and the role of the women had

been largely that of drudges, now the female's economic contributions were of first importance. She participated—perhaps even predominated—in the planting and reaping of the crops, and, as the mother of life and nourisher of life, was thought to assist the earth symbolically in its productivity. (*Masks: Primitive*, p. 139)

Campbell goes so far as to associate hunting with a patriarchal stage of society and planting with a matriarchal one:

The second stage or type of primitive society recognized by this culture-historical school of ethnology is that of the large, totemistic hunting groups. . . . Moreover, there is considerable emphasis placed on the role and authority of the men, both in the religious and in the political organization of the symbolically articulated community. . . . A very different course of development is to be traced, however, in the sphere of the tropical gardening cultures, where a third type or stage of social organization matured that was almost completely antithetical to that of the hunting peoples. For in these areas it was the women, not the men, who enjoyed the magico-religious and social advantage, they having been the ones to effect the transition from plant-collecting to plant-cultivation. . . . Thus they won both economic and social power and prestige, and the complex of the matriarchy took form. (*Masks: Primitive*, pp. 319–320)

In *Masks: Primitive* patriarchy precedes matriarchy. In *Masks: Occidental*, however, matriarchy precedes patriarchy. Campbell's shifting views may reflect his shifting sources: in volume one of *Masks* he relies on the Austrian anthropologist Father Wilhelm Schmidt, who puts patriarchy first;[3] in volume three, though never cited, on the Swiss classicist and jurist J. J. Bachofen, who puts matriarchy first.

Campbell is interested in patriarchal and matriarchal societies not in themselves but as explanations of myths: patriarchy for him explains myths in which the chief gods are male; matriarchy, those in which the chief gods are female. When, in *Masks: Occidental,* he reverses the chronology of patriarchy and matriarchy, matriarchy explains myths that assume either the past or the present dominance of female gods; patriarchy, myths that assume either the present or the future dominance of male gods.

In equating planting with not only human but also divine matriarchy, Campbell breaks with James Frazer. For Frazer, the chief god of vegetation is always male, and the king, not queen, is either his representative or his outright incarnation.[4] To be sure, the ritual enacted by the king includes marriage to the queen. Indeed, it is from their mating—the planting of his seed in hers—that vegetation grows. Nevertheless, the supreme god of vegetation as well as his representative or incarnation on earth is always male. For Campbell, the supreme, if not sole, god of vegetation is always female.

Campbell associates hunting with not just male gods in general but tricksters in particular. He also associates hunting with shamans. Both tricksters and shamans act independently of the community and even in defiance of it. Campbell here thus reverts to his initial characterization of hunters as individualists. In associating planting in turn both with gods who uphold morality and with priests, he preserves his original view of planting as distinctively communal:

The contrast between the two world views [i.e., planting and hunting] may be seen more sharply by comparing the priest and the shaman. The priest is the socially initiated, ceremonially inducted member of a recognized religious organization, where he holds a certain rank and functions as the tenant of an office that was held by others before him, while the shaman is one who, as a consequence of a personal psychological crisis, has gained a certain power of his own. . . . This ambiguous, curiously fascinating character of the trickster appears to have been the chief mythological character of the paleolithic [i.e., hunting] world of story. A fool and a cruel, lecherous cheat, an epitome of the principle of disorder. . . . The Greek Titan, a sublimation of the image of the self-reliant, shamanistic trickster, . . . is neither condemned in his intransigent defiance of Zeus nor mocked as a fool by the Greek playwright, but offered, rather, as a tragic pattern of man's relationship to the governing powers of the natural universe. Whereas the Bible, in its spirit of priestly piety, recognizing equally the tension between God and man, stands on the side of God and breaks not only man's will but the serpent's too. (*Masks: Primitive,* pp. 231, 273, 279)

The Hieratic City State

Planting for Campbell culminates in the formation of what he calls the "hieratic city state," in which the mystical bond linking all members of the planting community gets magnified. The community, itself enlarged from village to city, becomes the earthly counterpart to a perfectly regulated cosmic order in which everything has a fixed place:

> The whole city, not simply the temple area, was now conceived as an imitation on earth of the cosmic order, a sociological "middle cosmos," or mesocosm, established by priestcraft between the macrocosm of the universe and the microcosm of the individual, making visible the one essential form of all. The king was the center, as a human representative of the power made celestially manifest either in the sun or in the moon, according to the focus of the local cult; the walled city was organized architecturally in the design of a quartered circle, . . . centered around the pivotal sanctum of the palace or ziggurat; . . . and there was a mathematically structured calendar to regulate the seasons of the city's life according to the passages of the sun and moon among the stars—as well as a highly developed system of liturgical arts, including music, the art rendering audible to human ears the world-ordering harmony of the celestial spheres. (*Masks: Primitive*, p. 147)

The hieratic city state originated in Sumer and spread from there nearly everywhere else: to Egypt, Crete, Greece, India, China, and even Peru and Mexico. While Campbell attributes planting myths, like hunting myths, to the independent economic experiences of each planting society, he attributes to diffusion the similarities among those planting myths that assume the hieratic outlook.

When, in subsequent volumes of *Masks*, Campbell describes the Eastern view, it involves four basic beliefs: (1) human matriarchy, (2) divine matriarchy, (3) human as well as divine immortality, and (4) the mystical unity of gods with humans. Planting in general embodies the first three of these beliefs. The hieratic city state embodies the fourth. It is, then, easy to see how Campbell can proceed to associate planters with the East.

To whatever extent Campbell in *Masks: Primitive* is not collapsing hunters into planters, he is praising planters and scorning hunters: planters for their participation in a social and cosmic community, hunters for their self-centered individuality. To whatever extent in the next two volumes of *Masks* he is not collapsing the West into the East, he is similarly lauding the East and damning the West on comparable grounds. Yet in volume four of *Masks* Campbell *celebrates* the individuality of the modern West and castigates its absence in other societies. To whatever extent Campbell in *Masks* is associating hunters with the West and planters with the East, his new praise of the West over the East means new praise for hunters over planters. In a separate essay[5] he most fully associates the outlook of the modern West with that of primitive hunters, and in praising the one he is therefore praising the other.

NOTES

[1]On primitive hunters and planters see also Campbell, *Flight of the Wild Gander,* ch. 5; *Myths to Live By,* pp. 30–42, 55–56, 175–178; "Joseph Campbell on the Great Goddess," *Parabola,* 5 (November 1980), pp. 75–81; "Myths from West to East," in Alexander Eliot, *Myths,* with contributions by Mircea Eliade and Campbell (New York: McGraw-Hill, 1976), pp. 34–35; *Atlas,* I–II.

[2]See, for example, Campbell, *Masks: Creative,* pp. 71–72.

[3]Strictly, Schmidt distinguishes three stages. The most primitive, which Campbell skips, is that of hunters, but both male and female; the next, still primitive, is of exclusively male hunters, whose rule constitutes patriarchy; the third is of female farmers, whose rule constitutes matriarchy.

[4]See James G. Frazer, *The Golden Bough,* one-vol. abridgment (London: Macmillan, 1922), chs. 24–26.

[5]See Campbell, ''The Symbol without Meaning,'' in his *Flight of the Wild Gander,* ch. 5.

... with ... ... from their ...
... Camp [illegible] ... ... pp. ... ...

CHAPTER FIVE

THE MASKS OF GOD: OCCIDENTAL MYTHOLOGY

Masks: Occidental Mythology appeared after *Masks: Oriental Mythology,* but it is closer in spirit to the first volume of *Masks* and will therefore be considered next.

In *Masks: Occidental* Campbell argues that the differences between the myths of the West and those of the East[1] reflect differing kinds of societies. Rather than investigating any societies themselves, Campbell analyzes their myths, which he takes for granted reflect the societies that produced them. Even though he continually lambastes those who read myths as history,[2] he himself uses myths to reconstruct at least the values of the societies that created them.

Western Mythology as Patriarchal

Eastern mythology, according to Campbell, reflects a matriarchal society,[3] for the chief gods are female. Western mythology reflects a patriarchal society because its chief gods are male. At the same time Eastern society is egalitarian. More precisely, it is undifferentiated into males and females, for male and female gods are somehow also mystically one. By contrast, Western society is divided as well as hierarchical, for male gods are necessarily distinct from their female subordinates (*Masks: Occidental*, pp. 26–27, 254).

Eastern mythology espouses the identity not just of male with female gods but also of all gods with humans, who are therefore gods themselves. Western mythology, by contrast, maintains a rigid division not just between male and female gods but also between gods and humans, whose worst offense is to seek to become gods themselves:

> But the ultimate realizations differ, according, on one hand, to those [Eastern] cults in which divinity is seen as at once immanent and transcendent, and on the other, to the orthodox [Western] Zoroastrian, Jewish, Christian, and Mohammedan liturgies, where the ontological distinction is retained between God and Man, Creator and Creature. In cults of the former type the two strengths, "outside" and "within," are finally to be recognized as identical. The savior worshiped as without, though indeed without, is at the same time one's self. "All things are Buddha things." Whereas in the great Near Eastern orthodoxies no such identity can be imagined or even credited as conceivable. The aim is not to come to a realization of one's self, here and now, as of one mystery with the Being of beings, but to know, love, and serve in this world a God who is apart. . . . (*Masks: Occidental*, p. 254)

From the identity of humans with gods comes, for Campbell, the Eastern belief in immortality. The West bars this belief because of the Western stress on the divide between humans and gods. For both East and West, to be divine is to be immortal.

Campbell defines immortality narrowly. For him, gods are immortal because they never die. Humans are immortal either whenever they, too, never die, as would have happened to Adam and Eve if they had not disobeyed, or when, having died, they are reborn into other bodies, as much of the East believes. For Campbell, humans are merely mortal either when the soul alone survives the death of the body, as in Hades and in popular Christian conceptions of the afterlife, or when the soul is reunited with its former body, as in the Biblical conception of the resurrection. Others would consider both of these fates cases of immortality.

Western Mythology as Originally Matriarchal

On the one hand Campbell says that Western mythology is patriarchal. On the other hand he argues that the West was originally matriarchal. He contends that even if archaic and classical Greece were patriarchal, primitive Greece was matriarchal. Likewise the ancient, or most ancient, Near East was matriarchal:

Jane Ellen Harrison demonstrated over half a century ago that in the field festivals and mystery cults of Greece numerous vestiges survived of a pre-Homeric mythology in which the place of honor was held, not by the male gods of the sunny Olympic pantheon, but by a goddess, darkly ominous, who might appear as one, two, three, or many, and was the mother of both the living and the dead. . . .

Thus we perceive that in this early mythic system of the nuclear Near East—in contrast to the later, strictly patriarchal system of the Bible—divinity could be represented as well under feminine as under masculine form. . . . (*Masks: Occidental*, pp. 13, 17)

The Biblical opposition to immortality represents a later, patriarchal aversion to a more ancient matriarchal belief in it:

No one familiar with the mythologies of the goddess of the primitive, ancient, and Oriental worlds can turn to the Bible without recognizing counterparts on every page, transformed, however, to render an argument contrary to the older faiths. In Eve's scene at the tree, for example, nothing is said to indicate that the serpent who appeared and spoke to her was a deity in his own right, who had been revered in the Levant for at least seven thousand years before the composition of the Book of Genesis. . . . The wonderful ability of the serpent to slough its skin and so renew its youth has earned for it throughout the world the character of the master of the mystery of rebirth. . . . (*Masks: Occidental*, p. 9)

Conflicts within myths between female and male gods Campbell interprets as expressions of the transition from matriarchy to patriarchy. For the male gods invariably defeat the female ones. To cite two of his examples, both the Babylonian creation story, the *Enuma Elish,* and the Greek creation story, the *Theogony,* begin with female rule and end with male rule:

The best-known mythic statement of this victory of
the sun-god over the goddess and her spouse is the
Babylonian epic of the victory of Marduk over his
great-great-great-grandmother Tiamat, which appears to have been composed either in, or shortly
following, the period of Hammurabi himself.
(*Masks: Occidental*, p. 75)

We have already watched [in Hesiod's *Theogony*]
Olympian Zeus conquer the serpent son and con-
sort of the goddess-mother Gaea. Let us now ob-
serve his behavior toward the numerous pretty
young goddesses he met when he came, as it were,
to gay Paree. Everyone has read of his mad turning of himself into bulls, serpents, swans, and
showers of gold. . . . The particular problem
faced by Zeus . . . was simply that wherever the
Greeks came, in every valley, every isle, and
every cove, there was a local manifestation of the
goddess-mother of the world whom he, as the
great god of the patriarchal order, had to master
in a patriarchal way. (*Masks: Occidental*, pp. 148–
149)

In candor, one must point out that in both myths the
chief conflict is less between females and males than
between one generation and another. In the *Enuma
Elish*[4] it is Apsu, Tiamat's husband, who starts the
conflict: he seeks to kill the younger gods because of
the noise they are making. Even though their noise is
disturbing his wife as well, she, as their mother, ob-
jects to the proposed solution. Discovering the scheme,
the male Ea, one of the younger gods, kills the male
Apsu and imprisons his vizier, the male Mummu. Only
upon the death of Apsu does Tiamat turn against the
younger gods. Even if the younger gods are all male—
they are repeatedly identified as Apsu and her

"sons"—not all of the gods on Tiamat's side are female. Notably, Kingu becomes her husband after the death of Apsu. Even if the male Marduk, upon defeating Tiamat, rules alone, he has defeated a combination of male and female gods. The conflict is more "generational" than sexual: the older gods, male and female alike, cannot stand the noise of the younger ones.

The prime conflict in the *Theogony*[5] is even more "generational." In the *Enuma Elish* the principal antagonists are at least female and male: Tiamat and Marduk, her great-great-grandson. In the *Theogony* the principal antagonists are fathers and sons, and the main conflict is Oedipal: fathers, fearing toppling by their sons, try to keep their children from being born. The sons retaliate and topple their father. Zeus' chief adversary is thus his father, Cronus, not his mother, Rhea, just as his father's prime adversary had been his father, Sky, not his mother, Earth. Certainly there is matrimonial as well as generational conflict: both between Earth and Sky and between Rhea and Cronus. But the matrimonial strife is the consequence of the generational one: the mother sides with her children against their father. Even if by the end male supremacy has replaced female, Zeus rules not alone, like Marduk, but with many wives: the initial power of the females, while subordinated to that of Zeus, remains. As much a synthesis as a revolution has occurred: male gods rule alongside female gods, not in place of them.

For Campbell, the evidence of the completeness of the triumph of the male gods is their ability to perform the female function of birth:

In the patriarchal cosmogonies, for example, the normal imagery of divine motherhood is taken over by the father, and we find such motifs as, in India, the World Lotus growing from the reclining [male] god Vishnu's navel. . . . Or in the Classical image of Zeus bearing Athene from his brain: . . . as the woman gives birth from the womb, so the father from his brain. Creation by the power of the Word is anther instance of such a transfer to the male womb: the mouth the vagina, the word the birth. (*Masks: Occidental,* p. 157)

Likewise in Genesis (1.2) God has supplanted his female opponent, the deep (*Masks: Occidental,* pp. 85–86).

Female gods get reduced to not just the subordinates of males but their evil nemeses:

In the older mother myths and rites the light and darker aspects of the mixed thing that is life had been honored equally and together, whereas in the later, male-oriented, patriarchal myths, all that is good and noble was attributed to the new, heroic master gods, leaving to the native nature powers the character only of darkness—to which, also, a negative moral judgment now was added. (*Masks: Occidental,* p. 21)

Campbell equates femininity with changelessness and passivity and masculinity with change and ambition. As he says of the gods of the *Enuma Elish:*

In the [matriarchal] triad of Apsu, Mummu, and Tiamat . . . the non-dual state antecedent to creation is symbolized, out of which all forms . . . are derived. But in the new [patriarchal] mythology of the great gods the plane of attention has been shifted to the foreground figures of duality and combat, power, profit and loss, where the mind of the man of action normally dwells. Whereas the aim of the earlier mythology had been to support a state of indifference to the modalities of time and identification with the inhabiting non-dual mystery of all being, that of the new was just the opposite: to foster action in the field of time. . . . (*Masks: Occidental,* p. 78)

Campbell goes so far as to associate masculinity with the ego itself, so that, by contrast, Eastern mythology expresses a yearning to dissolve the ego and return to the unconscious:

In both Greece and India a dialogue had been permitted to occur between the two contrary orders of patriarchal and matriarchal thought, such as in the biblical tradition was deliberately suppressed in favor exclusively of the male. However, although in both Greece and India this interplay had been fostered, the results in the two provinces were not the same. In India the power of the goddess-mother finally prevailed to such a degree that the principle of masculine ego initiative was suppressed, even to the point of dissolving the will to individual life; whereas in Greece the masculine will and ego not only held their own, but prospered in a manner that at that time was unique in the world. . . . (*Masks: Occidental,* pp. 173–174)

Where the masculine goal is to break free of the mother goddess and establish one's independence, the feminine goal is to return to her and become mystically reunited with her:

. . . neither to the patriarchal Aryans nor to the patriarchal Semites belong the genial, mystic, poetic themes of the lovely world of a paradise neither lost nor regained but ever present in the bosom of the goddess-mother in whose being we have our death, as well as life, without fear. (*Masks: Occidental*, p. 54)

Western Mythology as Really Matriarchal

Just as Campbell distinguishes sharply between hunting and planting mythologies yet collapses hunting into planting, so he distinguishes rigidly between Western and Eastern mythology yet reduces Western mythology to an artifice "masking" its true, Eastern nature. Western mythology at once reflects the triumph of patriarchy over matriarchy and expresses the inevitable return of matriarchy.

On the one hand Campbell thus says, as noted, that Hesiod's *Theogony* describes the triumph of male gods, led by Zeus, over once dominant female gods, led by Earth. On the other hand he says that the triumph is an illusion. Female gods remain powerful:

The victory of the patriarchal deities over the earlier matriarchal ones was not as decisive in the Greco-Roman sphere as in the myths of the Old Testament. . . . For in Greece the patriarchal gods did not exterminate, but married, the goddesses of the land, and these succeeded ultimately in regaining influence, whereas in biblical mythology all the goddesses were exterminated—or, at least, were supposed to have been. However, as we read in every chapter of the book of Samuel and Kings, the old fertility cults continued to be honored throughout Israel, both by the people and by the majority of their rulers. (*Masks: Occidental*, pp. 28–29)

In the *Theogony* the Titans, presently imprisoned in Tartarus, may one day escape and challenge Zeus anew. As the enemies of the patriarchal Zeus, they get tied by Campbell to matriarchy. Even after his earlier defeat of them Zeus had to defeat Earth's son Typhon, who similarly remains merely imprisoned, not dead. Zeus will one day have to fight the prophesied son of Metis. Earth herself remains both free and, either directly or through her present successor, Hera, in power. Whether it is female gods or older ones who retain power is, however, still the question.

In the Babylonian *Gilgamesh Epic* as well, according to Campbell, female gods retain power even after their seeming defeat by male gods. The goddess Aruru gets revenge on Gilgamesh, the agent of male gods, by denying him immortality:

"The plant is like a buckthorn," Ut-napishtim had told him. "Its thorns will tear your hands; but if your hands can pluck it, you will gain new life." At a point midway, the boat paused. Gilgamesh tied heavy stones to his feet, which drew him down into the deep. He spied the plant. It tore his hands. But he plucked it, cut away those stones, and returning to the surface, boarded, and made for shore. . . . But when he had landed and was on his way, he paused by a freshet for the night; and when he went to bathe, a serpent, sniffing the fragrance of the plant, came out of the water, took the plant, returned to its abode and, consuming it, shed its skin. Whereat Gilgamesh—sat down and wept. And that is why the Serpent Power of Immortal Life, which formerly was known as a property of man, was taken away and now remains apart—in the keep of the cursed serpent and defamed goddess, in the lost paradise of the innocence of fear. (*Masks: Occidental*, p. 92)

Yet again in candor, one must note that in the *Gilgamesh Epic*,[6] as in the *Enuma Elish* and the *Theogony*, the central issue is not gender. The myth does not say that the chief gods were once female; that even the present chief gods are necessarily male; that there is any conflict between male and female gods; that Gilgamesh is the representative of male gods; that the female Aruru is his enemy; that Aruru creates his rival Enkidu for any reason other than to placate Gilgamesh's subjects, male and female alike; that the serpent, which steals the plant bestowing eternal youth, is an agent or symbol of Aruru; that humanity possessed immortality during matriarchy and that a defeated matriarchy withdrew immortality to punish humanity when patriarchy displaced it; or that Gilgamesh individually loses the chance for immortality as punishment by any gods. On the contrary, the story is arguing that humans are by nature mortal, have always been so, and must accept the fact, as Gilgamesh is continually urged to do and in the end may do. Gilgamesh's inability to remain awake for six days is meant to say that he could never have secured immortality.

Utnapishtim is an exception: alone saved from the Flood because he was the favorite of Ea, he and his wife got immortality only because Enlil felt guilty for having destroyed humanity and, in addition, wanted sacrifices. Utnapishtim did not get immortality as a reward, and Gilgamesh did not lose it as punishment. The gods *could* have created humans immortal but chose to make them mortal in order to preserve divine superiority. Mortality is therefore the human condition, not simply the present one, let alone one resulting from the revenge of spiteful fallen gods.

Campbell interprets the Garden of Eden story (Genesis 3) as a similar expression of continuing challenges to patriarchy. Equating Eve with a female god, he maintains that her rebellion against God represents an attempt by defeated female gods to regain their rule—the male serpent and Adam somehow being a part of the rebellion. Campbell does grant that this particular rebellion fails. Keeping the trio from becoming gods themselves, God thereby re-establishes patriarchy:

> Thus Yahweh cursed the woman to bring forth in pain and be subject to her spouse—which set the seal of the patriarchy on the new age. And he cursed, also, the man who had come to the tree and eaten of the fruit that she presented. (*Masks: Occidental*, p. 29)

But Campbell then suggests that the earth to which Adam and Eve will, as dust, be returning at death symbolizes the mother goddess, who, in receiving back her children, triumphs over God. Campbell even suggests that at death Adam and Eve will again become one—Eve having emerged from Adam's rib. The reunion of male with female is simply an alternative to female dominance as the expression of triumphant matriarchy:

But the ground, the dust, out of which the punished couple had been taken, was, of course, the goddess Earth, deprived of her anthropomorphic features, yet retaining in her elemental aspect her function of furnishing the substance into which the new spouse, Yahweh, had breathed the breath of her children's life. And they were to return to her, not to the father, in death. Out of her they had been taken, and to her they would return. Like the Titans of the older faith, Adam and Eve were thus the children of the mother-goddess Earth. They had been one at first, as Adam; then split in two, as Adam and Eve. . . . "The man," we read, "called his wife's name Eve, because she was the mother of all living." As the mother of all living, Eve herself, then, must be recognized as the missing anthropomorphic aspect of the mother-goddess. And Adam, therefore, must have been her son as well as spouse: for the legend of the rib is clearly a patriarchal inversion (giving preference to the male) of the earlier myth of the hero born from the goddess Earth [i.e., Eve], who returns to her to be reborn. (*Masks: Occidental*, pp. 29–30)

Even if the Bible were somehow interpretable as depicting the ultimate victory of matriarchy over patriarchy, would it also be interpretable as praising rather than condemning that victory? If not, is not the Bible still preaching patriarchy? There *are* interpretations of the Bible, above all by ancient heretical Christians called Gnostics,[7] which make God an evil power and the serpent the savior of humanity. Those interpretations support Campbell's, though even they do not make the conflict one of gender. But they seem to be more rewritings than reinterpretations.

Aware of this difficulty, Campbell argues that the

Bible does not understand its own true nature. The capacity of later Christians to extract from the story the doctrine of the "fortunate fall" proves to him that the Bible is really praising Adam and Eve for rebelling against a tyrannical god. The condemnation of them is only a later, patriarchal invention, which "masks" the true, pristine, matriarchal endorsement of them:

> . . . it is certain that the ninth- and fourth-century
> B.C. shapers of this tale had no such adventurous
> thought in mind—though something similar is implicit in the Roman Catholic idea that "the essence of the Bible story is that the Fall, the disintegration, is permitted in order that a greater good may come." (*Masks: Occidental,* p. 110)

Just as Campbell detects a matriarchal message in Genesis 3, so he detects one in Genesis 1. From the verse "God created man in his own image; . . . male and female he created them" (1.27), he, like many other interpreters, infers that God himself is both male and female: "And finally, if, when made in the image of Elohim, Adam and Eve appeared together, then Elohim must have been not male alone but androgyne . . ." (*Masks: Occidental,* p. 112). Because that unity of male and female is for Campbell an alternative to female dominance as a form of matriarchy, the androgyny of God makes God himself a matriarchal rather than patriarchal figure.

If Campbell can show that even the Hebrew Bible, for him the staunchest bastion of patriarchy, sanctions matriarchy, then he can show that matriarchy is truly panhuman and that all mythology, which reflects society, is therefore at heart matriarchal as well.

Patriarchal and Matriarchal Heroism

In *Hero* all heroes may be male, but they are not therefore all Western. On the contrary, they are universal.
Because Campbell in *Masks: Occidental* equates masculinity with the West, heroism, as a distinctively male
endeavor, now becomes a distinctively Western one as
well:

> Hence, the early Iron Age literatures both of Aryan
> Greece and Rome and of the neighboring Semitic
> Levant are alive with variants of the conquest by a
> shining hero of the dark and—for one reason or
> another—disparaged monster of the earlier order of
> godhood, from whose coils some treasure was to
> be won: a fair land, a maid, a boon of gold, or
> simply freedom from the tyranny of the impugned
> monster itself. (*Masks: Occidental,* p. 22)

In *Hero* heroism means less conquest than boldness:
the hero is heroic not because he defeats enemies but
because he ventures to an unknown land. Indeed, far
from defeating its occupants, he becomes one with
them. In *Masks: Occidental* heroism means conquest,
of female gods above all. In *Hero* the hero is selfless—
he returns home only to aid his countrymen. In *Masks:
Occidental* the hero is self-centered—he fights only for
himself.

Yet when, as quoted (*Masks: Occidental,* p. 30),
Campbell calls Adam, an agent of Earth, a "hero,"
he is clearly no longer restricting heroism to patriarchy
and is in this respect reverting to the universal view

of *Hero*. But in characterizing Adam's heroism as that of conquest rather than adventurousness, he is retaining the outlook of *Masks: Occidental*: Adam is heroic because he steals what God has forbidden him to take. Campbell even types him as a heroic slayer of monsters:

> There is an interesting use of the One Forbidden Road motif in certain primitive monster-slayer myths, where the young hero deliberately violates the taboo, which has been given to protect him, and so enters the field of one or more malignant powers, whom he overcomes, to release mankind from their oppression. One could reread the episode in the Garden from such a point of view and find that it was not God but Adam and Eve to whom we owe the great world of the realities of life. (*Masks: Occidental,* p. 110)

In the irenic *Hero* God would be beckoning Adam to partake of the Trees of Knowledge and Life and thereby become divine himself: divinity would be the "boon" to be disseminated to the rest of humanity. In the bellicose *Masks: Occidental* Adam is, like Prometheus, at war with God, who opposes his quest for divinity. Yet Adam, as a matriarchal hero, remains at peace with the mother goddess, to whom, as quoted (*Masks: Occidental,* p. 30), he longs to return. While Campbell does say that the hero returns to her in order to be reborn, Campbell's stress on the hero's mystical oneness with the mother goddess undercuts any striving for independence suggested by rebirth:

> . . . the sense of accord remained between the questing hero and the powers of the living world, who, like himself, were ultimately but transforma-

tions of the one mystery of being. Thus in the Buddha legend, as in the old Near Eastern seals, an atmosphere of substantial accord prevails at the cosmic tree, where the goddess and her serpent spouse give support to their worthy son's quest for release from the bondages of birth, disease, old age, and death. (*Masks: Occidental,* p. 16)

The hero's mystical goal in *Masks: Occidental* is actually no different from that in *Hero.* In *Hero* the hero seemingly seeks to leave the strange new world and return to the everyday one, but in fact he returns only because he finds there the new world, in which case he is not really returning at all. If the hero in *Hero* really did break free of the new world, he would be breaking free of the mother and thereby of the equivalent in *Hero* of matriarchy. One could, then, call him a patriarchal hero. Because the hero actually remains bound to the new world, he remains bound to the equivalent of matriarchy. In *Hero* Campbell never characterizes either liberation or return as either patriarchal or matriarchal because he deems the hero the ideal of every society, not just either patriarchal or matriarchal ones. But the goal is the same mystical, hence matriarchal, one of *Masks: Occidental.*

Campbell and Bachofen on Matriarchy

Campbell's distinction between matriarchy and patriarchy derives ultimately from the classic distinction first drawn in the nineteenth century by J. J. Bachofen. Even though Campbell oddly never mentions Bachofen in *Masks*, he later wrote the introduction to a selection of his writings.[8] In *Mutterrecht* and other works Bachofen argues that prior to the present state of patriarchy, which has existed for so long as to seem natural, there was a state of matriarchy, or "mother right"—a term Campbell uses in *Masks: Occidental* (pp. 22, 34) but never attributes to Bachofen. Like Campbell, Bachofen associates matriarchy with the East and patriarchy with the West. For Bachofen, matriarchy existed in not only Asia and Africa but also the Near East and Greece until the emergence of Israel and Athens. Patriarchy began in classical Greece and established itself firmly in Rome, from which it spread elsewhere.

Bachofen characterizes matriarchy and patriarchy in ways comparable with Campbell's. In matriarchy the chief gods are female; in patriarchy, male. Although Bachofen stresses the point far more, for him, as for Campbell, female gods are earth gods and male gods sky and sun gods. For Bachofen, Demeter is the classic matriarchal god and Apollo the classic patriarchal one.

Bachofen, like Campbell, characterizes femininity and masculinity in stereotyped ways. For both, the prime matriarchal values are changelessness, passivity, peace, selflessness, and equality. The prime patriarchal ones are change, activity, ambition, fighting, self-centeredness, and hierarchy. If matriarchy means female dominance, it also means the equality of males and females. Campbell carries matriarchal equality further than Bachofen to outright unity, and the unity of humans with gods as well as of male with female gods. Because matriarchy for Bachofen does not espouse unity, it is far less mystical than it is for Campbell. Bachofen, for his part, carries selflessness further than Campbell to universal love. For both, patriarchal hierarchy means the subordination both of females to males and of humans to gods. Bachofen equates self-centeredness with nationalism.

In *Hero* the myths of even exclusively male heroes preach matriarchal values. In *Masks: Occidental* hero myths are, as for Bachofen, conspicuously patriarchal: they applaud the grandest strivings of their always male protagonists. Where, as noted, Campbell allows for matriarchal heroes, those heroes seek only to return to the pristine state of unity with the mother goddess.

Bachofen is interested in the matriarchal and patriarchal societies that produced their accompanying myths. Campbell, while assuming that the myths reflect the societies that produced them, is far more interested in the myths themselves. Hence he is not at all, like Bachofen, interested in matriarchal and patriarchal institutions—for example, those of inheritance and law. Campbell views matriarchy and patriarchy as less political than psychological entities: they represent aspects of all humans. Matriarchy means the primacy of the female side in all humans; patriarchy, the primacy of the male.

Bachofen deems the shift from matriarchy to patriarchy a real one. Campbell deems it a superficial one. While there have been patriarchal societies, which patriarchal myths reflect, they have been artificial departures from the essentially matriarchal character of males and females alike. The attempt to deny that character is vain, so that Campbell, unlike Bachofen, is concerned to show myths in which matriarchy finally triumphs. Where for Campbell patriarchy only seemingly triumphs, for Bachofen it actually does.

For example, Bachofen interprets Aeschylus' trilogy, the *Oresteia,* as a depiction of the actual triumph of patriarchy over matriarchy: Apollo, Athena, and ultimately Zeus vanquish the Furies, who, if placated, nevertheless cede their matriarchal revenge. By contrast, Campbell would surely interpret the place accorded the Furies as evidence of their ultimate triumph.

For Campbell, matriarchy alone fulfills human nature. For Bachofen, despite his undeniable yearning for the lost matriarchal age, patriarchy is higher. It represents the elevation of spirit over matter, of reason over emotion, and of striving over passivity.

Western and Hunting Mythologies, Eastern and Planting Ones

It is not clear whether Campbell is outright equating Western mythology with that of primitive hunting and Eastern mythology with that of primitive planting. Seemingly, the pairs are distinct. Hunting and planting mythologies are those of nonliterate cultures. Western and Eastern mythologies are those of literate ones. Campbell ties hunting and planting mythologies to economics. He treats Western and Eastern mythologies as autonomous sets of beliefs.

Still, the beliefs of hunting and planting mythologies are at least close to those of Western and Eastern mythologies. Campbell associates both hunting and Western mythologies with patriarchy, divine and human alike. Because he does not link Western and Eastern mythologies to economics, he does not link Western mythology to a male occupation, the way he considers hunting a male preserve. But he does associate both hunting and Western mythologies with politics: males rule both in heaven and on earth. Similarly, Campbell associates both planting and Eastern mythologies with matriarchy, divine and human alike. Even if he does not associate Eastern mythology with planting, he does deem the chief gods of both mythologies gods of earth and fertility (*Masks: Occidental,* pp. 22, 26, 29).

Furthermore, Campbell associates both hunting and Western mythologies with aggression and both planting and Eastern mythologies with peace. Where hunters kill for food, planters grow theirs. Though again Campbell draws no economic parallels, he does say analogously that where patriarchy in Western mythology requires the violent toppling of an original matriarchy, Eastern matriarchy, while fighting back, rules peacefully during its tenure. Since in *Masks: Primitive* Campbell considers patriarchy an earlier and not, as in *Masks: Occidental,* a later stage than matriarchy,[9] he does not there appeal to the means of its emergence as an argument for its tie to violence.

Campbell also links both hunting and Western mythologies to self-centeredness and individuality and both planting and Eastern mythologies to selflessness and community. Where hunters hunt individually, planters plant in a group. Where the Western hero fights only for himself, the Eastern one, if there is one, fights for others.

Where hunters and hunted stand pitted against each other, planters and planted are part of a single community. There is a mystical bond not just between planters and planted but also between them and the sacrifices offered by them to spur the growth of plants—a bond that, as noted, Campbell in turn attributes to hunters and hunted as well. Analogously, where in Western mythology male gods stand above not only female gods but also all humans, in Eastern mythology female gods are mystically one with not only male gods but also humans. Confining himself to the relations between primitives and the sources of their food, Campbell does not discuss the relations between primitives and gods. Whether it is possible to extrapolate from the one relationship to the other it is hard to say, in which case it is hard to say whether the beliefs of hunting and planting mythologies match those of Western and Eastern ones.

Finally, Campbell associates both hunting and Western mythologies with mortality and both planting and Eastern mythologies with immortality. Where the hunted dies, the planted is annually reborn— further distinctions that, as noted, Campbell then qualifies if not virtually denies. Where in Western mythology humans are distinct from gods and are therefore, by Campbell's definition, mortal, in Eastern mythology they are gods themselves and are therefore immortal. Because, again, Campbell concentrates on the relations between primitives and the sources of their food, he deals with the longevity of those sources themselves, not of humans. Whether it is possible to extrapolate from the longevity of those sources to that of humans themselves it is hard to say, in which case it is, again, hard to say whether the beliefs of hunting and planting mythologies truly parallel those of Western and Eastern ones. If they do, and if Campbell is saying that planters are really hunters and Westerners really Easterners, and if, in addition, he is saying that what he calls "creative mythology" is really only a revival of primitive hunting mythology, then he is indeed saying in *Masks* that all mythology is one.

One assertion that Campbell makes at the outset of *Masks: Occidental* does identify the East with primitive planting. He says that primitive planting culminated in the "hieratic city state" of Sumer, from which it spread to both the West and the East. But he also says that the East, unlike the West (*Masks: Occidental*, p. 7), was untouched by Semitic and Aryan invaders and thereby retained the outlook of the hieratic city state:

> Nothing quite of the kind has ever seriously troubled the mentality of the Orient east of Iran, where the old hieratic Bronze Age cosmology of the ever-circling eons—static yet turning ever, in a round of mathematical impersonality, from everlasting to everlasting—endures to this day as the last word on the universe and the place of man within it. . . . [T]his Bronze Age image of the cosmos, still intact in the Orient, renders a fixed world of fixed duties, roles, and possibilities: not a process, but a state; and the individual, whether man or god, is but a flash among the facets. (*Masks: Occidental*, p. 6)

Here Campbell is explicitly equating the East with planting, whether or not the West with hunting.

Yet Campbell also typically argues that the planting outlook was never really extinguished by the Semitic and Aryan conquerers of the Near East and Europe. Rather, the Westerners were themselves assimilated,[10] so that the planting, which is to say Eastern, outlook remained. The Eastern outlook thus proves universal—save for any surviving descendants of primitive hunters.

NOTES

[1] On the differences between the West and the East see, in addition to *Masks*, Campbell, *Flight of the Wild Gander*, pp. 195–207; *Myths to Live By*, chs. 4, 5; "The Occult in Myth and Literature," in *Literature and the Occult*,, ed. Luanne Frank (Arlington: University of Texas at Arlington, 1977), pp. 4–12.

[2] See, for example, Campbell, *Myths to Live By*, ch. 1.

[3] Yet in his essay "Joseph Campbell on the Great Goddess" (*Parabola*, 5 [November 1980], p. 77) Campbell declares, most surprisingly, that while through planting "the prestige of women in the villages became enlarged," he "doubts" that "there was ever anything on earth like a matriarchy. . . ."

[4] See "The Creation Myth," tr. E. A. Speiser, in *Ancient Near Eastern Texts*, ed. James B. Pritchard, third ed. (Princeton, NJ: Princeton University Press, 1969), pp. 60–72.

[5] See Hesiod, *Theogony*, tr. Richmond Lattimore, in *Hesiod*, ed. and tr. Lattimore (Ann Arbor: University of Michigan Press, 1959), pp. 119–186.

[6] See "The Epic of Gilgamesh," tr. E. A. Speiser, in *Ancient Near Eastern Texts*, ed. Pritchard, pp. 72–99.

[7] See, for example, Hans Jonas, *The Gnostic Religion*, second ed. (Boston: Beacon, 1963), pp. 92–94.

[8] Campbell, introduction to *Myth, Religion, and Mother Right: Selected Writings of J. J. Bachofen*, tr. Ralph Manheim (Princeton, NJ: Princeton University Press, 1967), pp. xxv–lvii. Campbell also mentions Bachofen in his introduction to Helen Diner, *Mother and Amazons*, ed. and tr. John Philip Lundin (New York: Julian, 1965), pp. vii–ix.

[9] In "Joseph Campbell on the Great Goddess" (pp. 75–82) Campbell in effect resolves this seeming inconsistency by arguing for three stages: first, that of primitive hunters, who are patriarchal; next, that of both primitive planters and

their Eastern descendants—both being matriarchal; and then that of Western warriors. In *Masks: Occidental,* as already quoted (pp. 5–6), Campbell says that the East continues the tradition of primitive planters, but only in ''Joseph Campbell on the Great Goddess'' does he in effect fuse the two stages into one.

[10]But in ''Joseph Campbell on the Great Goddess'' (pp. 82–84) Campbell says that the Semitic tradition differed from its Indo-European counterpart in resisting the assimilation.

CHAPTER SIX

THE MASKS OF GOD: ORIENTAL MYTHOLOGY

In *Masks: Oriental* Campbell makes the same basic distinctions as in *Masks: Occidental*, but his emphases are different. In *Masks: Occidental* the fundamental difference between West and East is that between patriarchy and matriarchy. From this difference, which for Campbell is one of values rather than of form of society, derive all the other differences:

(1) the stress in the West on the domination of male gods over female gods and of gods over humans; the stress in the East on the equality of all gods and of gods with humans;

(2) hierarchy aside, the stress in the West on the distinction between male and female gods and between gods and humans; the stress in the East on the mystical oneness of all of them;

(3) the emphasis in the West on human mortality; the emphasis in the East on immortality;

(4) the stress in the West on ambition and aggression; the stress in the East on passivity and peace;

(5) the commitment in the West to heroism; the indifference to it in the East, at least when heroism takes the form of ambition and striving; and

(6) in psychological terms, the desire in the West to

develop a strong, independent ego; the desire in the East to dissolve the ego and return to sheer unconsciousness.

In *Masks: Oriental* Campbell gives much less emphasis to the difference between Western patriarchy and Eastern matriarchy. While he does contrast the Western division into male and female to the Eastern unification of the two, he contrasts far more the Western division into divine and human to the Eastern unification of them. He ascribes this difference not to patriarchy and matriarchy but to the stress in the West on distinctions and in the East on the rejection of them. From this fundamental difference come all others, including the difference between patriarchy and matriarchy.

In *Masks: Oriental,* in contrast to *Masks: Occidental,* Campbell does not proceed to deny the differences he enumerates between the West and the East. He does grant that there are exceptions to the distinctions, but he retains the distinctions themselves. As he bluntly puts it, "Two completely opposed mythologies . . . have come together in the modern world" (*Masks: Oriental,* p. 9). Critics might even say that Campbell exaggerates the differences between West and East. For example, they might note the presence of Genghis Khan and the Samurai in the would-be peaceful East. Or they might broaden Campbell's Eastern definition of human immortality as reincarnation to allow as well for Western survival of the soul after the death of the body or resurrection of the dead body.

Differences in
the Concept of Time

The West, according to Campbell, makes distinctions of all kinds. Temporarily, it distinguishes the present from the past and the future from the present. These distinctions permit, if not create, a sense of progress: "A progressive, temporally oriented mythology arose, of a creation, once and for all, at the beginning of time, a subsequent fall, and a work of restoration, still in progress" (*Masks: Oriental*, p. 7). On the one hand the physical world was created rather than is preexistent. There is therefore a distinction between the time before its creation and the time since. On the other hand the physical world will one day be purified rather than dissolve, and the purified world will be different from the pre-fallen one. There is therefore a distinction between the time before its purification and the time after. As Campbell says of the Western outlook of Zoroastrianism:

. . . the Zoroastrian version of the world course presents a creation by a god of pure light into which an evil principle entered, by nature contrary to and independent of the first, so that there is a cosmic battle in progress; which, however, is not to go on forever, but will terminate in a total victory of the light: whereupon the process will end in a perfect realization of the Kingdom of Righteousness on Earth, and there will be no continuation of the cycle. There is no idea here of eternal return. (*Masks: Oriental*, p. 244)

The East, says Campbell, makes no distinctions among past, present, and future. More precisely, it makes no distinction between the past and the future, for the future is only a return to the past. Time is, then, cyclical rather than progressive:

> The myth of eternal return, which is still basic to Oriental life, displays an order of fixed forms that appear and reappear through all time. The daily round of the sun, the waning and waxing moon, the cycle of the year, and the rhythm of organic birth, death, and new birth, represent a miracle of continuous arising that is fundamental to the nature of the universe. We all know the archaic myth of the four ages of gold, silver, bronze, and iron, where the world is shown declining, growing ever worse. It will disintegrate presently in chaos, only to burst forth again, fresh as a flower, to recommence spontaneously the inevitable course. There never was a time when time was not. Nor will there be a time when this kaleidoscopic play of eternity in time will have ceased. (*Masks: Oriental*, p. 3)

Even if there is a distinction between the time before creation and the time since, and even if there is a distinction between the time since and the time of the envisioned end, there is none between the time before creation and the time of the envisioned end. For the end envisioned is the dissolution of creation and the return to the time before it.

Differences in
the Concepts of God and Humanity

According to Campbell, West and East differ over not only temporal distinctions but also spatial and, even more, metaphysical ones. Where in the West god is transcendent, in the East god is immanent. Where in the West god is distinct from humans, in the East humans are identical with god. Where in the West humans strive to obey god, in the East they strive to become god. More precisely, they strive to realize their innate divinity:

> In the Indian version it is the god himself that divides and becomes not man alone but all creation; so that everything is a manifestation of that single inhabiting divine substance: there is no other; whereas in the Bible, God and man, from the beginning, are distinct. Man is made in the image of God, indeed, and the breath of God has been breathed into his nostrils; yet his being, his self, is not that of God, nor is it one with the universe. . . . God is transcendent. . . . The goal . . . has to be, rather, to know the *relationship* of God to his creation, or more specifically, to man, and through such knowledge, by God's grace, to link one's own will back to that of the Creator. (*Masks: Oriental,* pp. 10–11)

This distinction between West and East does not seem exaggerated. The West does stress the gap between humanity and god and is therefore largely non-mystical: ordinarily, its ideal is proximity to god, not union with god. Undeniably, there are both Western mystics and Eastern nonmystics, but mysticism is still an overwhelmingly Eastern phenomenon. Defining the term ''mysticism'' more loosely, many scholars argue that most Western ''mystics'' seek only an encounter with god, not oneness with god. Meister Eckhart and the Gnostics may seek outright oneness, but St. Teresa and St. John of the Cross do not. Even scholars who maintain that Western as well as Eastern mystics seek oneness grant that mysticism is a minor activity in the West and a central one in the East.

For Campbell, a consequence of the separation in the West between humanity and god is that kings are merely human. In the East they are divine. In the West kings may be the representatives of gods and may therefore be higher than other humans, but human they remain. In the East, by contrast, kings are simply humans who have realized their divinity. Campbell thus contrasts the merely human status of later Sumerian kings—earlier ones being part of the Eastern outlook— to the outright divine one of Egyptian kings, whom he considers Eastern:

> For the Mesopotamian [i.e., later Sumerian] kings were no longer, like those of Egypt, gods in themselves. That critical dissociation between the spheres of God and man which in time was to separate decisively the religious systems of the Occident from those of the Orient, had already taken place. The king was no longer a god-king . . . but only the ''vicar'' . . . of the true King, who was the god above. (*Masks: Oriental*, p. 107)

As a striking case of the belief in the divinity of kings Campbell cites (*Masks: Oriental*, pp. 4–5) James

Frazer's description of the ritualistic killing of kings to ensure the continuing health of the god of vegetation residing in them and therefore of vegetation itself.[1] But where Frazer himself considers this practice universal, Campbell restricts it to the East, for it presupposes the belief in the divinity of the king. Where Campbell assumes that in the East all humanity is divine, Frazer restricts divinity worldwide to the king, who for that reason is the only one killed.

Differences in the Concept of Heroism

In *Masks: Oriental*, as in *Masks: Occidental*, heroism is an exclusively Western phenomenon. Where in *Masks: Occidental* Campbell roots heroism in patriarchy and its absence in matriarchy, in *Masks: Oriental* he attributes heroism to the belief in the separation between humanity and god and its absence to the belief in their identity. Striving makes little sense when one is already united with the object of one's striving. Campbell's most telling example of this difference between West and East is the contrast he draws between the individualistic striving of the Aryan invaders, who are Western, and the yearning by the conquered pre-Aryan inhabitants, who are Eastern, for absorption in the cosmos:

> Now, as we have seen, the mythological foundation of the Indus Civilization overthrown by the Aryans appears to have been a variant of the old High Bronze Age vegetal-lunar rhythmic order, wherein a priestly science of the calendar required of all

submission without resistance to an ungainsayable
destiny. The goddess mother in whose macrocos-
mic womb all things were supposed to live their
brief lives was absolute in her sway; and no such
puny sentiment as heroism could hope, in the field
of her dominion, to achieve any serious result. "She
is self-willed," said Ramakrishna, "and must always have her own way." Yet for those children
who submit without tumult to their mother's will,
"she is full of bliss." (*Masks: Oriental*, p. 179)

Differences in
the Concepts of Reality

For Campbell, the West preaches a division not only
between humans and god but also within humans between their bodies and their souls. That division, or
dualism, is a microcosm of the cosmic division between the physical world and a nonphysical one. By
contrast, says Campbell, the East preaches the identity
of the body with the soul. That identity, or monism,
is in turn a microcosm of the identity of the physical
with the nonphysical world.

In fact, the Western outlook is not quite uniformly
dualistic. Insofar as there is dualism in the West, it
typically takes mild rather than radical form. For example, in most of Plato, in Aristotle, and in the Gos-
pels of Matthew and Mark, to cite some central works
of Western culture, the aim of life is merely to subordinate the body to the soul. The aim is to harmonize
the parts of a human being. Where, less often, the
dualism is radical, the aim is to reject the body for the
soul. The aim is to disentangle the parts. Some classic

examples of radical dualism in the West are Plato's *Phaedo*, Apuleius' *Golden Ass,* aspects of the Gospel of John, the Desert Fathers, and above all Gnosticism.

Much of the West, however, is monistic rather than dualistic. Ordinary monism recognizes the existence of only the body. There is barely, if any, soul. Homer, Hesiod, and most of the Hebrew Bible evince ordinary monism. Values are worldly. The aim of life is prosperity, health, power, or even something intangible but still worldly like honor. There is no asceticism. There is a scant afterlife. Hades, for example, is really only a pale shadow of life before death. The body in this life is the prime reality. Where there is a yearning to escape from the body, it is because life is painful, not, as in radical dualism, because life is trivial or meaningless.

Just as dualism represents a stage beyond ordinary monism, so radical monism represents a stage beyond dualism. Like dualism, radical monism takes two forms. Far more frequent in the West, in which radical monism of any kind is hardly plentiful, is radical monism of the tame kind. Here the soul alone is real, and the body is illusory—the reverse of ordinary monism. Valentinian Gnostics and Christian Scientists are examples. Both dismiss the body as not just inferior or even evil but unreal.

The radical variety of radical monism says that the single substance that exists is neither immateriality nor matter but rather a fusion of the two. Immateriality and matter, soul and body, prove to be one and the same. Western believers in this radical form of radical dualism include Meister Eckhart and William Blake.

Dualism, radical or mild, may well, as Campbell says, be far more prevalent in the West than in the East, but in the West ordinary monism may be even more prevalent. Doubtless radical monism is, as Campbell says, the prevailing belief in the East. The tame version is the more common. Virtually all of Hinayana Buddhism and the dominant, Vedantic branch of Hinduism preach the freedom of the soul from the body, which is not, as in dualism, merely inferior or even evil but illusory. Mahayana Buddhism and Tantrism, among various other branches of Hinduism, espouse the radical variety of radical monism. They thereby preach not the rejection of the body for the soul but the experience of the soul in the body—better, of the soul *as* the body.

Masks and Hero

In *Masks* Campbell interprets Eastern myths the way in *Hero* he interprets all myths. Contrary to *Hero*, he now limits heroism to the West. Also contrary to *Hero*, he interprets heroism as striving for individual attainment rather than for absorption in the whole. In *Masks* Campbell says that only the East seeks unity and that heroism assumes individuality.

Yet Campbell's characterization of what in *Hero* he calls universal heroism is almost identical with what in *Masks* he calls distinctively Eastern nonheroism. In both cases the ideal is the radical form of radical monism: the experience of the oneness of the material with the immaterial world and of the body with the soul. As Campbell says of India, which for him, as for others, is the heart of the East:

. . . although the holy mystery and power have been understood to be indeed transcendent, . . . they are also, at the same time, immanent. . . . It is not that the divine is every*where:* it is that the divine is every*thing.* So that one does not require any outside reference, revelation, sacrament, or authorized community to return to it. (*Masks: Oriental,* pp. 12–13)[2]

In *Hero* all but the hero are ordinary monists: they are oblivious to even the possibility of a world beyond the everyday, material one. They scorn the hero for believing otherwise. Before the call even he is oblivious. Were the hero's quest to end with his permanent separation from the everyday world, hero myths would be preaching either radical dualism or the tame variety of radical monism. If they preached that the everyday world is real but simply trivial or even evil, they would be preaching radical dualism. If they preached that the everyday world is outright illusory, they would be preaching radical monism of the tame variety.

For Campbell, hero myths preach instead return to the everyday world. Seemingly, Campbell says that the hero returns wholly selflessly to inform others of the existence of a higher reality, which they should seek by forsaking the everyday one. In that case hero myths would still be espousing either radical dualism or the tame version of radical monism. In actuality, Campbell says that the hero, even in returning selflessly, stays because he discovers the higher reality within the everyday one. Still, "within" can mean distinct from the everyday world, just intertwined with it or even trapped within it. In that case hero myths would clearly be preaching radical dualism. For Campbell, the hero in *Hero* really discovers that the higher reality exists not within but *as* the everyday reality. He discovers that the two realities are one—the radical brand of radical monism that in *Masks* Campbell deems the distinctively Eastern view.

An Illustration of the Different Concepts of Reality

A famous tale from one of the Hindu *Upanishads* best illustrates these different outlooks:

> "Explain more to me, father," said Svetaketu.
>
> "So be it, my son."
>
> "Place this salt in water and come to me tomorrow morning."
>
> Svetaketu did as he was commanded, and in the morning his father said to him: "Bring me the salt you put into the water last night."
>
> Svetaketu looked into the water, but could not find it, for it had dissolved.
>
> His father then said: "Taste the water from this side. How is it?"
>
> "It is salt."
>
> "Taste it from the middle. How is it?"
>
> "It is salt."
>
> "Taste it from the side. How is it?"
>
> "It is salt."
>
> "Look for the salt again and come again to me."
>
> The son did so, saying: "I cannot see the salt. I only see water."
>
> His father then said: "In the same way, O my son, you cannot see the Spirit. But in truth he is here."[3]

Ordinary monists would, strictly, not even taste the salt, which corresponds to immateriality, and would experience only the water, which corresponds to matter. Better, they would not distinguish between the salt and the water. They would consider it all mere water, which simply happened to be salty.

Dualists would distinguish between the salt and the water. They would consider the salt an addition to the water. Mild dualists would merely care more about the salt than about the water. Radical dualists would seek to extricate the salt from the water, which they would then discard.

Radical monists of the tame sort would deny the reality of the water. They would claim that all was salt—the water being an illusion. Extreme radical monists would claim that the two substances were really one: that salt and water were really a single, salt-watery substance, not a mixture of once distinct salt and water.

Svetaketu is preaching this extreme brand of radical monism to his son, who till now has likely been a dualist. Admittedly, the metaphor of salt and water is less than perfect: after all, salt can be added to water and perhaps even extracted from it, and both salt and water are material substances. Still, the point is clear: just as salt ordinarily seems inextricable from water, so immateriality is inextricable from matter, in which case they constitute a single substance.

Only in passing in *Masks: Oriental* does Campbell associate Western mythology with patriarchy and Eastern with matriarchy. Indeed, only by implication does he associate the West with patriarchy, and he links the East less to a matriarchal society than to the supremacy of the mother goddess. As quoted (*Masks: Oriental,* p. 179), he contrasts the independence of the mother sought by the West to the absorption in her sought by the East. In *Masks: Oriental,* as in *Masks: Occidental,* Campbell occasionally ties the East to planting but even less frequently, if at all, the West to hunting.

Campbell "psychologizes" myth far less in any of the volumes of *Masks* than in *Hero.* In *Masks* he uses psychology more as a metaphorical description of myth than as an actual technique for analyzing it. Still, he does say in *Masks: Oriental,* as in *Masks: Occidental* (1964, pp. 173–174), that the Western goal corresponds to the development of the ego and the Eastern one to its dissolution: ". . . spiritual maturity, as understood in the modern Occident, requires a differentiation of *ego* from *id,* whereas in the Orient . . . ego . . . is impugned as the principle of libidinous delusion, to be dissolved" (*Masks: Oriental,* p. 15). Where in *Masks* the dissolution of the ego is a distinctively Eastern goal, in *Hero* it is the universal one.

NOTES

[1] See James G. Frazer, *The Golden Bough,* one-vol. abridgment (London: Macmillan, 1922), chs. 24–26.

[2] To be sure, since Campbell says that the East espouses radical monism of the tame as well as the strong form, to the West's striving in the physical world he sometimes contrasts the East's utter rejection of that world rather than identification of it with the nonphysical world: see his *Masks: Oriental,* pp. 232–233, 244–245.

[3] Chandogya Upanishad, in *The Upanishads,* tr. Juan Mascaro (Harmondsworth, Middlesex, England: Penguin, 1965), pp. 117–118.

CHAPTER SEVEN

THE MASKS OF GOD: CREATIVE MYTHOLOGY

In one central respect *Masks: Creative Mythology* constitutes a break with the rest of *Masks* and a return to *Hero:* in its endorsement of heroism. While Campbell does not discuss heroism in the first volume of *Masks,* in volumes two and three he denigrates it as the epitome of the divisive, self-centered, futile striving of the individualistic West. In contrast to it stands the passive absorption in the whole wisely sought by the East. In volumes two and three of *Masks* the hero strives to conquer the world, not to help others. His striving assumes a gap which he is seeking to overcome: a gap not only between him and others but also between him and god. Ultimately, the hero is seeking to become god. Because the East assumes the identity of not only all humans with one another but also humans with god, it denies the gulf that heroism yearns to overcome.

In *Hero,* by contrast, heroism is a universal, not merely Western, enterprise. The hero is striving for oneness with the cosmos rather than for control over it. He is seeking to realize the oneness he innately has. He is seeking not to become god but to realize his divinity. He is, moreover, acting on behalf of others, not or not just himself. He is still heroic, for he must still undertake a daring journey to an unknown land, but his heroism is peaceful rather than hostile. It evinces the very beliefs that volumes two and three of *Masks* applaud as Eastern and nonheroic.

In several ways volume four of *Masks* represents a return to *Hero*. First, heroism again is universal rather than particularly Western. Second, heroism again is mystical: the hero seeks to realize his oneness with the cosmos rather than to gain control over it. Third, heroism again is selfless rather than self-centered: the hero seeks to share his discovery with others. Fourth, heroism again requires a dangerous trek to a strange world and return from it.

Masks: Creative is not, however, a simple return to *Hero*. Heroism now is "creative." The new, creative hero is not the protagonist of hero myths but his creator.

Following others, Campbell characterizes the period of creative mythology, the middle of the twelfth century on, as one of a loss of faith, at least faith in orthodox, institutionalized Christianity. The modern loss of faith conventionally ascribed to the rise of science Campbell considers a continuation of this earlier one. The consequence of the loss of faith in the late medieval period was the loss of traditional myths, which for Campbell had always been tied to religion. Where, according to Campbell, previous humanity, primitive and Eastern as well as Western, had existing myths to guide it, Westerners since 1150 or so have had to invent their own:

> In the context of a traditional mythology, the symbols are presented in socially maintained rites, through which the individual is required to experience . . . certain insights, sentiments, and commitments. In what I am calling "creative" mythology, on the other hand, this order is reversed: the individual has had an experience of his

own—of order, horror, beauty, or even mere exhil-
aration—which he seeks to communicate through
signs; and if his realization has been of a certain
depth and import, his communication will have the
value and force of living myth—for those, that is to
say, who receive and respond to it of themselves,
with recognition, uncoerced. (*Masks: Creative,*
p. 4)

It is, then, the mythmakers themselves who are
Campbell's *modern* heroes. Chief among them are
Gottfried von Strassburg, author of *Tristan;* Wolfram
von Eschenbach, author of *Parzival;* James Joyce; and
Thomas Mann. As Campbell declares elsewhere,
"Perhaps the artist is the best prototype of the modern
hero. James Joyce or Thomas Mann, for instance, have
[sic] created a new mythology."[1]

Because Campbell considers only the later medieval
and modern West to be bereft of traditional myths, he
considers only it to be capable of creative mythology.
Repeatedly, he contrasts the originality and individuality of the later West to the rigidity and conformity
of not just the earlier West but also the East and primitive peoples:

And so we may say in summary at this point that
the first and absolutely essential characteristic of
the new . . . mythology that was emerging in the
literature of the twelfth and thirteenth centuries was
that its structuring themes were not derived from
dogma, learning, politics, or any current concepts
of the general social good, but were expressions of
individual experience: what I have termed Libido
as opposed to Credo. . . . Traditional mythologies,
that is to say, whether of the primitive or of the
higher cultures, antecede and control experience;

whereas what I am here calling Creative Mythology
is an effect and expression of experience. (*Masks:
Creative*, pp. 64–65)

Campbell goes much further in praise of creative
mythology. He credits it with not just a new set of
heroes but also a new definition of heroism. Despite
his praising both universal heroism in *Hero* and the
nonheroism of the East in *Masks: Occidental* and *Oriental* for exactly their affirmation rather than rejection
of the everyday, material world, Campbell now singles
out creative mythology as alone affirming the physical
world, which, he now says, all past mythologies reject. The epitome of this affirmation is for him courtly
love, as represented by not only *Tristan* but also *Parzival*. Whether Campbell in fact views creative mythology, any more than other mythologies, as affirming
rather than rejecting the physical world is a question
to be considered.

Gottfried's *Tristan*

At the outset of his analysis of *Tristan*[2] Campbell expresses amazement that anyone could interpret the
work as Gnostic, which is to say as radically dualistic
rather than radically monistic:

I find it impossible to understand how anyone who
had really read both the literature of Gnosticism
and the poetry of Gottfried could suggest—as does
a recent student of the psychology of *amor*—that
not only Gottfried but also the other Tristan poets,
and the troubadors as well, were Manichaeans.
(*Masks: Creative*, p. 175)

Where the Gnostics reject the material world, Tristan accepts it:

> . . . whereas according to the Gnostic-Manichaean view nature is corrupt and the lure of the senses to be repudiated, in the poetry of the troubadors, in the Tristan story, and in Gottfried's work above all, nature in its noblest moment—the realization of love—is an end and glory in itself; and the senses, ennobled and refined by courtesy and art, temperance, loyalty and courage, are the guides to this realization. (*Masks: Creative*, p. 176)

Invoking a distinction that he applies more fully to the Grail legend, Campbell asserts that the Tristan story defines the ideal form of love as neither *eros* nor *agape* but *amor. Eros,* as lust, amounts to worldliness and so to ordinary monism. *Agape,* as selfless, brotherly love, is equivalent to otherworldliness and so to radical dualism. *Amor* somehow combines the two to constitute the radical variety of radical monism:

> It is amazing, but our theologians still are writing of *agape* and *eros* and their radical opposition, as though these two were the final terms of the principle of "love": the former, "charity," godly and spiritual, being "of men toward each other in a community," and the latter, "lust," natural and fleshly, being the "urge, desire and delight of sex." Nobody in a pulpit seems ever to have heard of *amor* as a third, selective, discriminating principle in contrast to the other two. (*Masks: Creative*, p. 177)

According to Campbell *Tristan* espouses radical monism in its radical form because it fuses heaven with earth, the soul with the body. For it finds the soul in the body rather than beyond it. One need not transcend the body to find the soul:

> For there is no such thing as a love that is either purely spiritual or merely sensual. Man is composed of body and spirit (if we may still use such terms) and is thus an essential mystery in himself; and the deepest heart of this mystery (in Gottfried's view) is the very point touched and wakened by— and in—the mystery of love, the sacramental purity of which has nothing whatsoever to do with a suspension or suppression of the sensuous and the senses, but includes and even rests upon the physical realization. (*Masks: Creative*, p. 248)

Campbell does not deny that the love of Tristan and Isolde leads to their deaths. Death, he laments, is simply the price of love. He denies the radically dualistic view of Richard Wagner and others that the couple's love culminates after death in a necessarily otherworldly, nonphysical form—a form that, despite his past characterization of the East as world-affirming, he now labels "Oriental":

> And so there came to pass that death of both, of which Brangaene had foretold: Tristan of love, Isolt of pity. She stretched her body to his, laid her mouth to his, yielded her spirit, and expired. Which is the death that Wagner rendered as the love-death—with an Oriental turn, however, borrowed from Schopenhauer, of the transcendence of duality in extinction. (*Masks: Creative*, p. 255)

Not all scholars would concur in Campbell's interpretation. Most would agree that the love of Tristan

and Isolde ceases with their deaths. Whatever fulfillment the two secure must be secured on earth, which
is what makes their continuing separation so poignant.
But few scholars therefore conclude that love and life
happily coincide. Few conclude that *Tristan* espouses
the radical form of radical monism rather than radical
dualism.

For if, as Campbell himself grants, love leads to
death, then love and life, which means life in this
world, are incompatible. The love of Blancheflor for
Rivalin does heal him, but she nearly dies when Rivalin tells her that he is going off to war, and she does
die in a premature childbirth indirectly induced by her
grieving over his death in battle. Tristan, the son conceived during Blancheflor's healing of Rivalin, is thus
the product of both love and death.

The potion that Isolde's mother brews for her daughter and King Mark at once intensifies, if not outright
causes, the love of Tristan and Isolde and certainly
causes their deaths. Indeed, they would have died at
the outset from their separation if Isolde's servant
Brangane had not consented to their union. Once
united, they cannot bear further separation, which
constitutes a living death. The literal death of one
causes the same in the other: Tristan dies of a broken
heart upon being falsely informed that Isolde has not
come to heal him, and Isolde dies upon discovering
his body.

The opposition between life in the cave and life in
society underscores the opposition between love and
life. Tristan and Isolde must flee society for the cave,
located deep in the forest, in order to consummate
their love. To say that society opposes only adultery,
not physical love itself, is to miss the point: that
courtly love, which Campbell deems the finest expres-

sion of worldly love, is inherently adulterous.[3] To note that the pair return voluntarily to society is to miss the point as well: that they return only out of duty, which remains at odds with their loves. Indeed, Tristan must eventually flee Mark's court altogether.

Undeniably, Tristan and Isolde attain spiritual bliss *through* physical intercourse. But sex is only the means, not the end, which is wholly spiritual. Indeed, the pair seek to transcend their bodies, which stand in the way of their final goal: not just reaching but unifying their souls. Life in the body thus precludes the attainment of this goal even in the cave. In short, *Tristan* lies closer to radical dualism than, as Campbell takes it, to the radical variety of radical monism.

Wolfram's *Parzival*

Campbell argues that Wolfram's version of the Grail legend,[4] like Gottfried's *Tristan,* espouses the radical form of radical monism: the soul lies within the body, ultimate reality within everyday reality. Better put: the soul *is* the body; ultimate reality *is* everyday reality. Campbell thus contrasts Wolfram's version, in which the hero is Parzival, to the radically dualistic one of the Cistercian Fathers' *La Queste del Saint Graal,*[5] in which the hero is Galahad:

> The Grail here [i.e., in Wolfram], as in the later *Queste,* is the symbol of supreme spiritual value. It is attained, however, not by renouncing the world or even current social custom, but, on the contrary, by participation with every ounce of one's force in the century's order of life in the way or ways dic-

tated by one's own uncorrupted heart. . . . (*Masks: Creative*, p. 564)

Certainly Parzival is a far more worldly knight than Galahad. Where Galahad is free of worldly values from the start, Parzival must be weaned away from them. Where Galahad immediately recognizes the other-worldly meaning of the Grail, Parzival grasps it only slowly. Where Galahad, upon partaking of the Mass with the Grail, ascends to heaven, Parzival remains on earth as the successor to the Fisher King.

Where, above all, Galahad is celibate, Parzival is married. For Campbell, Parzival's ability to secure the Grail without forsaking his wife epitomizes the ideal blend of otherworldliness and worldliness that constitutes radical monism, which henceforth will mean in its radical form. Indeed, Campbell characterizes Parzival's relationship to Condwiramurs, his wife, as one of *amor* rather than either *eros,* which Gawain embodies, or *agape,* which not only Galahad but also the later Parzival of both Wagner and Alfred Lord Tennyson represent:

> Condwiramurs, like Parzival, stood for a new ideal, a new possibility in love and life: namely, of love *(amor)* as the sole motive for marriage and an indissoluble marriage as the sacrament of love— whereas in the normal manner of that period the sacrament was held as far as possible apart from the influence of *amor,* to be governed by the concerns only of security and reputation, politics and economics: while love, known only as *eros,* was to be sublimated as *agape,* and if any such physical contact occurred as would not become either a monk or a nun, it was to be undertaken dutifully, as far as possible without pleasure, for God's pur-

pose of repopulating those vacant seats in Heaven
which had been emptied when the wicked angels
fell. (*Masks: Creative*, p. 456)

The duty that Parzival rejects thus involves not only
abstinence but also social convention: Parzival rejects
the daughter of the knight Gurnemanz as his wife because he does not love her.

Campbell views the Parzival story as the legacy of
a pre-Christian, Celtic, radically monistic tradition.
The Galahad story represents a later "Christianizing"
of the Parzival version by radically dualistic monks.[6]

At the same time Campbell considers Wolfram the
creator of a secular mythology, if somehow still a
Christian one:

Moreover, he [Wolfram] applied his interpretations
consciously to an altogether *secular* mythology, of
men and women living for *this* world, not "that,"
pursuing earthly, human, and humane (i.e., in Wolfram's terms, "courtly") purposes, and supported
in their spiritual tasks not by a supernatural grace
dispensed by way of sacraments but by the *natural*
grace of individual endowment and the worldly virtue of loyalty in love. That is what gives to his work
its epochal significance as the first example in the
history of world literature of a *consciously developed secular Christian myth*. (*Masks: Creative*,
p. 476)

In the name of radical monism, whether or not of
the Celtic outlook, Campbell may be going too far.
The Parzival version is incontestably more worldly
than the Galahad one, but it is at least as dualistic as
monistic. To begin with, Parzival must outright reject
many worldly values, not simply fuse them with oth-

erworldly ones. Most conspicuously, he loses the Grail the first time because, as Campbell himself stresses, he abides by knightly etiquette in refusing to query the Fisher King:

> The Round Table stands in Wolfram's work for the social order of the period of which it was the summit and consummation. The young knight's concern for his reputation as one worthy of that circle was his motive for holding his tongue when his own better nature was actually pressing him to speak; and in the light of his conscious notion of himself as a knight worthy of the name, just hailed as the greatest in the world, one can understand his shock and resentment at the sharp judgments of the Loathly Damsel and Sigune. However, those two were the messengers of a deeper sphere of values and possibilities than was yet known, or even sensed, by his socially conscious mind; they were of the sphere not of the Round Table but of the Castle of the Grail, which had not been a feature of the normal daylight world, visible to all, but dreamlike, visionary, mythic. . . . It had appeared to him as the first sign and challenge of a kingdom yet to be earned, beyond the sphere of the world's flattery, proper to his own unfolding life. . . . (*Masks: Creative,* p. 454)

Even if Parzival eventually returns to his wife, it is not clear how physical their relationship is. As Campbell himself notes (*Masks: Creative,* pp. 440–443), the pair establish a spiritual bond, one involving abstinence, before they establish a physical one, which at the least is therefore less important. Before meeting his wife, Parzival, in preparation for finding the Grail, must resist the temptation of sex with the wife of the knight Orilus. The objection here is seemingly to more than the fact of adultery. For Campbell himself judges the adulterous liaison of Tristan and Isolde *amor* rather than *eros*.

Parzival may return to rule over the Grail Kingdom rather than, like Galahad, ascend to heaven, but the Kingdom is otherworldly. Indeed, it is visible only to those who are ready for it.

Finally, Galahad, not Parzival, has always been the most popular hero of the Grail saga. It would therefore be hard to deem Parzival the representative Grail hero. Even if one judged the Parzival account radically monistic rather than dualistic, the Grail saga generally, as represented by Galahad, would therefore remain dualistic.

Because Wolfram considers the Grail itself a precious stone rather than, as in other versions, a cup, he is often assumed to be an alchemist. The stone would be the philosopher's stone, used to catalyze the transformation of base metals into gold or silver. In that case Wolfram would truly be a radical monist: because immateriality, for alchemists, lies latent in matter, the two substances are really one. Parzival would be discovering that the Grail Kingdom lies *in* the everyday, material world, not outside it. As Campbell puts it alchemically, "The stone . . . will bring us . . . back to the world—as gold" (*Masks: Creative,* p. 430).

But in likely associating Wolfram with alchemy, Campbell overlooks the far more common association of him with Catharism. As a form of medieval Gnosticism, the Cathar movement was uncompromisingly dualistic.[7] If Wolfram were a Cathar, he would be espousing the utter rejection of the material world for the immaterial godhead. He would hardly be preaching return to the material world.

Indeed, author Jessie Weston, whom Campbell cites approvingly (*Masks: Creative,* pp. 406–407, 457–458) for precisely her interpretation of the Grail story as originally pre-Christian and then heterodox Christian, views the saga as the continuation of an ancient, esoteric, otherworldly tradition, only the public, exoteric side of which—the sole side recognized by James Frazer—was worldly:

> The Grail story is not *du fond en comble* the product of imagination, literary or popular. At its root lies the record . . . of an ancient Ritual, having for its ultimate object the initiation into the secret of the sources of Life, physical and spiritual. This ritual, in its lower, exoteric form, as affecting the processes of Nature, and physical life, survives today. . . . In its esoteric "Mystery" form it was freely utilized for the imparting of high spiritual teaching concerning the relation of Man to the Divine Source of his being, and the possibility of a sensible union between Man, and God.[8]

Admittedly, Weston herself interprets the esoteric side of the Grail cult as merely far higher than the exoteric one rather than opposed to it, but so much higher is the esoteric side that the difference amounts to near-rejection of the exoteric, material side and is therefore almost identical with radical dualism. In fact, Weston deems the ancient practitioners of the esoteric side Gnostics.[9] To be sure, she does not say that these esoteric practitioners judged matter outright evil. Rather, they judged it merely inferior, but, again, so hopelessly inferior as nearly to be rejected altogether.

To the extent that Campbell relies on Weston's interpretation the Grail story is, then, preaching something far more akin to radical dualism than to radical monism. When he praises her for showing "that the aim of the Grail Quest was originally [i.e., as pre-Christian] the restoration to life, health, and fecundity of a land, its people, and its king,"[10] he is, in candor, reversing her main point.

In a long essay elsewhere on the Grail legend[11] Campbell, without mentioning Weston, does connect Wolfram to the Cathars, or Albigensians—a connection he never draws in *Masks*.[12] Yet he then characterizes the Albigensians as radical monists rather than radical dualists.

In *Masks: Creative* itself Campbell alternatively characterizes medieval Gnosticism as dualistic and as monistic. On the other hand he still says that the world-rejecting dualism of Gnosticism puts it even further afield of the radical monism of *Tristan* than the milder, if still radical, dualism of orthodox Christianity (*Masks: Creative*, pp. 175–176, 230). On the other hand he links courtly love, and so presumably both *Tristan* and *Parzival*, to Gnosticism (*Masks: Creative*, pp. 162–171), which he then links to the radical monism of the East (*Masks: Creative*, pp. 149–161):

Hence, although the usual Gnostic attitude was strictly dualistic, striving . . . to separate spirit from matter, with a strong sense of repugnance for the world, it is also possible to find in certain other Gnostic remains passages of inspiring affirmation; as, for instance, the words attributed to Jesus in the Gnostic Gospel "According to Thomas": "The Kingdom of the Father is spread upon the earth and men do not see it"; or again: "The Kingdom is within you and is without you. If you will know yourselves, then you will be known and you will know that you are the sons of the Living Father." . . . And, as we have learned from numerous Ma-

hayana Buddhist texts of exactly the period of these
Gnostic Perates, there is a "Wisdom of the Yonder
Shore," . . . which is, in fact, the ultimate wisdom
of Buddhist realization; namely, a knowledge beyond all such dualistic conceptions as matter and
spirit, bondage and release, sorrow and bliss.
(*Masks: Creative,* p. 157)[13]

Campbell assumes that because divinity, or immateriality, lies within the material world, immateriality
and matter are one, in which case there is radical monism. But in fact immateriality lies *trapped* in matter,
from which it is irremediably distinct. The two substances are not like salt and water in the tale from the
Upanishads. Christ is to be found not in the bodies
but in the souls of his followers. Their souls may exist
within their bodies, but, again, trapped in them and
therefore distinct from them. Not coincidentally, the
Gospel of Thomas preaches rejection of the body; rejection of the material world; rejection of the Hebrew
Bible for exactly its approval of this world; salvation
as the return of the immaterial souls to the immaterial
godhead, from which they originally fell; and doce-
tism, or the doctrine that Jesus, the Gnostic savior,
only seemingly had a body. When Campbell describes
another Gnostic group as believing that "since Christ,
the Son of the Father, is entrapped in the field of Matter, the whole universe is the cross on which the Son
is crucified" (*Masks: Creative,* p. 161), he is clearly
confusing entrapment with identity. Only by so doing
can he claim that even if orthodox Christianity of the
Middle Ages was radically dualistic, a sophisticated
elite, one including both Gottfried and Wolfram, was
radically monistic.

Mann and Joyce

Campbell regards Thomas Mann[14] and James Joyce[15] as the twentieth-century counterparts to Gottfried and Wolfram. He sees the heroes of "Tonio Kroger," *Buddenbrooks*, *The Magic Mountain*, *Joseph and His Brothers*, *A Portrait of the Artist as a Young Man*, *Ulysses*, and *Finnegans Wake* as persons daring enough not only to venture forth to a strange new world but also to return. Art rather than love is their entrée to that world. These heroes are not selfless. They return to the everyday world not because they want to spread the word to others but only because they discover the new world within the everyday one. Unlike radical dualists, they need not forsake the body for the soul, earth for heaven, or humanity for god. As radical monists, they find the soul in the body, heaven on earth, and god in humanity. More precisely, they find that the soul is the body, that heaven is earth, and that god is humanity. What Campbell says of the difference between Joyce's outlook and the orthodox Roman Catholic one applies equally for Campbell to the difference between Mann's outlook and the mainstream Protestant one:

> But between Joyce's and the Roman Catholic clergy's ways of interpreting Christian symbols there is a world of difference. The artist reads them in the universally known old Greco-Roman, Celto-Germanic, Hindu-Buddhist-Taoist, Neoplatonic way, as referring to an experience of the mystery beyond theology that is immanent in all things, in-

cluding gods, demons, and flies. The priests, on the other hand, are insisting on the absolute finality of their Old Testament concept of a personal creator God "out there," who, though omnipresent, omniscient, and omni-everything-else, is ontologically distinct from the living substance of his world. . . . (*Masks: Creative,* pp 260–261)

Specifically, Campbell contrasts the outlook of Hans Castorp, the hero of Mann's *Magic Mountain*, to that of his two would-be mentors: the optimistic, liberal, progressive, humanist Settembrini, and the pessimistic, cynical, Marxist, Jesuit Naphta. Where Settembrini preaches a worldly human improvement that corresponds to ordinary monism, Naphta espouses a world-rejecting religiosity that amounts to radical dualism:

One [i.e., Settembrini] is defending the glory of man and the spirit as revealed in the faculty of reason; the other [i.e., Naphta], God and the spirit transcendent, absolutely apart from and against fallen, natural man, his instincts, reason, pretensions to freedom, progress, science, rights, and all the rest. Naphta charges Settembrini with the heresy of [ordinary] monism; Settembrini, Naphta with [radical] dualism and world-splitting. (*Masks: Creative,* p. 380)

Hans does indeed learn from both, but he learns above all to reject the extremes they embody. On the one hand he learns that there exists more than the everyday world of ordinary monism, the world below that he has left behind for the sanitorium. On the other hand he learns that he, like Campbell's hero in *Hero,* need not reject the everyday world for the deeper, higher one. For the two worlds are really one. Hence Hans finally leaves the sanitorium for the world below:

> The young engineer [i.e., Hans] was able to recognize . . . in the arguments of Naphta . . . a depth of insight into the woes of the world that went beyond that of his other mentor, Settembrini. However, the separation by Naphta of the values of the spirit from those of living in this world with love for it as it is, left him unconvinced. Pain, sickness, death and corruption, indeed: but were these a refutation of life? (*Masks: Creative,* p. 382)[16]

Western Individualism, Eastern Collectivism

In volumes two and three of *Masks* the East is Campbell's ideal. Suddenly, in volume four, together with several essays in *The Flight of the Wild Gander* and *Myths to Live By*,[17] the West, from the twelfth century on, becomes his ideal, and the East becomes his nemesis. Where in volumes two and three of *Masks* Campbell praises the East for its nonheroic yearning for the absorption of the individual in the cosmic whole, now in *Masks: Creative* he condemns what he labels the East's oppressive, even totalitarian subordination of the individual to the whole, which here is as much social as cosmic. Where in volumes two and three of *Masks* Campbell scorns the West for its stress on the petty, selfish, and vain striving of the individual, now in *Masks: Creative* he upholds individuality as indispensably human. Elsewhere Campbell makes clear that he is outright endorsing, not merely describing, this romantic individualism:

It is my thought, that the wealth and glory of the Western world, and of the modern world as well (in so far as it is still in spirit Western), is a function of this respect for the individual, not as a member of some sanctified consensus through which he is given worth, . . . nor as an indifferent name and form of that "same perfection and infinity . . . present in every grain of sand, and in the raindrop as much as in the sea," . . . but as an end and value in himself, unique in his *im*perfection, i.e., in his yearning, in his process of becoming not what he "ought" to be but what he is, actually and potentially: such a one as was never seen before. (*Flight of the Wild Gander,* pp. 222–223)

Wolfram's *Parzival* marks the new age. That age at last frees humanity from submission to god:

In Wolfram's *Parzival* the boon is to be the inauguration of a new age of the human spirit: of *secular* spirituality, sustained by self-responsible individuals acting not in terms of general laws supposed to represent the will or way of some personal god or impersonal eternity, but each in terms of his own developing realization of worth. Such an idea is distinctly—and uniquely—European. (*Masks: Creative,* p. 480)

The new age frees humanity from submission to the group as well:

The Indian notion of *sva-dharma,* "one's own duty," [seemingly] suggests comparison: "Better is one's own dharma, imperfectly performed, than the dharma of another, performed to perfection," states the *Bhagavad Gītā.* However, the idea of duty there is of the duties of one's caste, as defined by

the timeless . . . Indian social order. The Westerner reading such a text might think of duties self-
imposed, self-discovered, self-assumed: a vocation
elected and realized. That is not the Oriental idea.
Nor is the Oriental "person" the same as ours. . . .
The "indwelling being" is the reincarnating mo-
nad; and the aim of a well-lived lifetime is not to
realize the unique possibilities of its temporal em-
bodiment, but on the contrary, to achieve such indifference to his body and its limitations,
potentialities, and vicissitudes, that, "completely
devoid of the sense of 'I' and 'mine,' one attains
peace." (*Masks: Creative,* pp. 480–481)

Campbell contrasts "creative" mythology to that of
not only the East but also primitives and the earlier
West. As he says of the individualistic tenets of creative mythology, "In the long course of our survey of
the mythologies of mankind we have encountered
nothing quite like this" (*Masks: Creative,* p. 480).
Still, he regards the East as the culture most fervently
opposed to individualism, though in at least a few
places[18] he castigates the earlier West—Judaism,
Christianity, and Islam—even more severely than it.

What accounts for the reversal of Campbell's views?
Campbell himself never says, though an interviewer
attributes it to Campbell's revulsion toward the India
he had long revered but not visited until 1954:

In 1954, after thirty years of being so immersed
in Eastern art, philosophy, and religion that he
considered himself "almost a Hindu," Campbell
traveled to India. And the gods played apple-
basket-turnover. He was so appalled by the caste
system and the lack of respect for the individual

that he returned a confirmed Westerner, celebrating the uniqueness of the person.[19]

Two critics of Campbell's[20] likewise struck by the abrupt reversal in Campbell's views attribute it to the Cold War. According to them, *Hero*, written at the end of World War II, displays the postwar American belief in world peace and unity. *Masks*, written in the fifties and sixties, expresses the subsequent American opposition to the totalitarianism of not only Russia but also the Third World.

It is true that Campbell voices his pro-Western, anti-Eastern convictions as early as the 1957 essay "The Symbol without Meaning."[21] But his praise of the East appears above all in volumes two and three of *Masks*, which were published as late as 1962 and 1964. The same chronology undercuts the attribution of Campbell's change of views to his visit to India in 1954. Conversely, Campbell's hostility to the East, while undeniably, if incongruously, found at the end of volume two of *Masks* (*Oriental*: ch. 9), peaks as late as 1968, when not only volume four of *Masks* but also the essay "The Secularization of the Sacred"[22] appeared. If by then the Cold War had not begun to ebb,[23] surely it had done so by 1975, when the interviews eventually published as *An Open Life* began. Yet even there Campbell's dislike of the collectivist East is unabated (*Open Life*, pp. 72–73). Changes in Campbell's views do not, then, parallel changes in American foreign policy. The source of the changes in Campbell's views remains a mystery.

Later Western and Primitive Hunting Mythologies; Earlier Western, Eastern, and Primitive Planting Ones

In volumes one and three of *Masks* Campbell parallels, if not quite equates, the mythology of primitive hunters with that of the West and the mythology of primitive planters with that of the East. At the outset of *Masks: Occidental* (pp. 5–6) Campbell goes so far as to characterize the Eastern outlook as the continuation of that of primitive planters, though not quite the Western one as the continuation of that of primitive hunters.

In above all his essay "The Symbol without Meaning" (*Flight of the Wild Gander*, ch. 5), which is otherwise largely a sketch of *Masks: Primitive*, Campbell proceeds to parallel, if likewise not quite equate, the mythology of primitive hunters with that of not the West per se but only the West from the twelfth century on: the West of individualistic striving free from the tyranny of either god or society. Where in *Masks: Creative* the individualism espoused by creative mythology is unprecedented, in "The Symbol without Meaning" it is a restoration of that of primitive hunters, who at least in *Masks: Primitive* possess the oldest brand of mythology. The forerunners of later Westerners, primitive hunters here are self-sufficient and rigidly independent:

. . . today, when the mandala itself, the whole structure of meaning to which society and its guardians would attach us, is dissolving, what is required of us all, spiritually as well as corporeally, is much more the fearless self-sufficiency of our shamanistic inheritance [i.e., hunters] than the timorous piety of the priest-guided Neolithic [i.e., planters]. . . . The creative researches and wonderful daring of our scientists today partake far more of the lion spirit of shamanism than of the piety of priest and peasant. (*Flight of the Wild Gander,* pp. 189, 192)

Where in volumes one and three of *Masks* Campbell proceeds to dismiss the very differences between hunters and planters and between West and East that he so labors to explicate, now, in volume four, he retains them. Where in volumes one and three Campbell not only denigrates but finally denies the would-be distinctive outlook of hunters and Westerners—consciously or unconsciously, hunters are really planters and Westerners Easterners—now he maintains that hunters and later Westerners have a distinctive, not to say superior, outlook. Primitive hunters and later Westerners are really, not just apparently, the opposite of primitive planters, earlier Westerners, and Easterners for all time.

In other works Campbell virtually identifies mythology with religion. For example, at one point he defines myths as "religious recitations conceived as symbolic of the play of Eternity in Time."[24] In *Masks: Creative* he severs myth from religion: creative mythology is secular rather than religious, even if Campbell simultaneously not only characterizes Mann and Joyce as religious but also labels *Parzival,* his prime example of creative mythology, a "secular Christian myth" (*Masks: Creative,* p. 476).

In other works Campbell does not, it is true, stress

the socializing function of myth, but as one of the four functions of myth he enumerates he certainly approves of it. In *Masks: Creative* he scorns this function as the subordination of the individual to society. That subordination is exemplified in medieval marriages based on convention rather than, like Parzival's, on love:

> . . . Wolfram solved the spiritual problem of his century first by setting the ideal of love above marriage and, simultaneously, the ideal of an indissoluble marriage beyond love. . . . As far as I know, he was the first poet in the world to put forward seriously this socially explosive ideal of marriage, which has become today, however, the romantic norm of the West, resisted and even despised in the Orient as anarchic, immoral, and insane. For through it are transcended the primitive, ancient, and Oriental orders of tribal and family marriage, where social, political, and economic considerations prevail over personal and romantic, and where the unfolding personality (which in the lore of this revelation is the flower of human life) is bound back, cropped and trained to the interests of a group. (*Masks: Creative,* pp. 567–568)

In fact, in all but volume one of *Masks* Campbell is indifferent to a social origin or function of myth. He considers mythology an autonomous set of beliefs—the product of neither the unconscious nor society. To be sure, in *Masks: Occidental* he ascribes the difference, or seeming difference, between the mythology of the East and that of the West to differing social organizations: matriarchy and patriarchy. But he never examines any societies themselves, only the beliefs expressed in their myths. It is ultimately not even clear whether for Campbell myth reflects society or vice versa. In *Masks: Oriental* he roots the mythological differences in differing beliefs themselves: the Eastern belief in the oneness of all things and the Western belief in the uniqueness of all things. The relationship between the individual and society is simply a consequence of the relationship between the individual and the cosmos. In *Masks: Primitive* Campbell does link mythological differences to economic ones, but the differing beliefs that myths express are so abstract and metaphysical as seemingly to transcend any possible economic roots. Certainly Campbell fails to provide the link.

In order to distinguish the secular, individualist, later Western outlook from the prior religious, collectivist one, Campbell argues that it represents the resurfacing of a pagan, pre-Christian tradition that Christianity had vainly tried to eradicate. Campbell labels this tradition distinctively European and identifies it with one of the strains forming the West: the strain composed of Greeks, Romans, Celts, and Germans *(Flight of the Wild Gander,* p. 215). The twelfth century represents the beginning of the continuing revolt by this secular, individualist strain against the religious, collectivist, Near Eastern one, composed of Jews, Muslims, and above all Christians:

> The great period of the breakthrough of the native European spirit against the imposed authority of decisions made by a lot of Levantine [i.e., Near Eastern] bishops at the Councils of Nicaea, Constantinople, Ephesus, and Chalcedon (fourth to eighth centuries A.D.), occurred in the twelfth and thirteenth centuries. . . . As I see it, this breakthrough followed as the consequence of the courage of an increasing number of people of great stature

to credit their own experience and to live by it against the dictates of authority. (*Flight of the Wild Gander*, p. 208)

Because Campbell considers *Tristan* and *Parzival* the greatest exemplars of this revolt, he argues that they constitute a rejection of Christianity, or otherworldly, institutionalized religion, in favor of worldly, individualistic experience:

> Though himself probably a cleric, and certainly learned in theology, Gottfried is openly disdainful of current Christian doctrines. . . . Chiefly, Gottfried's inspiration had sprung from his recognition in the Celtic legend . . . [of] an order of poetic imagery congenial to his own mode of experience. It was a legend rooted, like all Arthurian romance, in the most ancient native European mythological tradition—that of the old megalithic, bronze-age goddess of many names. . . . The Grail legend, also, had sprung from that pagan base. . . . [I]n rejecting absolutely the authority of the Church, these lovers and poets returned consciously and conscientiously to an earlier, pre-Christian, native European order of conscience, wherein the immanence of divinity was recognized in nature and its productions. . . . (*Flight of the Wild Gander*, pp. 216–217, 222)

When, finally, Campbell says that the secular individualism introduced by courtly love fully affirms rather than, as before, rejects the everyday world—the change to which the phrase "secularization of the sacred" refers—he has fully repudiated his heretofore relentless praise of the East for accomplishing exactly this end, which is that of the radical variety of radical monism:

> . . . this, after all, is the leading lesson of Arthurian romance in general. Within its fold the gods and goddesses of other days have become [human] knights and ladies, hermits and kings of this world, their dwellings castles; and the adventures, largely magical, are of the magic rather of poetry than of traditional religion, not so much miracles of God as signs of an unfolding dimension of nature. . . . (*Masks: Creative,* p. 566)

At times Campbell, like Jung, is unabashedly elitist: the distinctively later Westerner is not the average person of the period but the exception. Only the few are sensitive to the breakdown of tradition. The masses cling obliviously to traditional religion and so traditional myths, which therefore continue to work for them. Campbell thus says that "The traditional myths—Christian and otherwise—still offer support for large numbers of people in our society."[25] More often Campbell, unlike Jung, is egalitarian: science has undone traditional religion and therefore traditional myths for later Westerners generally.[26]

Ironically, even the egalitarian Campbell is far more contemptuous of traditional Christianity than the elitist Jung. *As* an elitist, Jung is wary of any venturing beyond tradition by all but the psychologically heartiest. He praises Catholicism above all for the regimen it offers adherents. By contrast, Campbell castigates his childhood Catholicism above all *for* its regimen. Jung turns anxiously to his own brand of psychology as a substitute for dying Christianity. By contrast, Campbell revels in the replacement of moribund Christianity by the "creative mythology" of unencumbered artists. For Jung, psychology at once replaces religion and interprets its extant myths. For Campbell, psychology recaptures the symbolic meaning of myths directly intuited by earliest humanity but missed ever since by their "churched" successors.

NOTES

[1]Campbell, interview with Sam Keen, in Keen, *Voices and Visions* (New York: Harper & Row, 1974), p. 77.

[2]On *Tristan* see Campbell, *Masks: Creative,* pp. 42–46, 65–67, 175–256; *Myths to Live By,* pp. 160–165; *Power of Myth,* pp. 190, 198–199, 200–203.

[3]Elsewhere (*Power of Myth,* p. 190) Campbell himself emphasizes the point.

[4]On the Grail legend see Campbell, *Masks: Creative,* pp. 405–570; *Flight of the Wild Gander,* pp. 209–222; *Myths to Live By,* pp. 166–171; "Indian Reflections in the Castle of the Grail," in *The Celtic Consciousness,* ed. Robert O'Driscoll (New York: Braziller, 1982), pp. 3–30; introduction to Helen Diner, *Mothers and Amazons,* ed. and tr. John Philip Lundin (New York: Julian, 1965), p. vii; *Power of Myth,* pp. 195–198, 199–200, 217–218; *Open Life,* pp. 32–34. For a summary of the versions see John Mathews, *The Grail* (New York: Crossroad, 1981).

[5]It is this version which Thomas Malory translates in his *Le Morte d'Arthur.*

[6]On the Parzival version as pre-Christian and Celtic see Campbell, *Flight of the Wild Gander,* pp. 217–222; introduction to Diner, p. vii.

[7]On Catharism see Steven Runciman, *The Medieval Manichee* (Cambridge, England: Cambridge University Press, 1947), ch. 4.

[8]Jessie L. Weston, *From Ritual to Romance* (Garden City, NY: Doubleday Anchor, 1957), p. 203.

⁹*Ibid.*, ch. 11. Furthermore, Weston derives her views from A. E. Waite, W. B. Yeats, and other members of the ascetic Hermetic Order of the Golden Dawn.

¹⁰Campbell, introduction to Diner, p. vii.

¹¹Campbell, "Indian Reflections in the Castle of the Grail," pp. 16–17.

¹²In *Masks* Campbell associates only *Tristan,* not *Parzival,* with Gnosticism, and, as quoted, associates it with opposition to Gnosticism.

¹³On the difference between medieval Gnostics and the East see Runciman, appendix IV.

¹⁴On Mann see Campbell, *Masks: Creative,* pp. 38–40, 308–333, 358–364, 366–367, 374–383, 636–645, 658–662; "Erotic Irony and Mythic Forms in the Art of Thomas Mann," *Boston University Journal,* 24 (1976), pp. 10–27; *Inner Reaches,* pp. 143–148; *Power of Myth,* p. 4.

¹⁵On Joyce see Campbell, *Masks: Creative,* pp. 38–40, 257–262, 274–277, 280–281, 283–285, 338–339, 364–373, 635–636, 639–642, 656–665; *A Skeleton Key to Finnegans Wake* (with Henry Morton Robinson) (New York: Harcourt, Brace, 1944); "Finnegan the Wake," *Chimera,* 4 (Spring 1946), pp. 63–80; "Contransmagnificandjewbangtantiality," *Studies in the Literary Imagination,* 3 (October 1970), pp. 3–18; *Inner Reaches,* ch. 3; *Power of Myth,* pp. 116–117, 220–221.

¹⁶Yet at the same time Settembrini's escape from the everyday world to the sanitorium, where talk takes the place of living, itself represents rejection of the world and so represents radical dualism.

¹⁷See Campbell, *Flight of the Wild Gander,* chs. 5 ("The Symbol without Meaning"), 6 ("The Secularization of the Sacred"); *Myths to Live By,* chs. 4 ("The Separation of East and West"), 5 ("The Confrontation of East and West in Religion").

¹⁸See, for example, Campbell, *Myths to Live By,* ch. 6.

¹⁹Sam Keen, interview with Campbell, p. 71.

²⁰Florence Sandler and Darrell Reeck, "The Masks of Joseph Campbell," *Religion,* 11 (January 1981), pp. 1–20.

[21]Campbell, "The Symbol without Meaning," *Eranos-Jahrbücher*, 26 (1957), pp. 415–476. Reprinted in partially revised form in *Flight of the Wild Gander*, ch. 6.

[22]Campbell, "The Secularization of the Sacred," in *The Religious Situation*, vol. 1 (1968), ed. Donald R. Cutler (Boston: Beacon, 1968), ch. 17. Reprinted in *Flight of the Wild Gander*, ch. 6.

[23]In *Myths to Live By*, ch. 4, which was first delivered as a lecture in 1961, Campbell is pro-Western but not anti-Eastern in particular. Rather, he opposes everything that is different from the later West: primitives and the earlier West as well as the East.

[24]Campbell, "Folkloristic Commentary" to *Grimm's Fairy Tales*, ed. Josef Scharl, tr. Margaret Hunt, rev. James Stern (New York: Pantheon, 1944), p. 841.

[25]Campbell, interview with Keen, p. 78.

[26]See, for example, *Myths to Live By*, pp. 8–9.

CHAPTER EIGHT

RECENT WORKS

The Mythic Image

In several respects *The Mythic Image* marks a return to *Hero*. Campbell no longer concerns himself with the differences among myths but seeks only the similarities. Where in *Masks* he stresses at least the surface differences between hunting and planting myths, between Western and Eastern myths, and between all other and later Western myths, now, as in *Hero*, he deems all myths the same. Moreover, myths are the same not just underneath, as Campbell argues in *Masks*, but on the surface. Even here Campbell grants that differences exist. In fact, he goes so far as to say that in them rather than in the similarities the "fascination resides" (*Mythic Image*, p. 11). But he then states that "it has been my leading thought in the present work to let sound the one accord through all its ranges of historic transformation, not allowing local features to obscure the everlasting themes . . ." (*Mythic Image*, pp. 11–12).

Where in *Masks* Campbell interprets myths almost entirely metaphysically, in *The Mythic Image*, as again in *Hero*, he interprets them psychologically as well. To use his new terms, he again interprets myths "microcosmically" as well as "macrocosmically" (*Mythic Image*, p. 221).

Whenever Campbell interprets myths psychologically, he compares them with dreams. In other works he then argues that both emanate from the unconscious,[1] in which case their true meaning, not to say origin and function, is psychological, even if also metaphysical. In *The Mythic Image* Campbell not merely interprets both myths and dreams psychologically but also interprets myths as dreamlike themselves. Where in other works Campbell distinguishes myths from dreams on the grounds that myths are the "consciously controlled" rather than "spontaneous products" (*Hero*, p. 256) of the unconscious now he views myths themselves as raw, spontaneous outpourings of the unconscious. Where in other works Campbell interprets myths as the formal arrangement of images in a logical, narrative sequence, now he sees myths as a series of disparate images themselves. Not coincidentally, he no longer discusses whole myths, only discrete images.

Where in other works myths abide by the ordinary rules of logic, now they heed their own, dreamlike logic. Where elsewhere myths preach the logical reconciliation of only apparent opposites, now they espouse a paradoxical reconciliation of real opposites. In so doing, they violate the law of noncontradiction, according to which A and not-A, be they human and god or matter and immateriality, cannot simultaneously be identical yet distinct:

However, as a mythological image transcending the popular notion of an absolute dichotomy of nature and spirit (*A* is not *not-A*: man is not God), it makes once again the point that had already been made (though canonically disregarded) in the doctrine of the Incarnation, where in the person of Jesus not only was the idea of the absolute distinction of the opposed terms God and man refuted, but the point was also made that one should realize, like Jesus, this coincidence of opposites as the ultimate truth and substance of oneself. . . . (*Mythic Image,* p. 62)

Where in other works myths are to be interpreted, now they are only to be experienced. Interpretation itself now proves part of only the ordinary, waking world. In claiming to interpret myths, both Freud and Jung have therefore missed the point. To transcend the bounds of the everyday, waking world, with which Campbell associates not only logic but also language, he now resorts to pictures, which supplement and finally replace words. *The Mythic Image* is largely a set of annotated pictures.

In other works Campbell uses Western psychology— Freud and Jung—to interpret myths. Now, despite his dismissal of interpretation per se, he employs the Eastern psychology of Kundalini yoga,[2] which underlies the beliefs of both Hinduism and Buddhism. As Campbell summarizes its precepts:

The basic thesis of the so-called Kundalini yoga system elucidated in this fundamental work is that there are six plus one—i.e., seven—psychological centers distributed up the body, from its base to the crown of the head, which can, through yoga, be successively activated and so caused to release ever higher realizations of spiritual consciousness and bliss. These are known as "lotuses," *padmas,* or as *chakras,* "wheels," and are to be thought of as normally hanging limp. However, when touched and activated by a rising spiritual center called the

Kundalini, which can be made to ascend through a mystic channel up the middle of the spine, they awaken to life and shine. The name of this power, *kundalini,* "the coiled one," is a feminine Sanskrit noun, here referring to the idea of a coiled serpent, to be thought of as sleeping in the lowest of the seven body centers. (*Myths to Live By,* p.110)

The aim is to advance from the first level to the seventh by the transformation, or sublimation, of spiritual energy. Not to advance is to become fixated. Each *chakra,* or level of consciousness, corresponds to a certain kind of myth. At level one, which lies midway between the genitals and the anus, persons take a wholly material view of themselves and the world. They believe in only "hard facts." They deny the existence of an innate mind and assume the sheer conditioning of humanity by the environment. Classical behaviorist psychology clearly lies here. As Campbell describes the outlook: "There is on this plane no zeal for life, no explicit impulse to expand [i.e., to grow]. There is simply a lethargic avidity in hanging on to [everyday] existence . . ." (*Mythic Image,* p. 341). Kundalini yoga thus provides a means of interpreting not only myths but also interpretations of myths.

At level two, that of the genitals, there is an innate mind, but it is composed entirely of material drives—the sexual one above all. Myths here describe the direct or indirect satisfaction of that drive. Freudian psychology obviously falls here:

When the Kundalini is active at this level, the whole aim of life is in sex. Not only is every thought and act sexually motivated, either as a means toward sexual ends or as a compensating sublimation of frustrated sexual zeal, but everything seen and heard is interpreted compulsively, both consciously and unconsciously, as symbolic of sexual themes. (*Mythic Image*, p. 345)

At level three, that of the navel, the psyche is composed of a less tangible and more assertive, hence more creative drive: the drive for power, though power still takes material form. "Here the energy turns to violence and its aim is to consume, to master, to turn the world into oneself and one's own" (*Mythic Image*, p. 350). The psychology of Alfred Adler lies here.

The satisfactions of the first three levels are not only physical but also external. They deal with the relationship of humans to the external world:

> Now all three of these lower chakras are of the modes of man's living in the world in his naive state, outward turned: the modes of the lovers, the fighters, the builders, the accomplishers. Joys and sorrows on these levels are functions of achievements in the world "out there": what people think of one, what has been gained, what lost. (*Mythic Image*, p. 356)

By contrast, levels four to seven deal with the relationship of humans to the internal world: the mind. Levels two and three do presuppose a mind, but the satisfaction of it is bodily. From level four on the satisfaction is spiritual. The shift from the first three levels to the last four is, in Jung's terms, the shift from the first half of life to the second.

At level four, that of the heart, persons merely discover or rediscover, the inner world. In so doing, they abandon the outer world. They do not yet connect the two. Jung's psychology, Campbell says elsewhere,[3] lies here: in the sheer rediscovery of the inner world. Doubtless the reason is that even though Jung certainly does insist on the reconnection of the inner world with the outer one, he does not preach their mystical fusion. Jung seeks a harmony but still a distinction between the inner and the outer. For Campbell, anything short of fusion likely constitutes less than even reconnection.

The fifth level, which corresponds to the larynx, is purgative: it serves to clear one's mind in preparation for the mystical experiences of the final two levels. The difference between the sixth and the seventh levels is that at the sixth level, which lies above and between the eyes, persons are still conscious of themselves vis-à-vis the world, inner and outer alike. Only at the seventh level, which lies at the crown of the head, do they lose all self-consciousness and become one with all things. Not only do they thereby become—better, prove to be—identical with both inner and outer worlds, but those worlds prove to be identical with each other. Kundalini yoga here certainly goes contrary to Jung, for whom the fusion of outer with inner, of ego with unconscious, would yield the sheer dissolution of the ego rather than a higher combination of it and the unconscious. The result, in Jungian terms, would ultimately be psychosis.[4]

For Campbell, the result is perfection. It is the realization of the radical brand of radical monism that he preaches: the fusion of all opposites into a single, higher unity. In *Hero* and half the time in *Masks* the attainment of that unity is the goal of all myths. In *The Mythic Image* it turns out to be the goal of just the highest category of myths, though likely only because the creators of lesser categories have yet to ascend to higher levels of consciousness. For

Campbell, the final message of myth is always the same: unity. Psychologically, the unity is of the ego with the unconscious. Metaphysically, it is of the individual with the cosmos and of all cosmic domains with one another. Psychologically, the yogi ascends through the levels of the yogi's consciousness. Metaphysically, the yogi ascends through the levels of the cosmos.

Historical Atlas
of World Mythology

Volume one of the *Atlas, The Way of the Animal Powers,* deals with primitive hunters and therefore corresponds to part three of volume one of *Masks.* Volume two, of which only the first of three planned parts has so far been published, deals with primitive planters and so corresponds to part two of volume one of *Masks.* It is entitled *The Way of the Seeded Earth.* Volume three, if it appears, will be entitled *The Way of the Celestial Light*; volume four, *The Way of Man.*

In the *Atlas,* as in *Masks,* geography determines economics, which determines myth. Campbell writes of "the sovereign role of geography in determining the destinies of races" (*Atlas,* II, pt. 1, p. 31). Primitives who live on the plains become hunters and view the world accordingly:

The landscape of the "Great Hunt," typically, was of a spreading plain, cleanly bounded by a circular horizon, with the great blue dome of an exalting heaven above, where hawks and eagles hovered and the blazing sun passed daily; becoming dark by

> night, star-filled, and with the moon there, waning
> and waxing. The essential food supply was of the
> multitudinous grazing herds, brought in by the
> males of the community following dangerous phys-
> ical encounters. And the ceremonial life was ad-
> dressed largely to the ends of a covenant with the
> animals, of reconciliation, veneration, and assur-
> ance that in return for the beasts' unremitting
> offering of themselves as willing victims, their life-
> blood should be given back in a sacred way to the
> earth, the mother of all, for rebirth. (*Atlas*, I, p. 9)

Primitives who live in the jungle become farmers
and likewise view the world accordingly:

> In contrast, the environment of jungle tribes is of
> a dense and mighty foliage, the trunks and branches
> of prodigious trees; no horizon; no dome of the
> sky; but above, a ceiling of leaves populated by
> screeching birds, and underfoot a rough leafage,
> beneath which may lurk scorpions and lethal fangs.
> Out of the rot of fallen wood and leaves, fresh
> sprouts arise—from which the lesson learned ap-
> pears to have been that from death springs life, out
> of death, new birth; and the grim conclusion drawn
> was that the way to increase life is to increase death.
> Accordingly, there has been endemic to the entire
> equatorial belt of this globe what can be described
> only as a frenzy of sacrifice, vegetable, animal, and
> human. . . . (*Atlas*, I, pp. 9–10)

Myths express the differing experiences of each group.
  In the *Atlas*, as in *Masks*, hunters are individualists
and planters are subordinate to their communities.
Also as in *Masks*, hunters are associated with male
rule, male gods, tricksters, and shamans; planters,
with female rule, female gods, ethical gods, and

priests. As in *Masks,* so here as well: Campbell characterizes hunting in contrary ways. Hunting means the death yet also the immortality of the hunter; the hunter's self-centered individuality yet also mystical oneness with his victim; the killing yet also the self-sacrifice of his victim: "And every hunter, in his sacrificial killing is . . . identified with the animal of his kill and at the same time guilty . . . with the primordial guilt of life that lives on life" (*Atlas,* I, p. 93).

Again as in *Masks*: Campbell similarly characterizes planting in somewhat contrary ways. Planting means mystical oneness yet also sacrificial killing: "Life lives on life," he says of both planting (*Atlas,* II, pt. 1, p. 37) and hunting (*Atlas,* I, p. 93). Campbell even ties planting to cannibalism: "Cannibalism is a feature commonly associated with the ceremonies of agricultural tribes recognizing the mythological image of a primal being whose body became and is now the universe. . . . [T]he universe is recognized as a living being from whose body all life and nourishment are drawn . . ." (*Atlas,* II, pt. 1, p. 44). Campbell says that the victim in planting, in contrast to that in hunting, is mystically one with its killer (*Atlas,* II, pt. 1, p. 44), but he says the same of the victim in hunting (*Atlas,* I, p. 93).

Once again, Campbell is thus arguing that hunters and planters, like Westerners and Easterners, are somehow at once different and the same. On the one hand he argues that the experiences, and so the myths, of hunters are the opposite of those of planters:

These, then, are two contrary orders of life, determinant of the lifestyles, mythologies, and rites of the most primitive peoples known: one, of the widespreading animal plains, the other of the sheltering forest. They were not arrived at by reason, but are grounded in fundamental experiences. . . . (*Atlas*, I, p. 112)

On the other hand Campbell argues that the experiences, and so the myths, of hunters and planters are, like those of all other humans, basically the same:

> Significant differences will be evident between the primary Paleolithic and recent ethnological materials; also, between the mythologies of hunting, foraging, planting, and herding tribes, no less than between those, generally, of the nonliterate and literate traditions. Nevertheless, through all these contrasts . . . there will be recognizable, also, a constellation of permanent, archetypal themes and motifs, which are as intrinsic to human life and thought as are the ribs, vertebrae, and cranial parts of our anatomy. (*Atlas*, I, p. 42)

In the *Atlas*, as again in *Masks*, Campbell parallels the individualistic, nonmystical side of hunting with Western religion and the communal, mystical whole of agriculture with Eastern (*Atlas*, II, pt. 1, p. 33). Also as in *Masks*, Campbell sometimes pits the West against the East and sometimes equates them. When he contrasts them, he argues that the Western desire to purify and control the physical world parallels the hunting outlook and that the Eastern yearning for absorption in the world parallels the planting outlook: in the West "One is not to put oneself in accord with [the] world, but to correct it"(*Atlas*, II, pt. 1, p.33).

To whatever extent hunters and farmers are really the same, so are Westerners and Easterners. In that case all peoples, and so all myths, are the same. All myths thereby preach mysticism. As Campbell says of all the volumes that will compose his *Atlas*, "The unfolding through time of all things from one is the simple message, finally, of every one of the creation myths reproduced in the pages of these volumes . . ." (*Atlas*, I, p. 10).

Though Campbell scorns them throughout his writings, in his *Atlas* he is especially contemptuous of "theologians." But where elsewhere he condemns them for interpreting myths literally and historically rather than symbolically and psychologically, now he berates them for interpreting myths at all. As part of his stress on the spontaneousness of mythology, Campbell maintains that myths express raw, unfiltered experience, which theologians artificially "interpret." Indeed, Campbell now argues for comparativism on the grounds that there is a single, universal mythic experience on which theologians, who are invariably Western, impose interpretations to fit the convictions of their specific religions:

> Whether either Bunjil of the Kurnai or the Yahweh specifically of Genesis 2 and 3 is actually equivalent to the "idea of God" of any respectable metaphysician today is a nice question for theologians; but in any case, the recognized sharing of such mythic themes by the simplest known religions with some of those we think of as the most advanced would seem, at least, to say something about the constancy of mythological archetypes. Whether interpreted theologically as supernatural revelations, or naturally as effects of the mind, they exist, endure, and undergo significant transformations on a plane [of experience] little affected, apparently, by any readily identifiable sociological or philosophical influences. (*Atlas*, I, p. 139)

Eastern theologians, if theologians they are, know that their gods and heroes are mere symbols of a universal god and hero rather than the symbolized themselves.

The Inner Reaches of Outer Space

In *The Inner Reaches of Outer Space* Campbell declares anew that the true meaning of myth is symbolic and that its symbolic meaning is both psychological and metaphysical: "Hence, the figurations of myth are metaphorical (as dreams normally are not) in *two* senses simultaneously, as bearing (1) *psychological,* but at the same time *metaphysical,* connotations" (*Inner Reaches,* p. 56). In the terms Campbell employs here, myth refers both to "inner space" and to "outer space."

Campbell similarly declares anew that the meaning of myth is mystical: "The universally distinguishing characteristic of mythological thought and communication is an implicit connotation through all its metaphorical imagery of a sense of identify of some kind, transcendent of appearances, which unites behind the scenes the opposed actors on the world stage" (*Inner Reaches,* p. 110). Metaphysically, not only is there an unknown part of the cosmos—the part discovered by the hero—but it and the known part are identical. Psychologically, not only is there an unknown part of the mind—again, the part discovered by the hero—but it and the known part turn out to be one. Indeed, the cosmos and the mind themselves are the same: "outer and inner space are the same" (*Inner Reaches,* p. 28).

Because Campbell always equates a symbolic meaning, psychological or metaphysical, with a universal one, he equates a literal meaning with a local one. Because he denies that the meaning of myth is at all literal, he denies that the meaning is at all local. Admittedly, Campbell continually *says* that the meaning is local as well as universal:

> Such a recognition of two aspects, a universal and a local, in the constitution of religions everywhere clarifies at one stroke those controversies . . . which forever engage theologians. . . . The first task of any systematic comparison of the myths and religions of mankind should therefore be (it seemed to me) to identify these universals . . . and as far as possible to interpret them; and the second task then should be to recognize and interpret the various locally and historically conditioned transformations of the metaphorical images through which these universals have been rendered. (*Inner Reaches*, pp. 11, 99)

But far more often he dismisses the local meaning. Hence he says that "the biblical mythologem of *The Fall* is but a variant of the universally known *Separation of Heaven and Earth*" (*Inner Reaches*, p. 61).

For Campbell, the local meaning adds nothing to the universal one. Specific symbols are either just a colorful way of expressing archetypes or, at most, a necessary means of conveying them. Even then, symbols are dispensable once the archetypes get conveyed. For Jung, by contrast, symbols not only are a permanently necessary means of conveying archetypes but also shape the archetypes they convey.

Put another way, Campbell effaces Jung's distinction between symbols and archetypes. He dissolves symbols into archetypes. For instance, where Jung would

say that a local conception of god as male rather than
female thereby discloses only the male side of an androgynous god, Campbell says that the Lord's Prayer,
though addressed to a male god, somehow manages to
transcend itself and reveal an androgynous entity:

> For example, at the opening of the Lord's Prayer
> ("Our Father, who art in Heaven . . .") the invo-
> cation, "Our Father," is metaphorical since the
> designated subject is not, in fact, a male parent,
> nor even a human being. . . . An equivalent prayer
> could as well have been addressed to "Our Mother,
> who art within or beneath the earth." (*Inner
> Reaches,* p. 58)

The transmission of the archetype is unaffected by the
symbol transmitting it.

Throughout his writings Campbell contends that traditional Western mythology, by which he means that
of the Bible rather than of Greece and Rome, is dead.
In *Masks: Creative* he argues that Biblical mythology
has been dead since the twelfth century. But in *Inner
Reaches,* as elsewhere, he argues that Biblical mythology has been dead only since the rise of modern
science centuries later. Taken symbolically, the Bible
refers to either metaphysical or psychological reality
and thereby runs askew to science, which deals with
physical reality. Taken literally, as Campbell assumes
the Bible continues to be taken, it covers the same
domain as science and thereby conflicts with science:

> For example: It is believed that Jesus, having risen
> from the dead, ascended physically to heaven (Luke
> 24:51), to be followed shortly by his mother in her
> sleep (Early Christian belief, confirmed as Roman
> Catholic dogma on November 1, 1950). It is also

written that some nine centuries earlier, Elijah, rid-
ing a chariot of fire, had been carried to heaven in
a whirlwind (2 Kings, 2:11). Now, even ascending
at the speed of light, which for a physical body is
impossible, those three celestial voyagers would not
yet be out of the galaxy. (*Inner Reaches*, pp. 30–
31)

In contrast to Campbell, Jung does not base the true
meaning of myth on something external to it like science. Doing so would rob myth of its autonomy. But
perhaps Campbell is no different. Perhaps he, like
Jung, is assuming that science provides the *opportu-
nity* rather than the *justification* for recovering the true,
symbolic meaning of myth. He would thereby be making an interpretive virtue out of an interpretive neces-
sity. But he would still have to justify the symbolic
meaning of myth as the true one. He could no longer
appeal to the rise of science *as* his justification.

In *Masks: Creative* Campbell says that modern
mythmakers are artists, who create myths for a culture
otherwise bereft of them. In *Inner Reaches* Campbell
compares the creative artist with the mystic, who pi-
oneers the route to ultimate reality, and contrasts both
to the priest, who merely perpetuates existing routes:

Carl Jung somewhere has written that the function
of religion is to protect us from an experience of
God. Some fifty percent of the mythic tales of
Ovid's *Metamorphoses* are of characters, ill-
prepared, who were unfavorably transformed by
encounters with divinities, the full blast of whose
light they were unready to absorb. The priest's
practical maxims and metaphorical rites moderate
transcendent light to secular conditions, intending
harmony and enrichment, not disquietude and dis-

solution. In contrast, the mystic deliberately offers himself to the blast and may go to pieces. Like the priest, the artist is a master of metaphorical language. The priest, however, is vocationally committed to a vocabulary already coined, of which he is the representative. He is a performing artist executing scripts already perfectly wrought, and his art is in the execution. Creative artists, in contrast, are creative only in so far as they are innovative. (*Inner Reaches,* p. 121)

Both the artist and the mystic are heroes: they undertake dangerous journeys to an unknown world and return home to inspire others to follow. Campbell acknowledges that the originality of many artists is one of technique rather than of vision. It is those with "innovative insights" (*Inner Reaches,* p. 121) whom he is comparing with mystics.

While Campbell lauds artists and mystics for transcending the everyday world—the world of "desire," "death," and "social duties, virtues, and commitments" (*Inner Reaches,* p. 136)—he nevertheless continues to insist on a return to that world. Because some mystics never return, they are inferior to artists, who, in their reliance on the senses, necessarily do:

The way of the mystic and the way of the artist are related, except that . . . the mystic may come to regard the [everyday] world with indifference, or even disdain. . . . Whereas the artist has been held by his craft in love to the world *as it is,* regarding with equal eye the brahmin, the dog, the eater of dogs, the slayer and the slain. . . . (*Inner Reaches,* p. 143)

Whether the world to which the artist, like the hero, returns is really the everyday one remains as much a question as it did in *Hero*.

In guiding others to ultimate reality, the modern artist is again like the hero of all ages. Campbell even laments that twentieth-century artists no longer occupy the public role that nineteenth-century ones did. Where nineteenth-century artists addressed their communities, twentieth-century, "alienated" artists reach only fellow alienated souls:

> . . . the proper artist [has] lost his public function. Today's pitiful contracts to invent monuments commemorating local-historical events and personages are hardly comparable to the earlier challenges of art, to break windows through the walls of the culture to eternity. Thus, the only true service of a proper artist today will have to be to individuals: reattuning them to forgotten archetypes. . . . (*Inner Reaches*, pp. 144–145)

In *Inner Reaches* Campbell goes further than in any other work in proclaiming myth true. Elsewhere his sheer enthusiasm for the mystical message of myth suggests mightily that he is endorsing as well as explicating that message. In *Inner Reaches* he commits himself explicitly. Having asserted that "proper" art conveys the same message as myth, he describes the truth it conveys: *"The way of art*, when followed 'properly' (in Joyce's sense), leads also to the mountaintop that is everywhere, beyond opposites, of transcendental vision, where, as Blake discovered and declared, the doors of perception are cleansed and every thing appears to man as it is, infinite" (*Inner Reaches*, p. 126). Campbell is saying that art, and therefore myth, are proper *because* they preach the ultimate oneness of all things.

The Power of Myth

The Power of Myth is an edited transcript of filmed conversations between Campbell and journalist Bill Moyers that took place in 1985 and 1986. The twenty-four hours of interviews were pared down to six for the Public Television series that aired nationwide in the spring of 1988.

Because of its interview format *The Power of Myth* is much more informal than Campbell's other writings. Campbell waxes autobiographical. He gives homey applications of his views on marriage, career, and misfortune. He tells more myths than he does in past works. Despite the division into titled chapters, topics crisscross chapter lines.

Campbell's views themselves remain unaltered. Indeed, it would be surprising if, in his early eighties, they changed. Once again, Campbell declares all myths, all peoples, and all things one. While continuing to acknowledge differences among myths—"Myths are so intimately bound to the culture, time and place" (*Power of Myth*, p. 59)—he stresses the similarities:

> That is one of the amazing things about these myths. I have been dealing with this stuff all my life, and I am still stunned by the accuracies of the repetitions. It is almost like a reflex in another medium of the same thing, the same story. . . . If you were not alert to the parallel themes [of myths],

you might think they were quite different stories, but they're not. (*Power of Myth,* pp. 104, 11)

Myths are the same because people are. While again acknowledging differences, differences due above all to geography, Campbell emphasizes the similarities:

> You've got the same body, with the same organs and energies, that Cro-Magnon man had thirty thousand years ago. Living a human life in New York City or living a human life in the caves, you go through the same stages of childhood, coming to sexual maturity, transformation of the dependency of childhood into the responsibility of manhood or womanhood, marriage, then failure of the body, gradual loss of its powers, and death. You have the same body, the same bodily experiences, and so you respond to the same images. (*Power of Myth,* p. 37)

Echoing *Hero,* Campbell, ever the ecumenist, appeals to the oneness of myths to spur the oneness of all peoples:

> We need myths that will identify the individual not with his local group but with the planet. . . . When you see the earth from the moon, you don't see any divisions there of nations or states. This might be the symbol, really, for the new mythology to come. That is the country that we are going to be celebrating. And those are the people that we are one with. (*Power of Myth,* pp. 24, 32)

Campbell is hardly unaware that on the surface myths differ. Once again, he assumes that those differences lie wholly at the literal level, which he dismisses as false. For him, the true meaning of myth remains symbolic. Campbell assumes that myth taken literally is myth taken historically and vice versa. For example, to take Genesis 3 literally is to believe that once upon a time a primordial couple resided in a place on earth called Eden. Campbell assumes that when one discovers that many other peoples have comparable myths of paradise, not to say of creation, the flood, ancestral heroes, and saviors, one will no longer be able to accept as historical, and so as literal, one's own myths: competing historical claims cancel each other out. Yet instead of spurning one's myths as false, one should, for Campbell, reread them as true symbolically: "Read myths. . . . Read other peoples' myths, not those of your own religion, because you tend to interpret your own religion in terms of [literal] facts—but if you read the other ones, you begin to get the [symbolic] message" (*Power of Myth,* p. 6).

Myths for Campbell continue to symbolize both the human mind and ultimate reality. A myth of paradise that literally describes a physical place initially occupied by the first human pair symbolically describes both the unconscious, the original portion of the mind from which consciousness arose, and invisible, immaterial reality, the original portion of the cosmos from which the created, material world emerged: "The Garden of Eden is a metaphor for that innocence that is innocent of time, innocent of opposites, and that is the prime center out of which consciousness then becomes aware of the changes" (*Power of Myth,* p. 50).

As the quotation presupposes, the symbolic meaning of myths also remains mystical. Myths pronounce all oppositions and all distinctions illusory:

MOYERS: Why do we think in terms of opposites?

CAMPBELL: Because we can't think otherwise.

MOYERS: That's the nature of reality in our time.

CAMPBELL: That's the nature of our *experience* of reality.

MOYERS: Man-woman, life-death, good-evil—

CAMPBELL: I and you, this and that, true and untrue—every one of them has its opposite. But mythology suggests that behind that duality there is a singularity over which this plays like a shadow game. (*Power of Myth,* p. 49)

Psychologically, myths say not only that there exists an unconscious as well as conscious mind but also that those two minds are really one. Metaphysically, myths say not only that there exists an immaterial world beyond the material one but also that those two worlds are actually one. Myths say that the human mind and the external world are themselves one as well.

The mysticism that all myths espouse is once again radical monism of the radical variety: myths preach not that everything is heaven rather than earth, soul rather than body, or god rather than the human but that heaven and earth are identical, soul and body identical, and god and human identical. Just as Campbell's hero returns to the everyday world to find within it the strange new world he assumed he had left behind, so all who heed the message of myth find the strange new world within, not beyond, the everyday one. As Campbell puts it, "Divinity informs the world" (*Power of Myth,* p. 31). Campbell typically condemns Biblical religions for teaching that "God is separate from nature" (*Power of Myth,* p. 32). He confirms Moyers' remark that "the supernatural, at least as you understand it, is really only the natural" (*Power of Myth,* p. 98):

> The idea of the supernatural as being something over and above the natural is a killing idea. . . . This is one of the glorious things about the mother-goddess religions, where the world is the body of the Goddess, divine in itself, and divinity isn't something ruling over and above a fallen nature. . . . However, our story of the Fall in the Garden sees nature as corrupt; and that myth corrupts the whole world for us. . . . You get a totally different civilization and a totally different way of living according to whether your myth presents nature as fallen or whether nature is in itself a manifestation of divinity, and the spirit is the revelation of the divinity that is inherent in nature. (*Power of Myth*, pp. 98–99)

Campbell's interpretation of myths worldwide scarcely tallies with conventional interpretations of the myths of Western religions. Christianity, Judaism, Islam, and ancient Greek and Roman religions do not ordinarily teach that god and humans are one. Mysticism is a minor strain in Western religions. Campbell's unruffled rejoinder remains unaltered: Western religions misconstrue their own myths. Even though many, though by no means all, Western myths are found within religions, Campbell once again distinguishes rigidly between myth and religion. He berates religion for reducing its myths from pristine expressions of universal, symbolic truths to degenerate pronouncements of local, literal pseudo-facts:

> Mythology is very fluid. Most of the myths are self-contradictory [at the literal level]. You may even find four or five myths in a given culture, all giving different versions of the same mystery. Then theology comes along and says it has got to be just

this way. Mythology is poetry, and the poetic language is very flexible. Religion turns poetry into prose. God is literally up there, and this is literally what he thinks, and this is the way you've got to behave to get into proper relationship with that god up there. (*Power of Myth*, pp. 141–142)

Campbell's hostility toward religion, by which he means institutionalized religion, never flags.

Campbell continues to take for granted that the conflict between religion and science stands unabated. But because myths for him are not meant literally, they are not intended to describe the material world and therefore do not conflict with science. Either myth and science run askew or, more typically, science is itself mythic:

> MOYERS: One of the intriguing points of your scholarship is that you do not believe science and mythology conflict.
> CAMPBELL: No, they don't conflict. Science is breaking through now into the mystery dimensions. It's pushed itself into the sphere the myth is talking about. It's come to the edge.
> MOYERS: The edge being—
> CAMPBELL: —the edge, the interface between what can be known and what is never to be discovered because it is a mystery that transcends all human research. (*Power of Myth*, p. 132)

Campbell once again assumes not only that the true meaning of myth is psychological, metaphysical, and mystical but also that the true meaning of myth is true: "No, mythology is not a lie, mythology is the penultimate truth—penultimate [only] because the ultimate cannot be put into words" (*Power of Myth*, p. 163). Campbell endorses the mysticism he says all myths preach. He is thus a mystic himself.

In *The Power of Myth*, as in various other works, Campbell sometimes bemoans and sometimes denies the absence of modern myths. Certainly he still takes for granted that traditional Western myths, by which he means Biblical ones, no longer work for many moderns. Taken literally, as he assumes most moderns take them, Biblical myths are undone by science. To cite again Campbell's favorite example:

> For example, Jesus ascended to heaven. The denotation would seem to be that somebody ascended to the sky. That's literally what is being said. But if that were really the meaning of the message, then we have to throw it away, because there would have been no such place for Jesus literally to go. We know that Jesus could not have ascended to heaven because there is no physical heaven anywhere in the universe. Even ascending at the speed of light, Jesus would still be in the galaxy. Astronomy and physics have simply eliminated that as a literal, physical possibility. (*Power of Myth*, p. 56)

At times Campbell says that in the wake of the demise of Biblical mythology "What we have today is a demythologized world" (*Power of Myth*, p. 9). He even ascribes social problems like crime to the absence of myths (*Power of Myth*, pp. 8–9). Campbell looks back nostalgically "to a time when these spiritual principles [of myth] informed the society" (*Power of Myth*, p. 95).

Other times Campbell says, as he does above all in *Hero*, that moderns are continuously creating myths:

MOYERS: Where do the kids growing up in the city—on 125th and Broadway, for example—where do these kids get their myths today?

CAMPBELL: They make them up themselves. This is why we have graffiti all over the city. These kids have their own gangs and their own initiations and their own morality, and they're doing the best they can. (*Power of Myth*, p. 8)

Campbell predicts that new myths, epitomized by the "Star Wars" saga, will come from technology:

Certainly *Star Wars* has a valid mythological perspective. It shows the state as a machine and asks, "Is the machine going to crush humanity or serve humanity?" Humanity comes not from the machine but from the heart. What I see in *Star Wars* is the same problem that *Faust* gives us: Mephistopheles, the machine man, can provide us with all the means, and is thus likely to determine the aims of life as well. . . . Now, when Luke Skywalker unmasks his father, he is taking off the machine role that the father has played. The father was the uniform. That is power, the state role. (*Power of Myth*, p. 18)

Whatever the source of new myths, artists, as Campbell says in *Masks: Creative* and *Inner Reaches,* will be the ones to create them (*Power of Myth*, p. 85).

An Open Life

Like *The Power of Myth, An Open Life* is an edited transcript of interviews with Campbell. These interviews were conducted over a ten-year period beginning in 1975. The interviewer was Michael Toms, host of the nationally broadcast "New Dimensions" radio show.

Like *The Power of Myth, An Open Life* has an informal, relaxed style. Restating his lifelong views, Campbell states anew that the true meaning of myth is neither literal nor historical—the literal and the historical being synonymous. A nonhistorical meaning is therefore a nonliteral one:

> TOMS: There are still millions who interpret the Bible literally.
>
> CAMPBELL: Well, literal interpretation of the Bible faces the problem of scientific and historical research. We know that there was no Garden of Eden; we know that there was no Universal Flood. So we have to ask, what is the spiritual meaning of the Garden of Eden? What is the spiritual meaning of the Flood? Interpreting Biblical texts literally reduces their value; it turns them into newspaper reports. So there was a flood thousands of years ago. So what? But if you can understand what the Flood means in terms of a reference to spiritual circumstances—the coming of chaos, the loss of balance, the end of an age, the end of a psychological posture—then it begins to talk to you again. (*Open Life*, p. 67–68)

The true meaning of myth is, once again, both psychological and metaphysical. Myth refers simultaneously to the human mind and the cosmos:

> When you think, for instance, "God is thy father," do you think he is [literally thy father]? No, that's a metaphor, and the metaphor points to two ends: one is psychological—that's why the dream is metaphoric; the other is metaphysical. Now, dream is metaphoric of the structures in the psyche, and your dream will correspond to the level of psychological realization that you are operating on. The metaphysical, on the other hand, points past all conceptualizations, all things, to the ultimate depth. And when the two come together, when psyche and metaphysics meet, then you have a real myth. (*Open Life*, pp. 21–22)

As Campbell says of the ancient Gnostic Gospel of Thomas, "It says specifically, definitely, and unquestionably that the kingdom of heaven is within, *in* you. And as I pointed out earlier, it also says that 'the kingdom of the Father is spread over the earth and men do not see it' " (*Open Life*, p. 95).

Taken literally, "god" is a personality separate from us. Taken merely psychologically, "god" is the unconscious within us. Taken metaphysically as well, "god" is both outside us and within us:

> Our Western religions tend to put the divine outside of the earthly world and in God, in heaven. But the whole sense of the Oriental is that the kingdom of heaven is within you. Who's in heaven? God is. Where's God? God's within you. And what is God? God is a personification of that world-creative en-

ergy and mystery which is beyond thinking and beyond naming. (*Open Life*, p. 64)

Whether psychological or metaphysical, the meaning of myth for Campbell remains mystical:

The main drift of mythology, if you want to put it into a sentence or two, is that the separateness that is apparent in the phenomenal world is secondary; beyond, and within, and supporting that world is an unseen but experienced unity and identity in us all. (*Open Life*, p. 52)

Yet Campbell, for all his advocacy of the realization of the oneness of all things, also advocates individuality—a topic first raised in *Masks: Creative*. In *An Open Life* he juxtaposes these views and argues for a balance between mysticism and individuality:

CAMPBELL: But then the opposite problem comes up: becoming too strongly linked to the commonalty—losing touch with your own individuality. Part of our loyalty to life is being loyal to our own lives, you see, not sacrificing your self, but letting oneself play in relation to the other in a prudent and positive way.

TOMS: Striking a balance.

CAMPBELL: Exactly that. Striking a balance. (*Open Life*, p. 53)

Whether Campbell actually reconciles the rejection of individuality inherent in mysticism with the rejection of mysticism assumed by individuality is another question. In fact, he himself, as in *Masks: Creative*, pits Eastern mysticism against Western individuality—as if the two were truly irreconcilable:

But, you see, the traditional Oriental idea is that the student should submit absolutely to the teacher. The guru actually assumes responsibility for the student's moral life, and this is total giving. I don't think that's quite proper for a Western person. One of the big spiritual truths for the West is that each of us is a unique creature, and consequently has a unique path. (*Open Life*, pp. 72–73)

Where the Campbell of *Hero* and the first three volumes of *Masks* would have chosen the Eastern route, the Campbell of *Masks: Creative* and *An Open Life* chooses the Western one. He calls this choice "following your bliss"—a phrase first used in *The Power of Myth*. The version of the Grail legend with Parzival rather than Galahad as the hero epitomizes this stance: "So the meaning of the Grail and of most myths is finding the dynamic source in your life so that its trajectory is out of your own center and not something put on you by society" (*Open Life*, pp. 33–34). In stressing the unique life plan of every person, Campbell is like Jung.

In *An Open Life* Campbell goes beyond other works in seeing all myths as hero myths. Asked by his interviewer to say when the notion of the hero first appeared in mythology, Campbell replies:

CAMPBELL: In mythology? That's the *essence* of mythology, I would say. The theme of the visionary quest; the one who goes to follow a vision. It appears one way or another in practically every mythology I know of.

TOMS: So it's the core of all myth.

CAMPBELL: Yes, because the Hero is the one who has gone on the adventure and brought back the message, and who is the founder of institutions—and the giver of life and vitality to his community. (*Open Life*, p. 23)

Campbell is saying not that all myths take the form of a heroic quest but that all myths make heroes out of those who heed them.

Doubtless the most appealing aspect of *An Open Life*, as of *The Power of Myth*, is the advice Campbell dispenses. The phrase "Follow your bliss" sums up the advice of both works. Campbell's boast that he has never regretted practicing this maxim himself makes the advice even more heartfelt:

> There's a wise saying: make your hobby your source of income. Then there's no such thing as work, and there's no such thing as getting tired. That's been my own experience. I did just what I wanted to do. It takes a little courage at first, but who the hell wants you to do just what you want to do; they've all got a lot of plans for you. But you can make it happen. I think it's very important for a young person to have the courage to do what seems to him significant in his life, and not just take a job in order to make money. But this takes a bit of prudence and very careful planning, and may delay financial achievement and comfortable living. But the ultimate result will be very much to his pleasure. (*Open Life*, p. 107)

Campbell thus urges his readers to be heroes themselves: "Each one has to be his own hero and follow the path that's no path" (*Open Life*, p. 109).

NOTES

[1] See, for example, Campbell, *Hero,* p. 4; "Bios and Mythos," p. 335; *Flight of the Wild Gander,* pp. 32–33.

[2] On Kundalini yoga see Campbell, *Mythic Image,* pp. 278–281, 303–305, 330–387; *Myths to Live By,* pp. 109–116; "Seven Levels of Consciousness," *Psychology Today,* 9 (December 1975), pp. 77–78; "The Interpretation of Symbolic Forms," in *The Binding of Prometheus,* eds. Marjorie W. McCune and others (Lewisburg, PA: Bucknell University Press, 1980), pp. 50–58; "Masks of Oriental Gods: Symbolism of Kundalini Yoga," in *Literature of Belief,* ed. Neal E. Lambert (Salt Lake City, UT: Brigham Young University Press, 1981), ch. 6, all but the first few pages of which are a reprinting of *The Mythic Image,* pp. 330–381; *Inner Reaches,* pp. 63ff.; *Power of Myth,* pp. 173–176.

[3] See Campbell, "Seven Levels of Consciousness," p. 78.

[4] For Jung's view of Kundalini yoga see Jung, "Psychological Commentary on Kundalini Yoga" (from the Notes of Mary Foote), *Spring* (1975), pp. 1–32; (1976), pp. 1–31. See also Harold Coward, *Jung and Eastern Thought* (Albany: State University of New York Press, 1985), ch. 6.

CHAPTER NINE

CAMPBELL AS A COMPARATIVIST

Myth is approachable as either a "particular" or a "universal." One can analyze a myth either as a specific myth—as the *Theogony* rather than the *Enuma Elish*—or as an instance of a class—the class of creation myths, hero myths, or all myths. One can ask either what distinguishes one myth from any other or what that myth shares with all others. The two approaches seem distinct and therefore compatible. They seem to be asking different questions: what makes myths different, and what makes them similar?

To draw an analogy, one can be interested in Socrates either as Socrates or as a member of the class of philosophers, Greeks, or human beings. If one is interested in Socrates as Socrates, one looks for exactly those qualities that distinguish him from other philosophers, Greeks, and human beings. If one is interested in Socrates as a philosopher, a Greek, or a human being, one looks for those qualities that he shares with others in his class. To single out Socrates' distinctive characteristics—for example, his skepticism—is not to deny his common ones but only to ignore them as irrelevant. Conversely, to focus on those characteristics that Socrates shares with others—for example, two arms and two legs—is only to ignore, not to deny, the ones that he alone possesses.

Yet in the case of myth, as in the cases of various other cultural phenomena, the two approaches, or at least their proponents, clash. Particularists do concede that even after all the differences have been explicated, some similarities remain: exactly those qualities that make any myth a myth. But particularists dismiss those similarities as too vague to be important. Universalists, for their part, do grant that even after all possible similarities have been explicated, differences remain: those qualities that make any two myths distinct. But universalists in turn reject those differences as trivial.

A Comparison of Two Hero Myths

A comparison of the myths about two ancient heroes, the Greek Odysseus and the Roman Aeneas, illustrates the difference between particularists and universalists.

Both Odysseus and Aeneas undertake a series of dangerous journeys to distant places. By Campbell's criteria, the two are heroic because they succeed where others would either fail or never try.

Particularists, however, would immediately cite the differences. Odysseus, they would note, is seeking to return home to Ithaca, which he left for the Trojan War. Aeneas, by contrast, is seeking a new home. His old home, Troy, has been razed by the Greeks. Odysseus is seeking to reestablish himself as husband, father, and ruler. Having lost his wife, his father, and his country, Aeneas is seeking to establish a new family and nation. Where Odysseus finally returns home,

Aeneas, *breaking* with Campbell's scheme, finally finds a new one.

Odysseus wants to return home for his own sake. By contrast, Aeneas leaves Troy only because he is commanded to go. Duty, not self-interest, impels him. Odysseus might have been acting selflessly in leaving Troy in the first place, but it is Aeneas, not Odysseus, who is selfless in leaving it now. He would have wished either to die at Troy during the fighting or to rebuild it on its ruins.

At the same time Odysseus is initially not so eager to return home promptly. He insists on seeing the world in the process. It is out of curiosity that he meets the Cyclops. His crew must beseech him to forsake Circe. Even though he declines Calypso's offer of immortality in exchange for remaining with her, she does tempt him. With her offer of wealth and power Nausicaa tempts him to stay, too. While most of the world he encounters is barbaric, some of it is alluring. Returning home requires resolve, as Campbell himself would stress.

With Aeneas, however, venturing forth in the first place requires resolve. Both his mother, Venus, and his dead wife, Creusa, must urge him to go. Once he leaves, his father, his mother, and other gods must prod him to continue his journey. Dido proves the strongest tempter—not, however, because she, like Calypso, offers him immortality in a supernatural world but, on the contrary, because she offers him the human domesticity that he was forced to abandon at Troy.

In the fashion of Campbell's pattern, Odysseus' adventures take him to a strange, barbaric, supernatural realm filled with monsters and other dangers. Aeneas encounters largely human foe. Once both reach their destinations, they must still defeat enemies: the suitors in the case of Odysseus, the Latins in the case of Aeneas. Yet even the suitors, while human, perpetuate the barbarism that Odysseus had encountered abroad. By contrast, Aeneas' enemies are much less barbaric.

Odysseus and Aeneas share above all a descent to the underworld. As a descent from the world of the living to that of the dead and back, the trek is doubtless the most extraordinary feat for both. But, again, particularists would note the differences. From his descent Odysseus learns his own personal destiny. From his descent Aeneas learns the destiny of his people. If Odysseus is at all transformed by his visit, the transformation does not spur him homeward but, in the wake of the mere shadowy existence he witnesses in Hades, intensifies his love of life. By contrast, Aeneas' undeniable transformation takes the form of strengthening his determination to proceed to Italy. Odysseus now treasures his old home even more. Aeneas is at last able to break with his.

Odysseus lands home alone, having lost all of his crew. In part he is heroic because he alone survives. Aeneas lands with virtually all of his followers save for those he left to establish a colony in Sicily. He is heroic because he makes it to Italy with his followers. Had he alone survived, he would have been considerably less heroic.

Odysseus' return is a personal triumph; Aeneas', that of a whole people. Odysseus is the ruler of one small kingdom within Greece, and even it he scarcely founded. Aeneas is the founder of a future civilization. In returning, Odysseus, contrary to Campbell's scheme, bestows no "boon" on his fellow Greeks or even Ithacans. The future of neither Greece nor even Ithaca rests with him. By contrast, Aeneas comes to

Italy precisely to bestow the greatest possible boon on his people: the founding of the greatest empire in the world.

Odysseus' success stems primarily from his own cunning and resourcefulness. Aeneas' stems from divine aid. While Odysseus, too, has divine help, he is far more independent than Aeneas.

Finally, Vergil is writing to present a Roman alternative to Homer's Greek heroism. His revulsion for Odysseus, whom he portrays as ruthless and treacherous, underscores the difference. Vergil's likely questioning of the worth of even Aeneas' feat puts his view of heroism even further afield of Homer's.

Against comparativists, particularists would say in sum that even when the adventures of Odysseus and Aeneas follow Campbell's heroic pattern, that pattern provides only an outline to be filled in differently by each mythmaker. The pattern is like an archetype for Jung: its meaning comes from the particular form it takes in any individual case. In response, comparativists would say that the common fact of heroism, as sketched by Campbell's pattern, far outweighs the idiosyncrasies of each case.

Campbell's Recognition of Differences

How staunch a comparativist is Campbell? Certainly he recognizes differences not only between one category of myth and another—for example, between creation and hero myths—but also between the myths of one society and those of another. "Myths" he says repeatedly, are "intimately bound to the culture, time and place" (*Power of Myth,* p. 59). He classifies mythologies worldwide as primitive distinctively Occidental, Oriental, or creative.

Even Campbell's hero pattern, by far his most elaborate, allows for variations. The hero need only leave the everyday world for an unknown one, encounter female and male gods, and return victoriously with some power for his countrymen. While the hero must be an adult male, he can be young or old, rich or poor, king or commoner, god or human. How and why he proceeds forth, how he gains entry to the new world, what boon he secures, how he secures it, and how he returns home are all open-ended:

> The mythological hero, setting forth from his commonday hut or castle, is lured, carried away, or else voluntarily proceeds, to the threshold of adventure. There he encounters a shadow presence that guards the passage. The hero may defeat or conciliate this power and go alive into the kingdom of the dark (brother-battle, dragon-battle; offering, charm), or be slain by the opponent and descend in death (dismemberment, crucifixion). Beyond the threshold, then, the hero journeys through a world of unfamiliar yet strangely intimate forces, some of which severely threaten him (tests), some of which give magical aid (helpers). When he arrives at the nadir of the mythological round, he undergoes a supreme ordeal and gains his reward. The triumph may be represented as the hero's sexual union with the goddess-mother of the world (sacred marriage), his recognition by the father-creator (father atonement), his own divinization (apotheosis). . . . The final work is that of the return. If the powers have blessed the hero, he now sets forth under their protection (emissary); if not, he flees and is pursued

(transformation flight, obstacle flight). (*Hero*, pp. 245–246)

Hero myths sometimes focus on only one or two elements of the pattern, sometimes fuse elements, and sometimes duplicate elements (*Hero*, p. 246). Campbell goes so far as to say that "The changes rung on the simple scale of the monomyth defy description" (*Hero*, p. 246).

Furthermore, Campbell grants that a mythic pattern or archetype expresses itself only through a particular form, never pure: ". . . universals are never experienced in a pure state, abstracted from their locally conditioned ethnic applications" (*Mythic Image*, p. 11). Campbell even says that in the differences, the "infinitely various metamorphoses" of universals, lies the "fascination" (*Mythic Image*, p. 11).

Moreover, Campbell is prepared not merely to note differences but also to explain them. Where he explains similarities psychologically, he explains differences socially and above all geographically: "Myths take into their domain the conditions and even the geographical idiosyncrasies of the various landscapes. One will be in a desert land, another in a jungle, and so on" (*Open Life*, p. 60). What Campbell says of initiation rites applies to myths, a term that he in fact uses broadly to encompass rituals as well as stories:

Hence, although the rites certainly have a psychological function and must be interpreted [i.e., explained] in terms of the general psychology of the human species, each local system itself has a long history behind it of a particular sort of social experience and cannot be explained in general psychological terms. It has been closely adjusted to specific, geographically determined conditions of existence. . . . (*Masks: Primitive,* pp. 90–91)

Again and again, Campbell states that a myth must be not only explained but also interpreted both locally and universally:

Such a recognition of two aspects, a universal and a local, in the constitution of religions everywhere clarifies at one stroke those controversies touching eternal and temporal values, truth and falsehood, which forever engage theologians. . . . The first task of any systematic comparison of the myths and religions of mankind should therefore be (it seemed to me) to identify these universals . . . and as far as possible to interpret them; and the second task then should be to recognize and interpret the various locally and historically conditioned transformations of the metaphorical images through which these universals have been rendered. (*Inner Reaches,* pp. 11, 99)

Campbell's Stress on Similarities

Yet even though Campbell acknowledges, if not stresses, the differences among myths, he finally dismisses them as trivial. As he puts it, "By casting off the [mere] shell of the local, historical inflection, one comes to the elementary idea which is the path to one's own innermost heart" (*Open Life,* p. 68). "Dissolving, the ethnic [i.e., local] ideas become transparent to the archetypes, those elementary ideas of which they [i.e., the ethnic ideas] are no more than the local masks" (*Atlas*, II, pt. 1, p. 111).

Myths for Campbell are fundamentally the same: in origin, function, and meaning. They constitute a *"philosophia perennis* of the human race" (*Myths to Live By*, p. 264):

> . . . in the face of the ubiquitous myth itself, its long persistence and the basic consistency of its lesson, all variations of detail must appear to be of only secondary moment; all finally conspire to inflect the single lesson. . . . [I]t is a story, therefore, which knows how to bend itself and reshape itself to the diverse needs of divers [sic] times and places; but there can be no doubt, it is one story. (*Where the Two Came to Their Father*, pp. 61–62)

"I have been dealing with this stuff all my life, and I am still stunned by the accuracies of the repetitions. It is almost like a reflex in another medium of the same thing, the same story" (*Power of Myth*, p. 104).

Typically, Campbell says on the one hand that the hero "evolves as the culture evolves" (*Power of Myth*, p. 135) but on the other hand that "Essentially, it might even be said [that] there is but one archetypal mythic hero whose life has been replicated in many lands by many, many people" (*Power of Myth*, p. 136). To cite an example, Campbell first stresses, not merely acknowledges, the differences in the myths about primordial androgynes. In Hinduism androgyny represents the mystical overriding of sexual and nonsexual distinctions. In Judaism androgyny symbolizes the prefallen state of humanity in Eden—division coming with the fall. In Aristophanes' speech in Plato's *Symposium* androgyny stands for the mystery of love: sexual attraction represents the reunification of the severed halves of once androgynous humans (*Masks: Primitive*, pp. 103–110). Yet after emphasizing these differences among the three mythologies, Campbell says:

> If we now allow all three of these versions—the Hindu, the Hebrew, and the Greek—to supplement and play against one another in our minds, we shall certainly find it difficult to believe that they have not been derived from a single common tradition. . . . (*Masks: Primitive*, p. 110)

Campbell's insistence on a common origin surely makes the similarities paramount.

The reason that all myths are finally the same is that humanity is. Like all modern social scientists, Campbell assumes the "psychic unity" of humanity: the notion that all humans are at heart alike. Campbell even faults those "dedicated to the proposition that mankind is not a species but an indefinitely variable dough, shaped by a self-creating demiurge, 'Society' " ("Bios and Mythos," p. 331). Campbell's advocacy of world unity rests on his assumption of psychic unity.

The Argument for Comparativism

What is Campbell's argument for the greater importance of similarities than differences? It is the fact itself of similarities:

> Comparative cultural studies have now demonstrated beyond question that similar mythic tales are to be found in every quarter of this earth. When

Cortes and his Catholic Spaniards arrived in Aztec Mexico, they immediately recognized in the local religion so many parallels to their own True Faith that they were hard put to explain the fact. . . . There was a High God above all, who was beyond all human thought and imaging. There was even an incarnate Savior, associated with a serpent, born of a virgin, who had died and was resurrected, one of whose symbols was a cross. . . . Modern scholarship, systematically comparing the myths and rites of mankind, has found just about everywhere legends of virgins giving birth to heroes who die and are resurrected. (*Myths to Live By*, pp. 7–8)

So striking for Campbell are the similarities that the meaning, not to add the origin and function, of myth must lie in them.

Needless to say, particularists would demur. They might well deny the existence of the similarities. They would certainly deny their importance. They would argue that the differences count far more. They would argue that the sheer presence in even all myths of gods, virgins, heroes, saviors, death, and rebirth would beg, not answer, the key question: whether these archetypes mean the same in each case.

The appeal to similarities themselves is the standard argument of all comparativists. For example, Edward Tylor argues that the similarities he finds in hero myths are too uniform to be coincidental, which for him means historical. The myths must therefore have a common source, which for him means a psychological one:

Of all things, what mythologic work needs is breadth of knowledge and of handling. Interpretations made to suit a narrow view reveal their weakness when exposed to a wide one. See Herodotus rationalizing the story of the infant Cyrus, exposed and suckled by a bitch; he simply relates that the child was brought up by a herdsman's wife named Spakô, . . . whence arose the fable that a real bitch rescued and fed him. So far so good—for a single case. But does the story of Romulus and Remus likewise record a real event, mystified in the self-same manner by a pun on a nurse's name, which happened to be a she-beast's? Did the Roman twins also really happen to be exposed, and brought up by a foster-mother who happened to be called Lupa? . . . [I]f we look properly into the matter, we find that these two stories are but specimens of a wide-spread mythic group, itself only a section of that far larger body of traditions in which exposed infants are saved to become national heroes.[1]

Lord Raglan argues the same. So common are the similarities he, too, finds in hero myths that the myths must have a common source, which for him means a ritualistic rather than historical one:

I doubt whether even the most fervent euhemerist would maintain that all these resemblances are mere coincidences; and if not, then three possibilities remain. The first is that all, or some, of the heroes were real persons whose stories were altered to make them conform to a ritual pattern; the second is that all, or some, of them were real persons in whose lives ritual played a predominant part; and the third [i.e., Raglan's view] is that they were all purely mythical [i.e., ritualistic].[2]

Like Tylor and especially Raglan, Campbell equates particularistic explanations with historical ones. At times he, like them, says that comparativist explanations render historical ones incredible: ''The idea of the Virgin Birth, for example, is argued as a historical fact, whereas in practically every mythology of the world instances have appeared of this elementary idea. American Indian mythologies abound in virgin births. Therefore, the intended reference of the archetypal image cannot possibly have been to a supposed occurrence in the Near East in the first century B.C.'' (*Inner Reaches*, p. 21). Other times he, unlike them, maintains that comparativist explanations render historical ones merely irrelevant, not incredible. Here a hero myth *can* have a historical figure behind it but simply need not:

> We may doubt whether such a scene ever actually took place. But that would not help us any; for we are concerned, at present, with problems of symbolism, not of historicity. We do not particularly care whether Rip van Winkle, Kamar al-Zaman, or Jesus Christ ever actually lived. (*Hero*, p. 230)

Any theorist of myth necessarily considers all myths basically the same. Theorists differ over what aspects of myth are the same: origin, function, or content. For Otto Rank, for example, the content as well as the origin and function of myth is the same: myth everywhere not only arises to release unconscious sexual wishes but, to do so, describes the realization of those wishes. Rank's, or Freud's, theory thus specifies the plot of myth.

For Campbell, too, the content as well as the origin and function of myth is the same—most clearly in the case of hero myths, where he provides a common plot, but in the cases of other kinds of myths as well. In *The Mythic Image* Campbell provides no common plot, but he does provide common motifs, or "images": sleep, dream, death, rebirth, child savior, virgin birth, world mountain, great goddess, cyclical time, *axis mundi*, primeval waters, serpent, sacrifice, awakening, and lotus. These images, or archetypes, are the counterparts to the archetypes that appear in hero myths: hero, call, journey, female and male gods, and return. But in *The Mythic Image* Campbell never interprets any of the archetypes, the way he does in *Hero*. He may therefore not be precluding differences in meaning from society to society.

At the outset of *Masks: Primitive* (ch. 2) Campbell enumerates universal experiences that constitute less the images than the topics of myths: suffering, gravity, alternation of light and dark, division into male and female, birth, breast feeding, excreting, Oedipus and Electra Complexes, puberty, and old age. While these shared topics constitute more of a common content than the sheer images of *The Mythic Image,* they do not add up to a common plot or a common meaning, which, as in *The Mythic Image,* may therefore vary from society to society.

Moreover, in much of the rest of *Masks,* as in the *Atlas* and other works, Campbell wavers back and forth between stressing the differing experiences of peoples and stressing the similarities. Whenever Campbell does say, as he does half the time, that hunters are at heart planters and Westerners at heart Easterners, he is coming close to saying that the meaning of all myths, which express those common experiences, is the same.

Comparativism and Symbolism

To say that the meaning of all myths is the same is not necessarily to make that meaning symbolic. Tylor, Raglan, and Vladimir Propp maintain that all hero myths have the same plot,[3] but none of them thereby deems the meaning of that plot symbolic. To qualify as a hero, a figure must, for all three, undertake the actions each prescribes, but none of the three says that in so doing the hero symbolizes something else. For all three, a hero is someone who literally, which does not mean historically, undertakes the adventures that his myth says he does.

By contrast, Campbell interprets heroism symbolically. Taken psychologically, a hero symbolizes the human ego, and his adventures symbolize the ego's encounter with the unconscious. Taken metaphysically, a hero symbolizes the human essence, and his adventures symbolize the encounter of that essence with the essence of the cosmos itself.

Because Tylor, Raglan, and Propp interpret hero myths comparatively yet literally, a comparativist interpretation need not mean a symbolic one. Campbell must therefore justify not only his comparativist analysis but, in addition, his symbolic one. To argue, as all comparativists do, that all heroes are fundamentally the same is to reduce individual heroes to mere instances of a class. It is not also to reduce that class to a symbol of something else.

From the fact of similarities at the literal level—the fact of heroes worldwide undertaking the same kinds of adventures—Campbell can at most conclude that all heroes are the same—the differences being trivial—but not also, as he does, that they are symbolic—the literal similarities somehow canceling out one another. Yet of not just hero myths but myths in general he typically says:

> Traditionally, . . . in the orthodoxies of popular faiths mythic beings and events are generally regarded and taught as facts; and this particularly in Jewish and Christian spheres. There *was* an Exodus from Egypt; there *was* a Resurrection of Christ. . . . When these stories are interpreted, though, not as reports of historic fact, but as merely imagined episodes projected onto history, and when they are recognized, then, as analogous to like projections produced elsewhere, . . . the import becomes obvious; namely, that although false and to be rejected as accounts of physical history, such universally cherished figures of the mythic imagination must represent facts of the mind. . . . And whereas it must, of course, be the task of the historian, archaeologist, and prehistorian to show that the myths are as facts untrue—that there is no one Chosen People of God in this multiracial world, no Found Truth to which we all must bow, no One and Only True Church—it will be more and more, and with increasing urgency, the task of the psychologist and comparative mythologist . . . to identify, analyze, and interpret the symbolized "facts of the mind. . . ." (*Myths to Live By,* pp. 10–11)

While Campbell can certainly continue to claim that "whenever a myth has been taken literally its sense has been perverted" (*Masks: Primitive,* p. 27), he must do so on more than comparativist grounds.

Finally, one might even question Campbell's assumption that believers who realize the existence of rival heroes worldwide can no longer accept their own alone. For believers may, like particularists, still be more impressed by the differences than by the similarities.

Comparativism and Historicity

If on the one hand Campbell, unlike Tylor and Raglan, at times grants that a symbolic hero can also be a historical one, on the other hand he, unlike them as well, assumes that a literal *interpretation* of a hero myth is also a historical one. As the earlier quotation (beginning "Traditionally") makes clear, Campbell assumes that to interpret myth literally is to interpret it historically. He abhors all historical interpretations because he also assumes that to interpret myth historically is to interpret it literally. Again, one might question Campbell's assumption. In any event he himself goes so far as to claim that myths get interpreted historically only once their pristine symbolic meaning either has been lost or is no longer believed:

> In the later stages of many mythologies, the key images hide like needles in great haystacks of secondary anecdote and rationalization; for when a civilization has passed from a mythological to a secular point of view, the older images are no longer felt or quite approved. . . . And in modern progressive Christianity the Christ—Incarnation of the Logos and Redeemer of the World—is primarily a historical personage, a harmless country wise man of the semi-oriental past, who preached a benign doctrine of "do as you would be done by," yet was executed as a criminal. His death is read as a splen-

did lesson in integrity and fortitude. Wherever the poetry of myth is interpreted as biography, history, or science, it is killed. The living images become only remote facts of distant time or sky. (*Hero*, pp. 248–249)

NOTES

[1]Edward B. Tylor, *Primitive Culture*, fifth ed. (New York: Harper Torchbooks, 1958), I (retitled *The Origins of Culture*), pp. 281–282.

[2]Lord Raglan, *The Hero* (New York: Vintage, 1956), p. 186. Neither Otto Rank nor Vladimir Propp explicitly says that the similarities he finds among hero myths proves that the heart of the myths lies in them, but any preoccupation with similarities rather than differences surely presupposes the view.

[3]Strictly, Propp confines himself to fairy tales rather than to myths. Following Campbell, I am using the term ''hero myth'' broadly to cover all stories about heroes.

CHAPTER TEN

THE ORIGIN OF MYTH

Having committed himself to comparativism, how does Campbell account for similarities in the myths? There are only two possible explanations for them: independent invention and diffusion. Either every society on its own creates myth, or else a single one does, from which it spreads to others. In some works Campbell attributes the similarities to independent invention; in others, to diffusion; in still others, to both.

The Hero
with a Thousand Faces

Despite his modest claim in *Hero* (p. 39, note 43) that he is seeking only to *establish* the similarities among hero myths, Campbell is in fact seeking to account for them as well: "Why," he asks, "is mythology everywhere the same, beneath its varieties of costume?" (*Hero*, p. 4) His answer is psychological: myths are the same because the mind, which creates them, is. That answer is a case of independent invention: it assumes that the human mind is everywhere the same, so that individuals everywhere will inevitably produce the same artifacts.

On the one hand Campbell says repeatedly that myths arise spontaneously from the "psyche," by which he means the unconscious: "For the symbols of mythology are not manufactured; they cannot be ordered, invented, or permanently suppressed. They are spontaneous productions of the psyche . . ." (*Hero*, p. 4). Whether the unconscious is created, as for Freud, or inherited, as for Jung, Campbell considers at length in *Masks* but not at all in *Hero*, though he does imply (*Hero*, p. 17) that it is inherited.

On the other hand Campbell distinguishes myths from dreams on exactly the grounds that myths are consciously created:

> But if we are to grasp the full value of the materials, we must note that myths are not exactly comparable to dream. Their figures originate from the same sources—the unconscious wells of fantasy— and their grammar is the same, but they are not the spontaneous products of sleep. On the contrary, their patterns are consciously controlled. (*Hero*, p. 256)

Moreover, Campbell continually maintains that ancients were aware of the true, symbolic, psychological meaning of myths. Only moderns, who invariably read myths literally, are not: "The old teachers knew what they were saying. Once we have learned to read again their symbolic language, it requires no more than the talent of an anthologist to let their teaching be heard" (*Hero*, p. vii). How, then, can Campbell still maintain that myths arise out of the unconscious?

Doubtless Campbell is distinguishing between the unconscious source of myths and the consciousness of that source. He is saying that ancient interpreters, like their modern, psychoanalytic counterparts, *recognized* the unconscious source of myths. Otherwise the true meaning of myths would have remained unknown.

Bios and Mythos

In "Bios and Mythos," his essay in the Festschrift for the Freudian anthropologist Géza Róheim, Campbell first contrasts those who stress the differences among myths—the anthropologist Bronislaw Malinowski and other functionalists—to those who, like Róheim, stress the similarities. Functionalists, he argues, fail to see the difference between function, where differences undeniably lie, and "homology," where similarities lie ("Bios and Mythos," pp. 330–336). How functionalists, who invariably maintain that myth serves the same function in every society, stress only differences Campbell does not make clear. Indeed, so intent are functionalists on finding similarities that they typically look for functional equivalents of myth like ideology in societies that lack myth itself. In subsequent works Campbell himself lists four functions that myth serves everywhere.

Unfortunately, it is no clearer what Campbell means by the homologies that unite myths than by the functions that divide them. Having in any case argued for similarities in the form of homologies, he argues for independent invention rather than diffusion as their cause. He does not deny that diffusion occurs. He merely relegates it to a secondary cause. It can account for similarities within a "culture sphere" but not for similarities cross-culturally:

However, it is important not to lose sight of the fact that the mythological archetypes (Bastian's Elementary Ideas) cut across the boundaries of these culture sphere and are not confined to any one or two, but are variously represented in all. For example, the idea of survival after death seems to be about coterminous with the human species; so also that of the sacred area (sanctuary), that of the efficacy of ritual, of ceremonial decorations, sacrifice, and of magic, that of supernal agencies, that of a transcendental yet ubiquitously immanent sacred power (mana, wakonda, śakti, etc.), that of a relationship between dream and the mythological realm, that of initiation, that of the initiate (shaman, priest, seer, etc.), and so on, for pages. ("Bios and Mythos," p. 333)[1]

By "archetypes," which is Campbell's most common term for the similarities among myths, he does not, like Jung, always mean inherited rather than acquired similarities.[2] Here, as elsewhere, he may be using the term for the products of similar experiences. As in *Hero*, so here: Campbell compares myths with dreams and deems both the product of the unconscious ("Bios and Mythos," p. 335). But in both works he does not consider the origin of that unconscious.

The Masks of God

In *Hero* Campbell deals primarily with whole myths. While he deals as well with individual archetypes like the hero, the call, and the mother goddess, he subsumes them under the stories in which they appear. By contrast, in *Masks*, as in the later *Mythic Image*,

Campbell deals primarily with archetypes themselves. He is interested less in the plots of myths than in the archetypal characters and events of which the plots are composed.

At the outset of *Masks: Primitive* Campbell attributes the archetypal similarities among myths to independent invention rather than diffusion. But independent invention must itself be explained. There are two possible explanations: heredity, Campbell's likely explanation in *Hero,* and experience. Where for Jung only inherited causes are archetypal, for Campbell, who thus uses the term far more loosely, even acquired ones can be.

By archetypes Campbell, like Jung, means not just recurrent mythological motifs but ones that stir emotion and propel behavior. Since, however, all genuine mythological motifs do so, all of them are archetypal.

In *Masks* Campbell invokes the studies of ethologists Niko Tinbergen and Konrad Lorenz to explain archetypes. Archetypes, he proposes (*Masks: Primitive,* pp. 21–131), are the releasers of what, according to these ethologists, directly prompt emotions and actions in animals: innate releasing mechanisms (IRM's).[3] Archetypes are the stimuli, or triggers, that activate IRM's, which in turn are the stimuli, or triggers,[4] that activate emotions and actions. Archetypes are to IRM's as IRM's are to emotions and actions. Yet archetypes themselves need to be activated, and it is concrete symbols that are the stimuli, or triggers, that activate them.

IRM's, believes Campbell, are found in humans as well as animals. The difference between the IRM's of humans and those of animals is that human ones respond to stimuli—archetypes—that are largely implanted by experience where animal ones respond to stimuli that are largely innate. Human stimuli are largely conditioned rather than unconditioned. Campbell cites the classic case of the innate response of newborn chicks to the sight of a hawk:

> Chicks with their eggshells still adhering to their tails dart for cover when a hawk flies overhead, but not when the bird is a gull or duck, heron or pigeon. . . . Here we have an extremely precise image—never seen before, yet recognized with reference not merely to its form but to its form in motion, and linked, furthermore, to an immediate, unplanned, unlearned, and even unintended system of appropriate action: flight, to cover. The image of the inherited enemy is already sleeping in the nervous system, and along with it the well-proven reaction. ("Bios and Mythos," p. 31)[5]

An actual hawk is a symbol. The category hawk is the archetype. The releaser of the emotion of fear and the action of flight is the IRM. Though the archetype needs an actual hawk to work, it itself is clearly innate. For the chick experiences fear and scurries for cover before it has ever encountered any hawks.

Campbell grants that some of the stimuli to which humans respond are innate.[6] In fact, he even grants that some of the stimuli to which animals respond are acquired.[7] His claim is that humans respond to far more acquired stimuli than do animals:

> But it must not be forgotten that the entire instinct structure of man is much more open to learning and conditioning than that of animals, so that when evaluating human behavior we have always a very much stronger factor of individual experience to consider than when measuring . . . the innate re-

leasing mechanisms (IRMs) of insect, fish, bird—
or even ape. (*Masks: Primitive*, p. 37)

Echoing Róheim, Campbell attributes this difference to the greater immaturity of humans at birth: "It
is by now a commonplace of biological thought to ob-
serve that man . . . is born at least a year too soon,
completing in the sphere of society a development that
other species accomplish within the womb" (*Masks:
Primitive*, p. 38). Because humans take longer to mature, they are more subject to experience and therefore
to imprinting: ". . . whereas even the animals most
helpless at birth mature very quickly, the human infant
is utterly helpless during the first dozen years of its
existence and . . . is completely subject to the pres-
sures of imprints of its local society." (*Masks: Primitive*, pp. 36–37)

The experiences that for Campbell have imprinted
the most powerful stimuli, or archetypes, on humans
are suffering, gravity, light and dark, male and female,
birth, breast feeding, excreting, Oedipus and Electra
Complexes, puberty, and old age (*Masks: Primitive*,
ch. 2). Some of these experiences are lifelong. Others
occur only at certain stages in life. Once imprinted, a
stimulus, upon activation by subsequent experience,
activates an IRM, which in turn impels the corresponding emotion and behavior. Without the archetype the subsequent experience would make much less
of an impact. The power of past experiences, imprinted in the form of an archetype, accounts for its
impact. Functioning as a symbol, subsequent experience activates the archetype and thereby begins the
process that ends in the manifestation of emotion and
behavior.

In his emphasis on acquired rather than innate stimuli,[8] Campbell is Freudian rather than Jungian. Jung stresses innate stimuli, to which, as noted, he restricts the term "archetypes." Neither Freud nor Jung has any notion of IRM's, which Campbell inserts between archetypes and the feelings and actions provoked.[9] For Jung, present experience activates the innate archetypes that in turn activate feelings and actions.[10] For Freud, present experience activates the equivalent of acquired archetypes, archetypes acquired through earlier experience. Where for Jung the experience of one's mother activates the innate archetype of the Great Mother, for Freud the experience of one's mother activates an impression—the equivalent of an acquired archetype—made by one's prior experience of her.[11]

As intent as Campbell is at the outset of *Masks* to prove that the similarities in myths stem from similar experiences,[12] no sooner does he make his case (*Masks: Primitive,* pt. 1) than he turns abruptly to differences in myths stemming from different experiences. Primitive hunters and planters have opposed kinds of experiences and therefore opposed kinds of myths. Furthermore, those experiences have nothing to do with any of the universal ones that Campbell presents in part one of *Masks: Primitive.* They are entirely economic. In subsequent volumes of *Masks* Campbell also stresses the difference in myths, but now he attributes them less to differing experiences of any kind than to differing metaphysical beliefs.

At the same time Campbell, in all but volume four of *Masks,* then denies the very differences that he has enumerated. Once again, as at the start of volume one of *Masks,* all myths prove to be the same, though because the beliefs rather than any experiences underlying the beliefs are the same. Beliefs shape experience rather than, as in volume one of *Masks,* vice versa.

Despite Campbell's initial stress on experience as the source of the similarities in myths, he soon turns instead to diffusion rather than experience as the source. He argues for the diffusion of myths within the West; within the East; from the East to the West; and above all from the "hieratic city state" of Sumer, the culmination of primitive planting, to all of the East. So obsessed is he with diffusion as the cause of similarities that many critics take him to be contradicting his initial, experiential explanation.

Perhaps there is no contradiction. Perhaps Campbell is attributing to diffusion only similarities in symbols—the pervasiveness of an Odysseus-like hero—and is still ascribing to experience similarities in archetypes—the pervasiveness of a hero per se. But the similarities he attributes to diffusion—notably, the concept of a hieratic city state—are so broad as to seem to be archetypes, not mere symbols.

In an essay devoted to explaining the similarities between the archetypes of a single Sioux Indian myth and those of other myths worldwide, Campbell juxtaposes diffusion with independent invention as equally plausible hypotheses:

> Who will say by what miracle—whether of history or of psychology—these two homologous images came into being, the one in India and the other in North America? It is, of course, possible that either one of the two paths of diffusion just described may have been followed. However, it is also possible that the two images were independently developed by some process of *convergence,* as an "effect," to use Frazer's words again, "of similar causes acting alike on the similar constitution of the human mind in different countries and under differ-

ent skies'': for in India, too, there was a meeting and joining of animal and plant cultures when the Aryans with their herds arrived in the Dravidian agricultural zone. Analogous processes may have been set in play—as in two separate alchemical retorts. (*Flight of The Wild Gander,* p. 104)

Here Campbell is clearly deeming diffusion and independent invention rival explanations, in which case diffusion, like independent invention, must be intended to account for archetypes, not just for symbols.

The Mythic Image

In *The Mythic Image,* as in both *Hero* and ''Bios and Mythos,'' Campbell compares myths with dreams and says that both come from the unconscious: ''This argument is, briefly, that through dreams a door is opened to mythology, since myths are of the nature of dream, and that, as dreams arise from an inward world unknown to waking consciousness, so do myths . . .'' (*Mythic Image,* p. xi). Whether the unconscious is acquired or inherited Campbell once again does not say. Taking the comparison between myths and dreams much further than he does in either *Hero* or ''Bios and Mythos,'' he contends that myths, like dreams, are composed less of plots than of images; have a logic of their own; and can only be experienced, not analyzed.

Yet in explaining the similarities among myths, Campbell, as surprisingly as in *Masks,* downplays the importance of independent invention, under which the unconscious falls, and focuses instead on diffusion. (*Mythic Image,* pp. 72–74). At the same time it is unclear what portion of myth get diffused. Are mythic "images," the elements that get diffused, the archetypes composing myths or only the symbols expressing those archetypes? What Campbell means by archetypes is clear: sleep, dream, death, rebirth, child savior, virgin birth, world mountain, great goddess, cyclical time, *axis mundi*, primeval waters, serpent, sacrifice, awakening, and lotus. Whether "mythic images" are these archetypes themselves or only the symbols expressing them is the question.[13]

While Campbell himself does not explicitly deny the possibility, it is unlikely that concrete symbols expressing archetypes are what come from the unconscious. It is much more likely that archetypes themselves do. If the images are archetypes themselves, then Campbell is simultaneously attributing archetypes both to diffusion, for it is the images that are diffused, and to the unconscious, for it is the archetypes that most likely stem from the unconscious. If, however, the images are the particular symbols expressing archetypes, then Campbell is attributing the archetypes to the unconscious, a form of independent invention, and is attributing their expression to diffusion. His prime example of diffusion, the recurrence of the number 432 and its multiples (*Mythic Image*, p. 74), is so specific as almost certainly to constitute a symbol rather than an archetype.[14] Images, the entities diffused, would therefore be symbols, not archetypes.

Whether it is symbols or archetypes that get diffused, it is from Mesopotamia that for Campbell high civilization spread to the rest of the world (*Mythic Image*, p. 74). As in *Masks*, so here: Mesopotamia—Campbell no longer specifies Sumer—developed the notion of a hieratic city state, in which everyone had a fixed place that mirrored the place everything had in the cosmos. Only Mesopotamian science, claims Campbell, was capable of making the observations on which the number 432 rests (*Mythic Image*, p. 74).

Historical Atlas of World Mythology

In the *Atlas*, as in both *Masks* and *The Mythic Image*, Campbell ascribes the similarities in myths to at once independent invention and diffusion. It is as likely here as in *The Mythic Image* that he is attributing similarities in symbols to diffusion and similarities in archetypes to independent invention. Hence one of the prime similarities he ascribes to diffusion, the widespread worship of the bear (*Atlas*, I, pp. 147–155), is far more likely the symbol of some archetype than an archetype itself.

Yet just as it is still not fully clear whether Campbell is attributing similar archetypes to independent invention or diffusion, so, as in all his other works save *Masks: Primitive*, it is not clear whether by independent invention he means experience or heredity. On the one hand he cites recurrent universal experiences: "For the phases of the moon were the same for Old Stone Age man as they are for us; so also were the processes of the womb" (*Atlas*, I, p. 68). Here Campbell reintroduces the concept of IRM's (*Atlas*, I, pp. 47–49), though he concentrates on the imprint made by the experience of death alone (*Atlas*, I, pp. 25, 47, 52–56) rather than by any of the other experiences he describes in part one of *Masks: Primitive*.

On the other hand, and in contrast to the stress in

part one of *Masks: Primitive* on perennial human experiences, Campbell cites wholly primitive experiences that still stir moderns:

> The animal envoys of the Unseen Power no longer serve, as in primeval times, to teach and to guide mankind. Bears, lions, elephants, ibexes, and gazelles are in cages in our zoos. Man is no longer the newcomer in a world of unexplored plains and forests, and our immediate neighbors are not wild beasts but other human beings. . . . Neither in body nor in mind do we inhabit the world of those hunting races of the Paleolithic millennia. . . . Memories of their animal envoys still must sleep, somehow, within us; for they wake a little and stir when we venture into [the] wilderness. They wake in terror to thunder. And again, they wake, with a sense of recognition, when we enter any one of those great painted caves. (*Atlas*, I, p.73)

Here Campbell echoes the early Jung, for whom subsequent humanity inherits the impact of the experiences of its forebears.

In volume two of the *Atlas* Campbell distinguishes *three* possible explanations of similarities in myths: diffusion, "convergence," and "parallelism." Convergence means independent invention through similar experiences of the environment: similar environmental conditions produce similar myths. Parallelism means independent invention through similarities in the mind: the "psychic unity" of humanity yields similar myths. Diffusion continues to mean the spread of myths from one culture to others.

Campbell accepts all three explanations. In those cases where contact between one culture and another is either known or plausible, he assumes diffusion.

Where "real or imagined geographical obstacles to such a vast diffusion are recognized" (*Atlas*, II, pt. 1, p. 18), he opts for independent invention. Where geographical similarities exist, he opts for convergence; where they do not, for parallelism. Campbell says that the similarities among hunting myths are attributable to diffusion where those among agricultural myths may result from convergence, parallelism, or diffusion (*Atlas*, II, pt. 1, p. 29).

The Inner Reaches of Outer Space

In *Inner Reaches* Campbell attributes the similarities in myths to, alternatively, independent invention and diffusion. Independent invention sometimes means the collective unconscious (*Inner Reaches*, pp. 80, 90–91) and other times means similar conscious experiences, as it does in part one of *Masks: Primitive*. Campbell singles out the conscious desires for food, sex, and power (*Inner Reaches*, pp. 13–16). Diffusion, which Campbell emphasizes even more than independent invention, accounts for similarities too detailed to have arisen independently (*Inner Reaches*, pp. 80, 91–92). He may be attributing to independent invention similarities in archetypes and to diffusion similarities in symbols, but it is far from clear that independent invention and diffusion are meant to account for different sets of similarities.

The Power of Myth

In *The Power of Myth* Campbell again attributes the similarities in myths at times to independent invention and at times to diffusion. By independent invention he here means the psychic unity of humanity—a unity that he now attributes to similarities in the body: "The psyche is the inward experience of the human body, which is essentially the same in all human beings, with the same organs, the same instincts, the same impulses, the same conflicts, the same fears. . . . You've got the same body, with the same organs and energies, that Cro-Magnon man had thirty thousand years ago" (*Power of Myth,* pp. 51, 37). Diffusion presupposes similar economic conditions: "Such a [farming] myth will accompany an agricultural or planting tradition. But you won't find it in a hunting culture" (*Power of Myth,* p. 52).

An Open Life

In *An Open Life* Campbell once again presents independent invention and diffusion as options: "Now the big question is: 'Do these [similarities in myths] arise in parallel independent ways, or is there actual diffusion to be recognized?' And of course, it will differ from case to case" (*Open Life,* p. 48). Yet Campbell usually opts for diffusion. He offers the standard argument of diffusionists: that the similarities are too detailed to be ascribable to independent invention. He explicitly *rejects* a Jungian account of detailed similarities:

> CAMPBELL: And I've indicated there what I do believe, namely, that the proposed evidence for influences from China, Northern Vietnam, and Cambodia of trans-Pacific diffusion of culture is *there*. That's all. So, we have a diffusion.
>
> TOMS: It's not attributable to the collective unconscious?
>
> CAMPBELL: No, this is diffusion. If you have one motif here, and the same element there, well, then, perhaps, yes. But if you have a constellation of about fifteen or twenty elements, or the whole range of the culture context—ideas, myths, actual details of costume, things like that—what are you going to do? (*Open Life*, p. 49)

NOTES

[1] When, in later works, Campbell argues for diffusion, he uses the term "zone of diffusion" rather than "culture sphere": see, for example, his *Masks: Primitive*, p. 387.

[2] Strictly, for Jung it is "archetypal images," not archetypes themselves, that are inherited.

[3] See Niko Tinbergen, *The Study of Instinct* (Oxford: Clarendon, 1951), esp. ch. 2; Konrad Lorenz, *Behind the Mirror*, tr. Ronald Taylor (New York: Harcourt Brace Jovanovich, 1977), esp. chs. 4–6. For a brief summary of the concept of innate releasing mechanisms see John Alcock, *Animal Behavior*, third ed. (Sunderland, MA: Sinauer, 1984), pp. 93–96.

[4] Besides "stimuli," Campbell calls archetypes "sign stimuli," "releasers," "images," "imprints," and "impressions."

[5] For other cases of innate stimuli in animals see Anthony Stevens, *Archetypes* (New York: Morrow, 1983), ch. 4.

[6]But see Campbell, *Masks: Primitive,* p. 48, where he questions whether any human stimuli are innate.

[7]See, for example, the contrast Campbell draws (*Masks: Primitive,* p. 35) between the acquired stimuli of ducks and the innate ones of chicks. For other cases of acquired stimuli in animals see Stevens, p. 51.

[8]IRM's that respond to only innate stimuli are called "closed," or "stereotyped"; those that respond to acquired ones as well are called "open": see Campbell, *Masks: Primitive,* pp. 35–36.

[9]To be sure, Campbell perhaps means that archetypes are the IRM's themselves. In his attempt to reduce Jung's irreducibly psychological archetypes to something physiological Stevens (p. 39) explicitly equates the two.

[10]Early Jung did believe that archetypes were acquired by prehistoric humans in response to their experience. The continual experience of the power of the sun, for example, eventually imprinted on prehistoric humans an archetype of it: see, for example, Jung, "The Structure of the Psyche," in his *The Structure and Dynamics of the Psyche,* The Collected Works, VIII, first ed. (New York: Pantheon, 1960), pp. 139–158. Later Jung came to believe that archetypes were innate in even prehistoric humans, whose experience of the sun reflected rather than, as Jung had initially assumed, shaped the corresponding archetype. Where archetypes originated Jung now considered a metaphysical rather than scientific question and declined to say. Yet even early Jung assumed that archetypes, once implanted in prehistoric humans, got transmitted to their descendants through heredity. Subsequent humanity thus inherited rather than acquired archetypes, though its experiences created new archetypes in turn.

[11]Freud scarcely denies that incestuous desires themselves are innate, but the Oedipus Complex involves one's *experience* of those desires, which includes the reaction of one's parents. One's encounter with them leaves an impression that constitutes, in Campbell's terms, an acquired stimulus.

Only if the impression existed independently of the child's contact with his parents would the stimulus be innate.

[12]Strictly, myths are not the same as the archetypes imprinted on the mind by experience. They are the stories in which archetypes get expressed.

[13]In Jung's terminology, "symbols" are distinct from "archetypal images," which are distinct from "archetypes."

[14]In fact, Campbell himself, (*Mythic Image*, p. 72) appeals to the specificity of the number 432 to argue for diffusion over independent invention, which would constitute too great a coincidence.

CHAPTER ELEVEN

THE FUNCTION OF MYTH

The Hero
with a Thousand Faces

In *Hero* Campbell is concerned less with the function or even the origin of myth than with its meaning. He wants to show that the meaning of myth is both psychological and metaphysical. Insofar as he considers the function, myth serves to reveal to humans the existence of a severed, deeper part of both themselves and the cosmos:

> . . . all the life-potentialities that we never managed to bring to adult realization, those other portions of ourself [sic], are there; for such golden seeds do not die. If only a portion of that lost totality could be dredged up into the light of day, we should experience a marvelous expansion of our powers, a vivid renewal of life. (*Hero*, p. 17)

The hero's rediscovery of the severed reality offers a model for others to emulate.

Myth for Campbell likely serves as a vehicle for actually encountering the severed reality, not just for learning of it. For myth does not just refer to archetypes but actually manifests them:

> For the symbols [i.e., archetypes] of mythology are not manufactured; they cannot be ordered, invented, or permanently suppressed. They are spontaneous productions of the psyche, and each bears within it, undamaged, the germ power of its source. (*Hero*, p. 4)

As Campbell puts it elsewhere: "Within each person there is what Jung called a collective unconscious. . . . We penetrate to this level by getting in touch with dreams, fantasies, and traditional myths; by using active imagination."[1]

The psychological and metaphysical functions of myth would seem to preclude a social one. If myth serves to reconnect humans with their severed selves, it operates solipsistically. If myth serves to reconnect humans with the cosmos as a whole, it either trivializes or outright dissolves any distinction between humans and anything else, including fellow humans.

Yet at least once in *Hero* Campbell does say that myth deals with society. Put negatively, social problems stem from psychological ones, from the failure to tend to the unconscious: ". . . every failure to cope with a life situation must be laid, in the end, to a restriction of consciousness. Wars and temper tantrums are the makeshifts of ignorance . . ." (*Hero*, p. 121). How the rediscovery of a severed part of either humans or the cosmos would abet one socially Campbell does not say.

Bios and Mythos

In "Bios and Mythos," his essay in the Festschrift for Géza Róheim,[2] Campbell deals entirely with the function, not the meaning, of myth. Here, as elsewhere, he cites Róheim's stress in *The Origin and Function of Culture* on the premature state of humans at birth. Humans for Róheim are born less developed than any other animal, are therefore more helpless, and are therefore more dependent on their mothers. Birth is traumatic exactly because it constitutes separation from the mother, unity with whom has heretofore shielded the child from the world into which the child is now thrust:

> Three factors are responsible for neurosis, a biological, a phylogenetic and a psychological factor. The biological factor is the protracted helplessness and dependence of the human infant. The intrauterine period is relatively too short as compared to most animals; human beings are born in an unfinished state. . . . [I]t is only from the object (the mother) that the infant can obtain protection against the dangers of a strange world and a prolongation of the intrauterine period of life. This biological factor is the basis of the primary danger situations it creates, the desire to be beloved, a desire which human beings can never give up.[3]

On the one hand all children remain dependent on their mothers until adolescence. On the other hand all children remain so traumatized by their initial separation from their mothers that they spend their lives

trying to overcome it. They try to overcome birth itself.

Yet Róheim distinguishes between a neurotic, childish means of restoring the prenatal bond and a normal,
adult one. Neurotics strive to restore their ties to their
actual mothers. They thereby remain fixated at birth.
Normal persons manage to break free not of the yearning itself, which is never transcended, but of the infantile means of satisfying it: the mother herself. They
find substitutes onto whom to displace or sublimate
their maternal attachment:

> We have compared neurosis and the sublimations
> which constitute the bulk of our civilization. In both
> cases we find the same defense mechanisms evolved
> on the basis of the infantile situation but while in
> neurosis the archaic objects are retained and the
> fate of the impulse must therefore be a frustration
> of some kind, the characteristic feature of a subli-
> mation is that the impulse is carried over to a sub-
> stitute object.[4]

From Róheim, all of culture, which provides these
substitutes, is a series of edifices constructed to keep
individuals from ever again facing the loneliness and
the terror of the separation experienced at birth:

> Civilization originates in delayed infancy and its
> function is security. It is a huge network of more
> or less successful attempts to protect mankind
> against the danger of object-loss, the colossal ef-
> forts made by a baby who is afraid of being left
> alone in the dark.[5]

Substitutes for the mother include both other persons—one's father, one's spouse, all of society—and

the external world—unity with the cosmos itself. Indeed, Róheim interprets magic, totemism, and rituals generally as means of achieving mystical oneness with the world.

In *The Origin and Function of Culture,* which is one of his later works, Róheim deals only in passing with myth. He deals more fully with it not only in his earlier, more orthodox Freudian works, in which myth fulfills the Oedipal desire for intercourse with one's mother, but also in other later ones, in which myth fulfills the infantile desire for reunion with her.[6] The mythic hero is still someone who dares to kill his father, and his father still threatens him with castration or death—not, however, because the father wants his wife for himself, as Róheim earlier argued, but because he wants his son to sever his infantile attachment to his mother and grow up.

Following the later Róheim, Campbell declares myth a second womb:

> Society, as a fostering organ is thus a kind of exterior "second womb," wherein the postnatal stages of man's long gestation—much longer than that of any other placental—are supported and defended. . . . Rites, then, together with the mythologies that support them, constitute the second womb, the matrix of the postnatal gestation of the placental *Homo sapiens.* . . . Mythology is the womb of mankind's initiation to life and death. ("Bios and Mythos," pp. 337, 339, 336)

How myth, which is not limited to hero myths, serves as a second womb Campbell neglects to say. Most likely, it explains the world and gives humans a firm place within it. Most likely, god takes the place of not, as for Freud in *the Future of an Illusion*, a child's father but an infant's mother.

Even if Róheim distinguishes between normal and neurotic means of preserving the prenatal bond, he, like Freud, still deems myth regressive. Where for Freud myth expresses the childhood, Oedipal desire for intercourse with one's mother, for Róheim it expresses the even earlier, infantile desire for absorption in the mother. The mythmaker or believer wishes not to satisfy the id but to dissolve the ego.[7]

While Campbell accepts Róheim's view of the substitutive function of culture, of which myth is a part, he also ventures beyond Róheim. For he envisions the possibility of breaking not just with the mother herself but even with substitutes for her. He envisions the possibility of transcending the need for a substitute and so, most strikingly, the need for mythology itself. Indeed, he argues that the ultimate aim in the East, in contrast to the West, *is* freedom from the mother and therefore from myth. Where the cowardly West seeks substitutes for the mother in order to continue to cling to her, the brave East seeks independence of even them. Where the West seeks permanent return to the womb, the East seeks return as only a means to an end, which is rebirth in turn. Hence Campbell contrasts the Eastern desire to be born again to the Western desire to undo birth altogether:

In India the objective is to be *born* from the womb of myth, not to remain in it, and the one who has attained to this "second birth" is truly the "twice born," freed from the pedagogical devices of society, the lures and threats of myth, the local *mores*, the usual hopes of benefits and rewards. He is truly "free" *(mukti)*, "released while living" *(ji-*

van mukti). . . . Within the Christian Church, however, there has been a historically successful tendency to anathematize the obvious implications of this idea, and the result has been a general obscuration of the fact that regeneration means going beyond, not remaining within, the confines of mythology. Whereas in the Orient . . . everyone is expected, at least in his final incarnation, to leave the womb of myth, to pass through the sun-door and stand beyond the gods, in the West . . . God remains the Father, and none can step beyond Him. This accounts, perhaps, for the great distinction between the manly piety of the Orient and the infantile of the recent Occident. In the lands of the truly "twice born" man is finally superior to the gods, whereas in the West even the saint is required to remain within the body of the Church and the "second birth" is read rather as being born [back] into the Church than born out of it. ("Bios and Mythos," p. 340)

In volumes two and three of *Masks,* however, Campbell reverses this interpretation of East and West: now the East preaches sheer return to the womb and the West return from it. More accurately, the East, too, preaches return from it, but a return so devaluing the world to which one returns that there is barely any return at all. Ironically, Campbell in *Masks: Oriental* and *Occidental* continues to praise the East and damn the West, but now for reverse reasons.

Even though in "Bios and Mythos" Campbell advocates a state beyond myth, he nevertheless considers myth necessary for achieving it: myth provides the necessary interim substitute for the mother. Like Róheim, Campbell labels neurotic anyone who lacks substitutes for the mother like it:

> Misbirth is possible from the mythological womb
> as well as from the physiological: there can be
> adhesions, malformations, arrestations, etc. We
> call them neuroses and psychoses. Hence we find
> today, after some five hundred years of the system-
> atic dismemberment and rejection of the mytho-
> logical organ of our species, all the sad young
> men, for whom life is a problem. Mythology leads
> the libido into ego-syntonic channels, whereas
> neurosis (to cite, once again, Róheim) "separates
> the individual from his fellows and connects him
> with his own infantile images." ("Bios and My-
> thos," pp. 342–343)

Campbell would simply proceed to label neurotic anyone who did not abandon myth in turn.

In *Hero* myth functions to restore a primordial tie.
In "Bios and Mythos" it functions to overcome one.
At the outset of *Hero* (pp. 6–7, 10–12) Campbell, cit-
ing Róheim's *Origin and Function of Culture*, does say
that myth functions to surmount the infantile attachment to the mother:

> It has always been the prime function of mythol-
> ogy and rite to supply the symbols that carry the
> human spirit forward, in counteraction to those
> other constant human fantasies that tend to tie it
> back. In fact, it may well be that the very high
> incidence of neuroticism among ourselves follows
> from the decline among us of such effective spir-
> itual aid. We remain fixated to the unexorcised
> images of our infancy, and hence disinclined to
> the necessary passages of our adulthood. (*Hero*,
> p. 11)

At the outset of *Hero* Campbell may be going so far
as to say, as he does not do even in "Bios and My-

thos,'' that ritual, which for him is always tied to myth, functions to surmount attachments to substitutes themselves for the mother:

> When we turn now, with this image in mind, to consider the numerous strange rituals that have been reported from the primitive tribes and great civilizations of the past, it becomes apparent that the purpose and actual effect of these was to conduct people across those difficult thresholds of transformation that demand a change in the patterns not only of conscious but also of unconscious life. The so-called rites of passage . . . are distinguished by formal, and usually very severe, exercises of severance, whereby the mind is radically cut away from the attitudes, attachments, and life patterns of the stage being left behind. (*Hero*, p. 10)

Nevertheless, Campbell's preoccupation in *Hero* is not with detaching humans from their infantile state but with returning them to it. Campbell's focus is not, as in ''Bios and Mythos,'' on the goal of the first half of life—separation from one's roots—but on the goal of the second half—reconnection with those roots. The attainment of the goal of the first half he simply takes for granted. Róheim himself would doubtless dismiss any return to one's roots in the second half of life as simply another vain attempt to return to the state prior to the first half, but Campbell does not. He distinguishes between an infantile attachment, which, contrary to Róheim, is surmountable, and an adult one, which is what his hero undertakes. Campbell's hero is heroic not because he manages to establish himself as an independent agent but because he dares to sacrifice his independence. In short, it is hard to see how

Campbell's invocation of Róheim, who argues that even the nonneurotic fails to achieve the goal of the first half of life, is compatible with either *Hero,* which espouses the goal of the second half, or even "Bios and Mythos," which espouses the goal of the first half. Since, however, the goal of the second half of life for Campbell turns out to be permanent return to the primordial state, the attainment of that goal would ironically put Campbell's hero in the same psychological state as Róheim's.

"Bios and Mythos" is a doubly incongruous piece: here alone Campbell not only restricts myth to the goal of the first half of life but in so doing seeks to transcend myth. Everywhere else he deems myth indispensable, and indispensable for above all the goal of the second half of life—his regressive characterization of that goal aside. Where in "Bios and Mythos" Campbell dismisses myth as childish, if still useful, everywhere else he defends it against precisely this kind of charge—usually by arguing that myth seems childish only when wrongly taken literally as history or science. In associating myth in "Bios and Mythos" with childhood and in arguing for the need to proceed beyond it, Campbell is closest to Freud and Rank.

The Masks of God

Because Campbell's analysis in part one of *Masks: Primitive* is so different from his analysis in the rest of *Masks,* the two analyses will be considered separately.

In part one of *Masks: Primitive* the function of myth becomes much more positive than it is in "Bios and

Mythos.'' First, myth ceases to be something to be superseded and becomes something to be used throughout life. The reason is that, second, myth ceases to serve merely as a substitute for the mother and becomes a means of breaking the attachment even to substitutes for her. Third, though Campbell still stresses human incompleteness at birth, the consequence shifts from human weakness—dependence on one's mother—to human strength—openness to change. Finally, myth ceases to deal merely with one's relationship with one's family and becomes a means of forging relationships with society and the cosmos as well.

In part one of *Masks: Primitive* archetypes function to activate IRM's, which in turn activate emotions and actions. Myths, like dreams and rituals, provide the symbols that activate archetypes. A myth about Horus or Apollo, for example, might trigger the archetype of the sun, which is clearly akin to one of Campbell's universal archetypes: the alternation of light and dark. To experience the sun would be to experience it as more than a natural object. It would be to experience the sun magnified, perhaps deified: as something overpowering or alluring. The sun would stir feelings of either awe or security and behavior of either avoidance or exposure.

Archetypes can be activated by natural as well as invented symbols—for example, by one's own mother as well as by a female character in a myth or painting. But some archetypes may require an activation so strong that only an invented symbol can stir it. As Campbell says of such ''supernormal'' symbols, or ''sign stimuli''—a term that he uses for both the archetypes activated and, as here, the symbols that activate them:

It was found, for instance, that the male of a certain butterfly known as the grayling *(Eumenis semele)*, which assumes [i.e., reacts by assuming] the initiative in mating by pursuing a passing female in flight, generally prefers [i.e., reacts to] females of darker hue to those of lighter—and to such a degree that if a model of even darker hue than anything known in nature is presented [as a stimulus], the sexually motivated male will pursue it in preference even to the darkest female of the species. . . . Evidence will appear . . . of the gods themselves [in myths] as [likewise] supernormal sign stimuli; . . . that is to say, as an organization of supernormal sign stimuli playing on a set of IRMs never met [i.e., triggered] by nature [which lacked the stimuli needed to release them] and yet most properly nature's own, inasmuch as man is her son. (*Masks: Primitive,* pp. 43–44)

Insofar as myths here serve to vent emotions and actions, their function is roughly Freudian—with the strong proviso that what is released need be neither repressed nor even unconscious. What is classically Freudian is the view of myth as a release.

But in part one of *Masks: Primitive* myth functions to do more than release emotions and actions. It also functions to interpret them. It interprets them in a variety of ways: psychologically, socially, and metaphysically. For example, the experience of the alternation of light and dark might, mythologically, become the dualism of soul and body or of good and evil—in oneself, society, or the cosmos. The experience of one's birth might become a metaphor for the experience of any transformation, or rebirth:

In the imagery of mythology and religion this birth (or more often rebirth) theme is extremely prominent; in fact, every threshold passage—not only this from the darkness of the womb to the light of the sun, but also those from childhood to adult life and from the light of the world to whatever mystery of darkness may lie beyond the portal of death—is comparable to a birth and has been ritually represented, practically everywhere, through an imagery of re-entry into the womb. (*Masks: Primitive,* pp. 61–62)

In part one of *Masks: Primitive* myth functions not only to trigger and to interpret emotions and actions but also to redirect them. Myths can wean one from one's mother and toward the external, adult world. In *Hero* initiation rites, which Campbell always deems mythological, likewise serve to replace the son's infantile attachment to his mother with an adult attachment to his father. But in *Hero* that goal becomes only a means to a mystical end: oneness with the father—and, indeed, with the mother as well. Moreover, that oneness is likely not with one's actual parents but with the archetypes they merely symbolize.

In part one of *Masks: Primitive,* by contrast, initiation rites serve to replace the son's infantile attachment to his actual mother with a mature attachment to his actual father, and to do so as a means to a social end:

So that, in sum, we may say that whereas the energies of the psyche in their primary context of infantile concerns are directed to the crude ends of individual pleasure and power, in the rituals of initiation they are reorganized and implicated in a system of social duty, with such effect that the individual henceforth can be safely trusted as an organ of the group. Pleasure, power, and duty: these are the systems of reference of all experience on the natural level of the primitive societies. And when such societies are in form, the first two are subordinated to the last, which, in turn, is mythologically supported and ritually enforced. Ritual is mythology made alive, and its effect is to convert men into angels. (*Masks: Primitive*, pp. 117–118)

In *Hero* myth initiates one into a strange, distant world, reachable only by leaving society. In part one of *Masks: Primitive* myth initiates one into society. Even if in *Hero* the proper hero returns to society, he values it only because he finds the new world within it. In part one of *Masks: Primitive* the initiate learns to value society for itself.

For Freud, as for Campbell in "Bios and Mythos," myth serves to satisfy childhood desires and thereby to keep one stymied in childhood. For Campbell in part one of *Masks: Primitive*, as for Jung, myth serves to lead one past childhood, not to say infancy, to adulthood. Campbell even now criticizes Freudians for interpreting myths as regressive (*Masks: Primitive*, pp. 64–65, 91).

After part one of *Masks: Primitive* Campbell becomes far more concerned with the meaning of myth than with its function. Where in part one he almost presupposes the meaning and focuses on its impact, after part one, as in *Hero*, he is concerned with the meaning itself.

In *Masks*, myths are no longer limited to stories, as they are in *Hero*. Where in *Hero* myths are *tied* to metaphysical beliefs, in *Masks* they seem to be beliefs themselves. Even where myths are still stories, as they are in *Masks: Creative* above all, Campbell is interested in them as sheer beliefs. In *Hero* Campbell is certainly concerned with the beliefs expressed by myths, but he is also concerned with the way myths, as stories, express those beliefs. He is concerned with the plot. In *Masks* Campbell is concerned with only the beliefs themselves.

In *Masks,* at least after part one of volume one, myth serves primarily to convey beliefs—but, in contrast to *Hero,* not necessarily beliefs heretofore unknown. Still, several times in *Masks,* and various places outside it, Campbell enumerates four other functions of myth.[8] First, he says, myth functions to instill and maintain a sense of awe and mystery before the world. It does so either by putting god in the world or, in the wake of science, by making the natural world more complicated and therefore more elusive.

Second, myth functions to explain the world, which, says Campbell, religion used to do but now science tries to do. More precisely, myth functions to provide a symbolic image for explaining the world—for example, the image of the Great Chain of Being. As Campbell puts it elsewhere, "A mythology is a system of affect-symbols, signs evoking and directing psychic energies. It is more like an affective art work than like a scientific proposition."[9]

Third, myth functions to maintain the social order. It does so by giving divine justification to social practices and institutions—for example, to the Indian caste system. Fourth and most of all, myth functions to harmonize persons with society, the cosmos, and themselves. It serves to link them with everything both outside and within themselves.

While Campbell presents these four functions several times in *Masks,* only at the end of *Masks: Creative* (pp. 608–624) does he actually apply them to any myths. Since in most of *Masks* Campbell is only concerned with myths as expressions of metaphysical beliefs, what connection any but the second, explanatory function has with them is not clear. The mystical oneness that in much of *Masks* all myths purportedly preach would seemingly efface the very distinctions that the other functions presuppose: between humans and the cosmos, humans and society, and humans and themselves.

When, at the end of *Masks: Creative,* Campbell evaluates "creative" mythology by these four functions, he concludes that the tentativeness of scientific explanations precludes the fulfillment of the second function, which demands certainty (pp. 611–621). Till now Campbell had scarcely associated creative mythology with science. Nowhere does he say what in science is mythological. Perhaps he means the models and images used. In an interview he says that it is the disparateness of individual sciences rather than the tentativeness of science generally that makes it inadequate as a mythological explanation:

> We don't have the idea of micro-macrocosm—the little cosmos of man, the big cosmos of nature, and then the middle cosmos of society which shows the laws that govern them all. We don't have that same unity anymore. Physics and psychology really are not the same science anymore, although in their outermost reaches they're beginning to bump into the same mysteries. Still, you wouldn't take Einstein's formula as a guide to marriage. So the two spheres have broken apart and this is part of the problem of modern man.[10]

Yet elsewhere Campbell is considerably more optimistic. Rather than lamenting that science precludes mythology, he insists only that an effective modern mythology accord with science:

> To be effective, a mythology . . . must be up-to-date scientifically, based on a concept of the universe that is current, accepted, and convincing. And in this respect, of course, it is immediately apparent that our own traditions are in deep trouble; for the leading claims of both the Old Testament and the New are founded in a cosmological image from the second millennium B.C., which was already out of date when the Bible was put together in the last centuries B.C. and first A.D.[11]

Still elsewhere Campbell says that the moon landing represents a potent contemporary mythic image:

> Let's look at the symbolic significance of the moon landing. Before Copernicus, man's images of the cosmos corresponded to what was visible. The sun rose and set and the earth was obviously the center of the cosmos. Then Copernicus created a theory that removed earth from the center and placed it as one planet among many in the heavens. Although this theory has been intellectually convincing, it lacked the emotional impact of a cosmological image that was visible. You couldn't experience the new world view. Now, suddenly, through the eyes of the astronauts and the marvels of technology, we can stand on the moon and watch the earth rise over the lunar horizon.[12]

Indeed, a refrain throughout Campbell's writing is that humans are continuously spinning myths, albeit private rather than public ones. Here the sole impediment to a modern mythology is obliviousness to the fact:

> In the absence of an effective general mythology, each of us has his private, unrecognized, rudimentary, yet secretly potent pantheon of dream. The latest incarnation of Oedipus, the continued romance of Beauty and the Beast, stand this afternoon on the corner of Forty-second Street and Fifth Avenue, waiting for the traffic light to change. (*Hero*, p. 4)

In *Masks: Creative* Campbell argues that the individualism espoused by creative mythology renders impossible the fulfillment of the third, social function of myth as well as the second one (pp. 621–623, 87). Elsewhere he says that relativism—the recognition of other customs and morals—makes it impossible to believe that the ways of any one society are divinely sanctioned by mythology.[13] In *Masks: Creative* Campbell may also be saying that the individualism inherent in creative mythology likewise precludes the fulfillment of the fourth, integrative function. One might ask why Campbell selects the four functions of myth that he does when the brand of mythology he himself touts above all fails to fulfill two or three of them.

The Mythic Image

In *The Mythic Image* Campbell concentrates much less on the function of myth than on its origin and meaning. Myth functions in the same way that it does in

Hero: both to reveal to humans the existence of a deeper reality, whether psychological or metaphysical, and to enable them to experience that reality. As virtually so in *Hero,* so wholly here: Campbell neglects any social function of myth. Myth deals with the relationship of humans to either themselves or the cosmos but not to society.

Historical Atlas of World Mythology

In the *Atlas* (I, pp. 8–10) Campbell enumerates the same four functions of myth that he does in *Masks* and elsewhere. To the first function, that of instilling and maintaining a sense of awe and mystery before the world, Campbell now adds a sense of participation in it. Since Campbell now denies that myth serves to explain the world (*Atlas,* I, p. 112), it is no longer clear what he means by the second, seemingly explanatory function. In *Masks* Campbell characterizes the fourth function as one of harmonizing individuals with society, the cosmos, and themselves. Now, as elsewhere, he introduces a chronological aspect: guiding individuals through the stages of life.

In *Masks* Campbell discusses the four functions most fully in the volume on modern Western mythology, which he doubts is capable of fulfilling two or even three of these functions. In the *Atlas* he is confident that primitive hunting mythology fulfills all four functions. Of the efficacy of planting mythology he has so far said nothing.

The Inner Reaches of Outer Space

In *Inner Reaches* myth serves the same four functions as elsewhere for Campbell: instilling and maintaining a sense of awe and mystery before the world, providing an image for explaining the world, upholding the social order, and guiding individuals through the stages of life *(Inner Reaches,* pp. 18, 20, 22).

The Power of Myth

In *The Power of Myth* myth again serves Campbell's four functions. As in earlier works, so here: the most important function is the fourth, which he now characterizes as "how to live a human lifetime under any circumstances. Myths can teach you that" *(Power of Myth,* p. 31). While Campbell does not say that myth can guide one in choosing a mate, he does say that myth, by presenting alternatives, can guide one in choosing a career:

> The big problem of any young person's life is to have models to suggest possibilities. . . . The mind has many possibilities, but we can live no more than one life. What are we going to do with ourselves? A living myth presents contemporary models. *(Power of Myth,* p. 150)

Myth can guide one through all the proverbial stages of life:

Mythology has a great deal to do with the stages of life, the initiation ceremonies as you move from childhood to adult responsibilities, from the unmarried state into the married state. All of those rituals are mythological rites. They have to do with your recognition of the new role that you're in, the process of throwing off the old one and coming out in the new, and entering into a responsible profession. (*Power of Myth*, pp. 11–12)

Myth can even guide one through the travails of life—not by denying misfortune but by putting it in perspective: "Myths tell us how to confront and bear and interpret suffering, but they do not say that in life there can or should be no suffering" (*Power of Myth*, p. 160). Myth puts sufferers in harmony with society and the cosmos:

> MOYERS: So the one great story [of myth] is our search to find our place in the drama?
> CAMPBELL: To be in accord with the grand symphony that this world is, to put the harmony of our own body in accord with that harmony. (*Power of Myth*, p. 55)

A cynic might question whether these homey lessons for life require a knowledge of myth. For Campbell they do. He assumes that, whether or not persons recognize it, they in fact employ myths in coping with life. He assumes that any who do not fail to cope.

An Open Life

In *An Open Life* Campbell discusses the functions of myth only in passing. He singles out the fourth of his four standard functions and once again credits myth with directing persons through the stages of life:

> TOMS: Myth also informs us about the stage of life we're in. Isn't that so?
>
> CAMPBELL: Yes. Actually, that's one of the main functions of myth. It's what I call the pedagogical: to carry a person through the inevitable stages of a lifetime. And these are the same today as they were in the paleolithic caves: as a youngster you're dependent on parents to teach you what life is, and what your relationship to other people has to be, and so forth; then you give up that dependence to become a self-responsible authority; and, finally, comes the stage of yielding: you realize that the world is in other hands. And the myths tell you what the values are in those stages in terms of the possibilities of your particular society. (*Open Life*, p. 32)

NOTES

[1]Campbell, interview with Sam Keen, *Voices and Visions* (New York: Harper & Row, 1974), p. 73.

[2]See also Campbell, ''Life's Delicate Child,'' review of Róheim, *The Origin and Function of Culture*, *Saturday Review of Literature*, 28 (October 13, 1945), pp. 56, 58.

[3]Géza Róheim, *The Origin and Function of Culture* (Garden City, NY: Doubleday Anchor, 1971), p. 27.

[4]*Ibid*, p. 122.

[5]*Ibid*, p. 131.

[6]Representative of Róheim's earlier work are *Australian Totemism* (London: Allen and Unwin, 1925) and *The Riddle of the Sphinx*, tr. R. Money-Kyrle (London: Hogarth, 1934), which stress the Oedipus Complex. Representative of his later work are *The Eternal Ones of the Dream* (New York: International Universities Press, 1945), and *Psychoanalysis and Anthropology* (New York: International Universities Press, 1950), which stress separation anxiety.

[7]While Freud originally downplayed the infantile relationship between mother and child in favor of the Oedipal one, he gradually came to recognize its importance. Still, he never accorded the fear of the loss of the mother the significance that he did the Oedipal fear of castration. Certainly he never gave it the importance that Róheim does. Róheim makes it not just the prime but virtually the sole human experience. He reinterprets the Oedipal conflict as the son's anger at the father for depriving him of unity, not sex, with the mother.

[8]On the four functions of myths see Campbell, *Masks: Occidental*, pp. 519–523; *Masks: Creative*, pp. 4–6, 608–624, 630; *Myths to Live By*, pp. 221–222; *Atlas*, I, pp. 8–10; *Inner Reaches*, pp. 18, 20; *Power of Myth*, p. 31; "Mythological Themes in Creative Literature and Art," in *Myths, Dreams, and Religion*, ed. Campbell (New York: Dutton, 1970), pp. 140–144; interview with Sam Keen, in Keen, *Voices and Visions* (New York: Harper & Row, 1974), p. 72; interview with Lorraine Kisly, *Parabola*, 1 (Spring 1976), p. 72.

[9]Campbell, interview with Kisly, p. 78.

[10]Campbell, interview with Kisly, p. 74.

[11]Campbell, "Mythological Themes in Creative Literature and Art," pp. 144-145.

[12]Campbell, interview with Keen, p. 84.

[13]See Campbell, "Mythological Themes in Creative Literature and Art," pp. 145-146.

CHAPTER TWELVE

CAMPBELL AS A JUNGIAN

Joseph Campbell is often labeled a Jungian.[1] He was certainly not a Jungian analyst and underwent no Jungian analysis. If he was a Jungian, it is because he shared Jung's view of myth.

Campbell does cite Jung approvingly throughout his writings, far more often than he cites any other theorist of myth. Again and again, he favorably contrasts Jung's understanding of myth to that of not only nonpsychologists—for example, those who read myth literally—but, most conspicuously, Freud:

> When I wrote *The Hero with a Thousand Faces,* they [Freud and Jung] were equal in my thinking: Freud served in one context, Jung in another. But then, in the years following, Jung became more and more eloquent to me. I think the longer you live, the more Jung can say to you. . . . Freud never says something new to me anymore; Freud tells us what myths mean to neurotics. On the other hand, Jung gives us clues as to how to let the myth talk to us in its own terms, without putting a formula on it. (*Open Life,* p. 121)

Campbell contrasts Jung's appreciation of the higher, adult meaning of myth to Freud's purported dismissive reduction of it to its childhood, sexual origins:

Myths, according to Freud's view, are of the psychological order of dream. . . . Both, in his opinion, are symptomatic of repressions of infantile incest wishes. . . . Civilization itself, in fact, is a pathological surrogate for unconscious infantile disappointments. . . . An altogether different approach is represented by Carl G. Jung, in whose view the imageries of mythology and religion serve positive, life-furthering ends. . . . [Myths] are telling us in picture language of powers of the psyche to be recognized and integrated in our lives. . . . Through a dialogue conducted with these inward forces through our dreams and through a study of myths, we can learn to know and come to terms with the greater horizon of our own deeper and wiser, inward self. (*Myths to Live by,* pp. 12–13)

More practically, Campbell edited *The Portable Jung* and the six-volume selection from the *Eranos-Jahrbücher,* which, while not always Jungian, is always Jungian in "spirit." Campbell himself twice gave lectures published in the *Jahrbücher.* Several volumes of his works appear in the Bollingen Series, which is similarly Jungian in spirit. Two of those works even constitute the inaugural and final entries in the Series. Campbell also edited other Bollingen volumes. Furthermore, he was both a fellow and a trustee of the Bollingen Foundation.

But is Campbell therefore a Jungian? He never calls himself one. He even denies that he is: "You know, for some people, 'Jungian' is a nasty word, and it has been flung at me by certain reviewers as though to say, 'Don't bother with Joe Campbell; he's a Jungian.' I'm not a Jungian!" (*Open Life,* p. 123). Campbell praises Jung rather than defers to him. At most, he says that Jung has come closest to grasping the meaning of myth: "As far as interpreting myths, Jung gives me the best clues I've got" (*Open Life,* p. 123). After lauding Jung over Freud, he adds, "But he's not the final word—I don't think there is a final word . . ." (*Open Life,* p. 121). If Campbell is truly a Jungian or even a kindred soul, he must surely share Jung's view of the origin and function, not just the meaning, of myth.

Jung's View of the Origin of Myth

The term "Jungian" is often used loosely. Merely to be interested in myth is not to be Jungian. Innumerable non-Jungians are no less interested in it. Merely to deem myth important is, for the same reason, insufficient. Even to find similarities in myths is not enough. All theorists of myth, as comparativists, do.

What *is* distinctively Jungian is the *explanation* of the similarities. There are, once again, two possible explanations: diffusion and independent invention. Diffusion means that myth originates in a single society and spreads elsewhere from it. Independent invention means that every society invents myth on its own.

Neither explanation assumes that the myths of any two societies are identical, only that they are similar enough to suggest a common cause. Diffusionists do often argue that the similarities they find are too detailed to be the product of independent invention. But even they grant that the myths of no two societies are identical. Diffusionists and independent "inventionists" alike seek only to account for the similarities, not to deny any differences.

If the prime argument of diffusionists is that the similarities are too precise to have arisen independently, the prime argument of independent "inventionists" is that diffusion, even when granted, fails to explain either the origin of myth in the society from which it spreads or the acceptance of myth by the societies to which it spreads.

To attribute the similarities in myths to independent invention rather than diffusion is not distinctively Jungian. Edward Tylor, James Frazer, and Freud, among other theorists of myth, do so as well. What *is* distinctively Jungian is the form independent invention takes. Here, too, there are, two possibilities: experience and heredity. Independent invention as experience means that every society creates myth for itself. Independent invention as heredity means that every society inherits myth.

Independent invention as experience does not mean that every member of a society creates myth. Every member may have the experiences that lead to its creation, but only a few members actually create it.

Independent invention as heredity means that every member of society not simply has the experiences that lead some members to create myth but, far more, has myth itself: every member is born with it. More accurately, every member is born with the elements that constitute the main content of myths: the similarities among myths that Jung calls archetypes.[2] Here, too, only certain members of society create actual myths, but what they do is far more limited: they turn innately archetypal material into specific myths—for example, turning the archetype of the hero into the myth of Odysseus.

Tylor, Frazer, and Freud ascribe independent invention to experience. Jung is distinctive in ascribing it to heredity—of a psychological, not biological, kind.

For Tylor,[3] everyone is born with a need to explain the world, but the explanations themselves are not innate. Everyone in primitive society, which alone has myth, doubtless experiences the same baffling phenomena that eventually lead to the creation of myths: the lifelessness of the body at death and the appearance of others in dreams. Similarly, every primitive doubtless seeks to explain these phenomena. But only a few postulate souls and then gods to explain them and finally spin myths to explain the actions of those gods. Because all primitives for Tylor experience the same perplexing phenomena, and because all primitive societies postulate gods to account for them, myths are bound to be similar. But each primitive society invents gods and myths on its own, in response to the similar experiences of its members.

For Frazer,[4] who is Campbell's grandest exemplar of independent invention through experience, everyone is born with a need not to explain the world but, more practically, to eat. No doubt everyone in society experiences hunger, but only the brightest members react by inventing first magic and then religion to explain how the world works and thereby how to secure food. There are no myths in the first, magical stage, which postulates mechanical, impersonal forces. Myth arises only in the next, religious stage, which postulates gods instead. On its own every society invents first magic and then religion. Every society invents its myths as part of its religion. As with Tylor, so with Frazer: similar causes are bound to yield similar effects, so that gods and therefore myths are bound to prove similar worldwide. Frazer puts the point in a line that Campbell repeatedly invokes as the clearest statement of independent invention through experience:

> . . . the resemblance which may be traced in this respect between the religions of the East and West is no more than what we commonly, though incorrectly, call a fortuitous coincidence, the effect of similar causes acting alike on the similar constitution of the human mind in different countries and under different skies.[5]

For Freud,[6] everyone is born with an incestuous drive that surfaces at age three to five. Everyone experiences that drive individually. From one's ancestors one inherits only the drive itself, not their experience of it. Everyone in society also experiences frustration in trying to satisfy that drive. Some members of every society invent myth as an indirect, disguised, compensatory outlet for the blocked drive, which dare not be vented directly or overtly. Again, similar experiences are bound to give rise to, in this case, similar heroes and thereby similar myths. Hence Otto Rank contends that all hero myths, if not all myths,[7] conform to the same pattern, one invented by each society on its own.

Like Tylor, Frazer, and Freud, Jung attributes the similarities in myths to independent invention. But unlike them he attributes independent invention to heredity rather than experience. He claims that everyone is born not just with a need of some kind that the invention of myth fulfills but with the myths, or the contents of myths, themselves. More precisely, everyone is born with the contents of myths already elevated to the level of myth.

For Tylor, for example, the true content, or subject, of myth is the physical world. Mythmakers transform the impersonal forces of the physical world into gods and the behavior of those gods into stories. For Frazer, the same is true. For Freud, the true subject of myth is a child and the child's parents. Mythmakers transform the child into a hero or heroine, the child's parents into royalty or nobility, and the conflicts between children and parents into stories.

For Jung, by contrast, the true subject of myth is the archetypes themselves of heroes and their adventures. The archetypes of the hero and his journey do not symbolize something else in turn. They are the symbolized. Because the archetypal level is the same as the mythic one, the mythic level is not invented but inherited. Everyone inherits the same archetypes, which together comprise what Jung calls the collective unconscious. In every society a few persons invent specific stories to express those archetypes, but mythmakers here are inventing only the manifestations of already mythic material. Odysseus, for example, gets either invented or appropriated to serve as a Greek expression of the hero archetype. Heroism itself is not invented, the way it is for Tylor, Frazer, and Freud. Only actual myths expressing it are.

For Tylor, Frazer, and Freud, experience, even if it is of innate needs, provides the impetus for the creation of myth. For Freud, for example, one's experience of one's parents' reaction to one's incestuous drives spurs the creation of myth. For Jung, by contrast, experience provides only an occasion for the expression of pre-existent archetypes. Archetypes *shape* experience rather than, as for Freud and the others, *derive* from it. The archetype of the Great Mother does not, as for Freud, result from the magnification of one's own mother but on the contrary expresses itself through her and thereby shapes one's experience of her.[8]

For Jung, as for Tylor, Frazer, and Freud, the differences among myths get transmitted by acculturation. But where for Tylor, Frazer, and Freud the similarities, as the product of the similar experiences of each society, do not get transmitted at all, for Jung they get transmitted by heredity. Again, the distinctiveness of Jung's explanation of the similarities in myth is not that he attributes them to independent invention rather than diffusion but that he attributes independent invention to heredity rather than experience.

Seemingly, independent invention through heredity is no invention at all. But independent invention does not require that every generation within a society invent myths anew. It requires only that one generation invent them rather than adopt those of another society. For Jung, every society experiences archetypes for itself and creates its own myths to express them.

Independent "inventionists" of both experience and heredity do allow for some borrowing among societies and therefore for some diffusion. They simply deny that diffusion can account for most of the similarities among myths—above all among societies too far removed from one another for any contact to have occurred. Thus Jung says:

Although tradition and transmission by migration certainly play a part, there are . . . very many cases that cannot be accounted for in this way and drive us to the hypothesis of "autochthonous [i.e., independent] revival." These cases are so numerous that we are obliged to assume the existence of a collective psychic substratum. I have called this the *collective unconscious.*[9]

The additional standard argument against diffusion, also given by Jung, is that even if diffusion can explain how contact takes place, it cannot explain how contact takes hold and remains:

> Now if the myth were nothing but an historical remnant [i.e., of diffusion], one would have to ask why it has not long since vanished into the great rubbish-heap of the past, and why it continues to make its influence felt on the highest levels of civilization. . . . [10]

Undeniably, Jung is saying that independent invention through heredity is far more important than diffusion, but he is at least acknowledging that diffusion occurs.

To maintain his distinction between archetypes, which are what get inherited, and their symbolic expressions, which get created by every society, Jung could say that independent invention accounts for the similarities in archetypes and diffusion for any similarities in symbols. Exactly because symbols are ordinarily the creation of each society, they usually differ from society to society: a Greek hero like Odysseus differs from a Roman one like Aeneas. Jung could therefore attribute to diffusion any similarities among specific heroes: the obvious influence of Homer's idea of heroism on Vergil. But in fact he attributes to similar archetypes and so to independent invention similarities within classes of symbols—for example, symbols of the cross per se—and attributes to diffusion only similarities in details—symbols of specific kinds of crosses.

Campbell's View of the Origin of Myth

Is Campbell's explanation of the similarities in myths Jungian? In both *Hero* and "Bios and Mythos" he attributes the similarities to the unconscious, which is a form of independent invention. In "Bios and Mythos" he even relegates diffusion to a mere secondary cause. But in neither work does he explain whether the similarities, which he calls archetypes in any case, are, as for Jung, inherited or, as for Freud, acquired. In *Hero* Campbell implies that the archetypes are inherited, but he never outright says so.

Campbell is less Jungian in *Masks* than in any other work except "Bios and Mythos." On the one hand he is so intent on tracing cultural influences that he might well seem to be attributing the similarities to diffusion rather than to independent invention. The possibility that he is attributing to diffusion only similarities in symbols and is thereby allowing for independent invention for archetypes does not seem to hold: the similarities he discusses are so general as surely to constitute archetypes rather than mere symbols.

On the other hand even if Campbell means to be attributing to diffusion symbols alone, the independent invention to which he would be attributing archetypes themselves is experience rather than, as for Jung, heredity. Campbell might here seem no different from early Jung, but for even early Jung the archetypes formed out of the experiences of prehistoric humans get inherited in turn. For Campbell, by contrast, each generation creates archetypes anew out of its own experiences. Imagination takes significant experiences and makes them mythical, or archetypal. Only the mechanisms for activating emotions and actions, the IRM's, are inherited. Archetypes themselves, which activate the IRM's, are not.

How close to Jung Campbell comes in *The Mythic Image* depends on what Campbell means by "mythic images." The images, he stresses, are the product of diffusion rather than heredity or experience, but it is not clear whether these images are archetypes themselves or mere symbols expressing them. If, as seems more likely, they are archetypes, then Campbell is breaking fundamentally with Jung. If, however, the images are symbols, then Campbell is compatible with Jung, even though, again, Jung attributes to diffusion only similarities in details. At the outset of *The Mythic Image* Campbell does say that myths come from the unconscious, but again he does not say whether its contents are inherited or acquired.

If, in the *Atlas,* Campbell is attributing the presence in myths of the same archetypes to diffusion, then once again he is clearly far afield of Jung. But if he is attributing the presence of those archetypes not just to independent invention in general but to heredity in particular (vol. I, p. 73), then he is obviously like Jung. Yet he would be closest to only early Jung since he would clearly still be claiming that prehistoric humans created, not inherited, archetypes and simply passed them on to their progeny (vol. I, p. 73).

In volume two of the *Atlas* Campbell alternatively attributes the similarities in myths to diffusion and to independent invention. He subdivides independent invention not into experience and heredity, as he does elsewhere, but into environment and the conscious, not unconscious, mind. None of his explanations here is, then, Jungian.

In *The Inner Reaches of Outer Space* Campbell alternatively ascribes the similarities in myths to independent invention and, more often, to diffusion. Independent invention sometimes means experience and sometimes means heredity. In *The Power of Myth* Campbell similarly alternates between independent invention, here exclusively of experience, and diffusion.

Since in *An Open Life* Campbell not only stresses diffusion as the source of similarities among myths but also contrasts that explanation to Jung's, he must be ascribing to diffusion similarities among archetypes, not just among symbols. Yet he also espouses the existence of a collective unconscious (*Open Life*, pp. 122–123) and, like Jung, says that diffusion explains only where similarities come from, not why they stick (*Open Life*, p. 43).

Jung's View of the Function of Myth

To be Jungian is not merely to ascribe the origin of myths, or their contents, to heredity but also to ascribe to myths various functions. For Jung, myth serves, first, to reveal the existence of the unconscious:

Myths are original revelations of the preconscious [i.e., collective] psyche, involuntary statements about unconscious psychic happenings. . . . Modern psychology treats the products of unconscious fantasy-activity as self-portraits of what is going on in the unconscious, or as statements of the unconscious psyche about itself.[11]

Whoever takes myth literally thinks that it is revealing the existence of something external like god, but in fact it is revealing the existence of the unconscious within.

Myth serves, second, to guide one in dealing with the unconscious. The lives of the characters described in myth become models to emulate:

> For instance, our ancestors have done so-and-so, and so shall you do. Or such and such a hero has done so-and-so, and that is your model. For instance, in the teachings of the Catholic Church, there are several thousand saints. They serve as models, they have their legends, and that is Christian mythology.[12]

Myth here assures one that others have had experiences like one's own.

Myth serves, third, not just to tell one about the unconscious but actually to open one up to it. Because one experiences the unconscious through only its symbolic manifestations, the symbols in myth serve as a conduit for encountering the unconscious. Myth simultaneously makes sense of any prior encounters and itself constitutes an encounter.

Campbell's View of the Function of Myth

While in *Hero* Campbell is concerned far less with the function than with the meaning of myth, the functions he does implicitly attribute to myth are snugly Jungian. Myth functions, first, to reveal the existence of a severed, deeper reality, which Campbell, going beyond Jung, deems metaphysical as well as psychological. Myth functions, second, as a vehicle for actually encountering that reality. Since myth describes the hero's own rediscovery of that reality, his story functions, third, as a model for others. But where for Jung myth fulfills these functions even when its meaning remains unconscious, for Campbell myth works only when "sages" reveal its meaning.

In *The Mythic Image,* in which Campbell is also less concerned with the function of myth than with its meaning, myth nevertheless serves the first two of the three Jungian functions that it serves in *Hero:* to reveal the existence of a deeper reality, whether psychological or metaphysical, and to enable humans to experience it. But Campbell here employs Kundalini yoga rather than Jungian psychology to interpret that reality.

In "Bios and Mythos" Campbell says *what* myth does but not *how* it does it. What myth does is far from Jungian. Though it helps one grow up, it ceases with the attainment of the goal of the first half of life. Going beyond the first half means going beyond myth itself, which Jung would scarcely grant. The attachment that, in the first half of life, myth helps overcome is, moreover, to one's mother herself, not, as for Jung, to the mother archetype projected onto her. Whether in any case myth helps break the attachment by, in Jungian fashion, providing a model Campbell never says.

Insofar as myths, in part one of volume one of *Masks*, serve to provide symbols for expressing archetypes, Campbell's view of their function parallels Jung's. But insofar as those symbols serve to activate archetypes, and in turn emotions and actions, Campbell's view is more Freudian than Jungian. For Jung, symbols in myths serve less to act out archetypes than to evince them. The payoff is not relief but understanding. Even though Campbell does not deem archetypes repressed or even unconscious, his stress on release puts him closer to Freud than to Jung. Still, his stress on myth as interpreting the archetypes it activates fits Jung's view of myth, however non-Jungian his interpretation of those archetypes.

Elsewhere in *Masks*, together with the *Atlas*, *Inner Reaches*, and *The Power of Myth*, Campbell lists four functions that all myths serve. The first two of those functions serve to link humans to the cosmos. The third serves to link them to society. The fourth alone singled out in *An Open Life*, serves to link them to everything, including themselves.

On the one hand Jung strongly opposes the rejection of the material world, including society, for the world of the unconscious. Ever seeking a balance between the one world and the other, Jung would applaud the third function, which, either intentionally or merely coincidentally, keeps humans anchored to something material. Indeed, Jung would doubtless contrast this effect to the rejection of the material world typically sought by Campbell. On the other hand Jung cares more about connecting humans to the unconscious than about connecting them to the material world, with which they have ordinarily not lost contact. Since only the fourth function deals with humans themselves, and since even it by no means necessarily deals with the unconscious, Jung would consider Campbell's four functions as a whole askew to his own.

Other Differences Between Campbell and Jung

Even if Campbell and Jung agreed fully on the origin and function of myth, they would remain far apart. Campbell, first of all, deems myth indispensable. No human being can survive without it. Jung values myth, but he does not consider it indispensable. Religion, art, dream, and what Jung calls the "active imagination" can serve as well, even if at times Jung, like Campbell, uses the term "myth" to encompass all of them. The functions that myth serves may themselves be indispensable, but myth is not indispensable to serving them.

For Campbell, to have a myth is to accept it wholly. It is to identify oneself with the myth—for example, with the protagonist of a hero myth or the divinity of a creation myth. It is to live out the myth.

Jung is more critical. To have a myth is valuable but limited. A myth provides entrée to a side of oneself, but to only one side. While a single myth can contain more than one archetype, no myth contains them all. An entire mythology like that of Christianity and Hinduism can cover the whole of one's personality, but no one myth can. One should therefore have many myths. At the same time one should identify oneself with none of them. To identify oneself with a myth is to lose touch with the rest of one's personality, not least one's ordinary, outward consciousness. Carried to an extreme, identification causes a breakdown rather than an enlargement of personality. Jung urges humans to learn from myth without abandoning themselves to it. More precisely, Jung urges humans to discover the range of meanings of a whole mythology before committing themselves to it. Properly understood, a complete mythology does accord a place to all sides of one's personality. One *should* live it out, but only upon recognizing its scope.

For Campbell, myth is not only necessary for the deepest human fulfillment but also sufficient. One needs nothing else, including therapy. In fact, therapy is only for those without myth.

Jung considers myth neither necessary nor sufficient for human fulfillment. Whenever myth is used, it should be used with therapy, which is an indispensable supplement, not alternative, to it. Primitives can never be fulfilled because they have no therapy, which is a modern invention.

Myth for Campbell contains all the wisdom humans need. They need only learn to interpret it. They need never venture beyond it. Moreover, myth is easy to interpret. It has a single meaning, even if "sages" are required to decipher that meaning.

Jung insists that humans reflect on myth, not blindly accept it. If myth can guide one through life, it can also lead one astray. If myth can help one evaluate one's life, one's life can also help evaluate it. Wisdom is to be found not just in myth but also in humans, who must nurture myth as well as be nurtured by it. There should be "give and take" between a myth and its adherents. A great person will not merely interpret but also transform a myth, the way Freud does the Oedipus myth and Jung himself the Job myth. Furthermore, myth has an inexhaustible array of meanings rather than a single one.

For Campbell, to interpret a myth is to identify the archetypes in it. To interpret the *Odyssey*, for example, is to classify it as a hero myth, to show how it conforms to a heroic monomyth.

Jung considers the identification of archetypes the first rather than the last step in the interpretation of a myth. One must proceed to determine the meaning of those archetypes in the specific myth in which they appear and the meaning of that myth in the life of the specific person who is stirred by it. The meaning of the myth is more than its general meaning for all humanity. One must analyze the person, not just the myth, to understand its significance. Hence the need for therapy. Hence Jung's distinction between archetypes, which are universal, and their symbols, which vary from case to case. Hence Jung's opposition to the adoption by the West of the specific myths of the East. Hence Jung's term for the ideal psychological state: "individua-tion." Many of Jung's disciples are like Campbell: they stop interpreting myth at the point of comparison, or "amplification."[13] But Jung himself does not. How ironic, then, that Campbell distinguishes himself from Jung on the grounds that he himself is interested in the differences as well as the similarities among myths (*Open Life*, pp. 51–52).

For both Campbell and Jung, myth functions above all to link humans to the unconscious. But they differ over the linkage. Campbell, whose knowledge of the unconscious derives from reading myths, has a detached, imperious attitude toward the unconscious. He seeks to *use* myth to enrich human lives. Jung, whose knowledge of the unconscious stems from a terrifying encounter with it, has a far warier and humbler stance. While he, too, seeks enrichment from the unconscious, he also fears the unconscious, which he realizes can overcome those who attempt to control it. Where Campbell can confidently advocate surrender to the unconscious, Jung, trepidatious at the prospect, promotes only a "dialogue" with the unconscious. Where Campbell assumes that the ego will somehow remain in place, Jung does not.

NOTES

[1]See, for example, Eric J. Sharpe: "The American scholar Joseph Campbell (b. 1907) has for many years been the major representative among students of comparative religion of the heritage of Jung. His industry has been remarkable, and he has in fact attempted a total Jungian interpretation of world mythology, particularly in the four volumes of *The Masks of God* . . ." (*Comparative Religion*, first ed. [New York: Scribner's, 1975], p. 212).

[2]Strictly, the similarities among myths are not of archetypes themselves, which are unobservable, but of "archetypal images," which manifest them, and which are manifested in turn in symbols. "Archetype" will be used here as shorthand for "archetypal image"—a shorthand used by Jung himself.

[3]See Edward B. Tylor, *Primitive Culture*, fifth ed. (New York: Harper Torchbooks, 1958), II (retitled *Religion in Primitive Culture*), esp. ch. 11.

[4]See James G. Frazer, *The Golden Bough*, one-vol. abridgment (London: Macmillan, 1922), esp. chs. 3–4.

[5]*Ibid.*, p. 448.

[6]See Sigmund Freud, *An Outline of Psycho-Analysis*, tr. James Strachey (New York: Norton, 1949), esp. ch. 7.

[7]See Otto Rank, "The Myth of the Birth of the Hero,"

in his *The Myth of the Birth of the Hero and Other Writings,* ed. Philip Freund (New York: Vintage, 1959), pp. 6–13.

[8]See, for example, Jung on the origin of the archetype of the divine child: see his Jung, *Symbols of Transformation,* The Collected Works, V, first ed. (New York: Pantheon, 1956), pp. 222, 328, 330, 417–420; ''The Psychology of the Child Archetype,'' in his *The Archetypes and the Collective Unconscious,* The Collected Works, IX, part 1, first ed. (New York: Pantheon, 1959), p. 161, note 21. To be sure, early Jung attributed archetypes to the imprinting of the experiences of prehistoric humans, who then transmitted to their descendants the memory of those experiences. Later Jung deemed archetypes innate in even prehistoric humans.

[9]Jung, ''The Psychology of the Child Archetype,'' p. 155.

[10]Jung, ''On the Psychology of the Trickster-Figure,'' in his *The Archetypes and the Collective Unconscious,* p. 262.

[11]Jung, ''The Psychology of the Child Archetype,'' pp. 154–155.

[12]Jung, reply, in Richard I. Evans, *Jung on Elementary Psychology,* rev. ed. (New York: Dutton, 1976), p. 67.

[13]See, most grandly, Erich Neumann, *The Great Mother,* tr. Ralph Manheim, first ed. (New York: Pantheon, 1955), though in his clinical practice Neumann likely went beyond amplification.

CHAPTER THIRTEEN

CAMPBELL THE ROMANTIC

Campbell's popularity requires scant documentation. His six-part PBS series with Bill Moyers attracted two and a half million viewers weekly. The video cassette version of the series has sold tens of thousands of copies. The book based on the series, *The Power of Myth*, remains ensconced on best-seller lists nationwide. Campbell's other books continue to sell feverishly. As *Newsweek* put it, "The hero is dead, but his message lives on."[1]

What accounts for Campbell's popularity? Many fans laud Campbell as above all a masterly storyteller. He does not simply know all the world's myths but also relishes reciting them. Yet in his writings he tells surprisingly few myths, at least whole ones. Instead, he cites portions of myths. In *Hero* Campbell presents barely one complete myth. In other works he plainly ignores the plot of myths and focuses instead on either the beliefs underlying the plot or else specific archetypes in the plot. The fact that myths for Campbell can be creeds and even rituals as well as stories underscores the limited role storytelling plays. Surely, then, Campbell's popularity does not stem primarily from his undeniable knack for telling tales.

In fact, Campbell himself would doubtless have been miffed if it had. For he sought not only to tell myths but even more to analyze them. He analyzes the origin, function, and meaning of myth. True, in *Hero* he states modestly that he is seeking only to *establish* a heroic pattern. But *analyze* that pattern he proceeds to do. In *The Mythic Image* he does boldly reject interpretation as an impediment to the unmediated experience of myth, but in all his other works he conspicuously deciphers, not just imbibes, myth. He is a *theorist* of myth.

Yet Campbell's popularity likely does not rest on his analysis of the *origin* and *function* of myth. In some works, including *Hero,* he discusses the origin and function only briefly. In other books he gives varied explanations.

By contrast, Campbell's interpretation of the *meaning* of myth is unchanging, and it is that interpretation which no doubt captivates Campbell's devotees. From first work to last the true meaning of myth is ahistorical rather than historical and symbolic rather than literal. The symbolic meaning is simultaneously psychological and metaphysical. Psychologically and metaphysically alike, the meaning of myth is mystical: myth preaches the oneness of at once consciousness with unconsciousness and the everyday world with the strange, new one.

Romantic and Rationalist Approaches to Myth

Campbell's view of the meaning, if also the function, of myth can loosely be called romantic and can be contrasted to a rationalist view—a view epitomized by the Victorian anthropologists Edward Tylor and James

Frazer. For rationalists, myth is an entirely primitive phenomenon. It constitutes a scientific-like explanation of the physical world. Indeed, it is the primitive counterpart to science, which is exclusively modern. Myth and science are not only incompatible in content but also redundant in function: both serve to account for the origin and the operation of the physical world. Myth invokes the wills of gods; science, the mechanical behavior of impersonal forces like atoms. There are no modern myths. In fact, "modern myth" is a contradiction in terms. Any would-be modern myth is a sheer relic: a story no longer believed, at least literally, though perhaps still told for entertainment and admired literarily.

For Campbell and other romantics, myth is an eternal possession. Nothing can supersede it. Where for rationalists science better serves its explanatory *function* than myth, for romantics nothing duplicates the psychological or metaphysical *content* of myth. Where for rationalists science makes it at once unnecessary and impossible for scientific "moderns" to harbor myth, for romantics science runs askew to myth, which moderns can therefore still have. Myth itself does not, like science, explain the physical world. Hence for Campbell myth at most provides only a symbolic image for an explanation—for example, the image of the Great Chain of Being.

In starkest contrast to rationalists, Campbell considers science itself mythic. While not, like Jung, going so far as to maintain that myth says the same thing as science, Campbell does, like Jung, contend that science gets transformed into myth. The "Star Wars" saga, for example, recasts the clash between humanity and technology into a heroic tale.

Where for rationalists the *function* served by myth

is indispensable, for romantics myth itself is indispensable to the serving of its function. The prime function is the revelation of the meaning of myth. All of the other functions enumerated by Campbell—for example, instilling and preserving a sense of the awe and mystery of the world—hinge on the revelatory one. Moderns as well as primitives not merely can have myth but must have it. For rationalists, humans without some explanation of the environment, be the explanation mythic or scientific, would be perplexed. For romantics, humans bereft of the message found exclusively in myth would be unfulfilled.

For rationalists, myth, like science, is effective, or functional, when it is believed to be true, but in fact it is false: myth is a cogent but nevertheless incorrect explanation of the world—science providing the correct one. For romantics, myth is effective not merely when it is accepted as true but only because it *is* true: the wisdom it offers would not, if false, be wisdom. The content of myth for romantics is thus far more tautly tied to the function than it is for rationalists. The chief function of myth for romantics is the revelation of not just some content but true content.

Campbell's Romantic Appeal

The first aspect of Campbell's romantic appeal is the elevated status he accords myth. Myth represents a collective Bible for all humanity. It alone contains the wisdom necessary for what amounts to salvation. Not only the array of functions Campbell ascribes to myth but also the scope of his definition of myth guarantees its irreplaceability. Ritual, art, ideology, and even science become varieties of myth rather than alternatives to it. An action as well as a belief can be mythic, and the belief need not take the form of a story, which itself can be of any kind.

Other theorists of myth both define myth more narrowly than Campbell and subsume it under a larger rubric like culture, religion, literature, and the mind. So broad is Campbell's definition of myth that these rubrics get subsumed under myth itself. Where others study culture, religion, literature, and the mind in order to understand myth, Campbell studies myth in order to understand culture, religion, literature, and the mind.

Because myth for Campbell is indispensable to the serving of its indispensable functions, he can declare unabashedly that without myth, even myth misinterpreted literally, humans are lost:

> For not only has it always been the way of multitudes to interpret their own symbols literally, but such literally read symbolic forms have always been the supports of their civilizations, the supports of their moral orders, their cohesion, vitality, and creative powers. With the loss of them there follows uncertainty, and with uncertainty, disequilibrium. . . . Today the same thing is happening to us. With our old mythologically founded taboos unsettled by our own modern sciences, there is everywhere in the civilized world a rapidly rising incidence of vice and crime, mental disorders, suicides and dope addictions, shattered homes, impudent children, violence, murder, and despair. These are facts; I am not inventing them. (*Myths to Live By*, pp. 8–9)

Because no one else relies on myth so much, no one else, not even Jung, is as much an evangelist for myth as Campbell.

The second aspect of Campbell's romantic appeal is the elevated status he accords primitives. Moderns can barely equal, let alone surpass, them. For rationalists, primitives, while scrupulously rational, are inferior intellectually to moderns: primitives invent myth, which is a childish as well as false explanation of the world; moderns create science, which is a mature as well as true explanation of the world. For Campbell, primitives are wiser than moderns: primitives know intuitively the mythic meaning that moderns need complicated techniques like Freudian and especially Jungian psychology to extricate. In fact, primitives know the meaning that moderns have altogether forgotten and need modern psychology to recollect. Campbell thus claims only to be rediscovering, not discovering, the real meaning of myth—a meaning fully known to the sages of yore. Jung himself, not to say Freud, never goes this far.

The third aspect of Campbell's romantic appeal follows from the second: if primitives already know the meaning of myth merely recovered by moderns, the meaning of myth is always the same. An unbroken tradition binds the hoariest myths to the latest ones. Contrary to rationalists, there *are* modern myths. Moderns no less than primitives are continuously creating them, and Campbell singles out the distinctively modern myths of space travel, as typified by "Star Wars." But modern myths have the same meaning as primitive ones. Individual myths may come and go with the cultures that produce them, but the meaning of all myths never changes. It is not coincidental that Campbell is an arch-comparativist: to say that the meaning of all myths is the same is to say that the differences among myths are trivial.

The fourth aspect of Campbell's romantic appeal parallels the third: not only do all myths bear one message, but the message borne is the oneness of all things. Myths not merely assume but outright preach mysticism. They proclaim humans one with one another: divisions into peoples and even persons are superficial. Campbell himself says at the outset of *Hero* that he hopes to foster world unity by demonstrating the oneness of all hero myths. Humans, according to myths, are, furthermore, one with their individual selves: divisions into consciousness and unconsciousness and into body and soul dissolve. Most grandly, humans are one with the cosmos: the division into oneself and the world proves illusory as well. No tenet is more staunchly romantic than the conviction that beneath the apparent disparateness of all things lies unity.

The fifth and final aspect of Campbell's romantic appeal is his assumption that the mystical message of myth is true. For Campbell, not only is the true meaning of myth the oneness of all things, but all things are truly one. Myth thus discloses the deepest truth about reality.

While those theorists who see myth as the ancient counterpart to modern science judge myth false, other theorists besides Campbell consider it true. Myth for them accurately depicts the mind, the environment, or society, if not quite ultimate reality. But for most of these theorists the function of myth is separate from its truth: in the process of, say, satisfying drives or preserving society, myth coincidentally evinces the nature of the mind or society. For other theorists, the function of myth is separate from its *falsity:* in the act of falsely explaining the world, myth actually fulfills instinct or bolsters society. To fulfill even those non-explanatory functions, not just the explanatory one, myth must be *believed* to be true but need not *be* true.

For Campbell, the utility and the veracity of myth are inseparable. Admittedly, when Campbell says that myth functions to keep society intact, its efficacy depends on only the *belief* in its veracity: myth can work as effectively when it is believed to be true as when it is true. But when Campbell says, far more effusively, that myth functions to reveal the ultimate nature of reality, to enable humans to experience that reality, and to guide them through the stages of life, its effectiveness depends on its correctness. To say that myth serves to reveal ultimate reality is surely to require that that reality exists. Even to say that myth serves to guide one through life is surely to presuppose that myth is sufficiently in touch in reality to be able to serve as a guide.

NOTES

[1] K. C. Cole, "Master of the Myth," *Newsweek,* 112 (November 14, 1988), p. 60.

BIBLIOGRAPHY

BY CAMPBELL

BOOKS

A Skeleton Key to Finnegans Wake. With Henry Morton Robinson. New York: Harcourt, Brace, and World, 1944. Paperback: New York: Viking Compass Books, 1961. Paperback reprint: New York: Penguin Books, 1977.

Edited:
The Works of Heinrich R. Zimmer:

Myths and Symbols in Indian Art and Civilization. Bollingen Series VI. New York: Pantheon Books, 1946. Paperback: New York: Harper Torchbooks, 1962. No second ed.

The King and the Corpse: Tales of the Soul's Conquest of Evil. Bollingen Series XI. New York: Pantheon Books, 1948. Second ed.: New York: Pantheon Books, 1956. Paperback: New York: Meridian Books, 1960.

Philosophies of India. Bollingen Series XXVI. New York: Pantheon Books, 1951. Paperback: New York: Meridian Books, 1956. No second ed.

The Art of Indian Asia: Its Mythology and Transformations. Completed by Campbell. 2 vols. Bollingen Series XXXIX. New York: Pantheon Books, 1955. Second ed.: New York: Pantheon Books, 1960.

The Hero with a Thousand Faces. Bollingen Series XVII. New York: Pantheon Books, 1949. Paperback: New York: Meridian Books, 1956. Second ed.: Princeton, NJ: Princeton University Press, 1968. Paperback of second ed.: Princeton, NJ: Princeton University Press, 1972.

Edited:
Myth and Man Series:
Carl Kerényi. *The Gods of the Greeks.* London and New York: Thames and Hudson, 1951.
Maya Deren. *Divine Horsemen: The Living Gods of Haiti.* London and New York: Thames and Hudson, 1953. With Foreword by Campbell.
Alan W. Watts. *Myth and Ritual in Christianity.* London and New York: Thames and Hudson, 1954.

Edited:
The Portable Arabian Nights. Viking Portable Library. New York: Viking Press, 1952.

Edited:
Papers from the Eranos Yearbooks, trs. Ralph Manheim and R.F.C. Hull. Bollingen Series XXX:
Vol. I: *Spirit and Nature.* New York: Pantheon Books, 1954. Paperback: Princeton, NJ: Princeton University Press, 1982.
Vol. II: *The Mysteries.* New York: Pantheon Books, 1955. Paperback: Princeton, NJ: Princeton University Press, 1979.
Vol. III: *Man and Time.* New York: Pantheon Books, 1957. Paperback: Princeton, NJ: Princeton University Press, 1983.
Vol. IV: *Spiritual Disciplines.* New York: Pantheon Books, 1960. Paperback: Princeton, NJ: Princeton University Press, 1985.
Vol. V: *Man and Transformation.* New York: Pantheon

Books, 1964. Paperback: Princeton, NJ: Princeton University Press, 1981.

Vol. VI: *The Mystic Vision*. Princeton, NJ: Princeton University Press, 1968. Paperback: Princeton, NJ: Princeton University Press, 1983.

The Masks of God:

Vol. I: *Primitive Mythology*. New York: Viking Press, 1959. Paperback: New York: Viking Compass Books, 1970. Paperback reprint: New York: Penguin Books, 1976.

Vol. II: *Oriental Mythology*. New York: Viking Press, 1962. Paperback: New York: Viking Compass Books, 1970. Paperback reprint: New York: Penguin Books, 1976.

Vol. III: *Occidental Mythology*. New York: Viking Press, 1964. Paperback: New York: Viking Compass Books, 1970. Paperback reprint: New York: Penguin Books, 1976.

Vol. IV: *Creative Mythology*. New York: Viking Press, 1968. Paperback: Viking Compass Books, 1970. Paperback reprint: New York: Penguin Books, 1976.

The Flight of the Wild Gander: Explorations in the Mythological Dimension. New York: Viking Press, 1969. Paperback: Chicago: Regnery Gateway Editions, 1972.

Edited:

Myths, Dreams, and Religion. New York: Dutton, 1970. Reprint: Dallas: Spring Publications, 1988.

Edited:

The Portable Jung, tr. R.F.C. Hull. Viking Portable Library. New York: Viking Press, 1971. Reprint: New York: Penguin Books, 1976.

Myths to Live By. New York: Viking Press, 1972. Paperback: New York: Bantam Books, 1973.

The Mythic Image. Assisted by M.J. Abadie. Bollingen Series C. Princeton, NJ: Princeton University Press, 1974. Paperback: Princeton, NJ: Princeton University Press, 1981.

Historical Atlas of World Mythology:
Vol. I: *The Way of the Animal Powers.* Alfred van der Marck Editions. New York: Harper & Row, 1983. Reprint: Part 1: *Mythologies of the Primitive Hunters and Gatherers.* New York: Alfred van der Marck Editions, 1988. Paperback of Part 1: New York: Harper & Row Perennial Library, 1988. Part 2: *Mythologies of the Great Hunt.* New York: Alfred van der Marck Editions, 1988. Paperback of Part 2: New York: Harper & Row Perennial Library, 1988.
Vol. II: *The Way of the Seeded Earth.* Alfred van der Marck Editions. Part 1: *The Sacrifice.* New York: Alfred van der Marck Editions, 1988. Paperback: New York: Harper & Row Perennial Library, 1988.

The Inner Reaches of Outer Space: Metaphor as Myth and as Religion. New York: Alfred van der Marck Editions, 1986. Paperback: New York: Harper & Row Perennial Library, 1988.

The Power of Myth. With Bill Moyers. Ed. Betty Sue Flowers. New York: Doubleday, 1988. Paperback: New York: Doubleday, 1988.

An Open Life. In Conversation with Michael Toms. Eds. John M. Maher and Dennie Briggs. Burdett, NY: Larson Publications, 1988.

ESSAYS, REVIEWS, ETC.

"Commentary" to *Where the Two Came to Their Father: A Navaho War Ceremonial,* given by Jeff King, text and paintings recorded by Maud Oakes, Bollingen Series I

(New York: Pantheon Books, 1943), pp. 51–84. Second ed. (with altered order): Princeton, NJ: Princeton University Press, 1969. Pp. 3–4, 7–8, 31–49.

"Folkloristic Commentary" to *Grimm's Fairy Tales*, ed. Josef Scharl, tr. Margaret Hunt, rev. James Stern (New York: Pantheon Books, 1944), pp. 833–864. Reprinted in Campbell, *The Flight of the Wild Gander*, ch. 1.

"Life's Delicate Child," review of Géza Róheim, *The Origin and Function of Culture*, *Saturday Review of Literature*, 28 (October 13, 1945), pp. 56, 58.

"Finnegan the Wake," *Chimera*, 4 (Spring 1946), pp. 63–80. Reprinted in *James Joyce: Two Decades of Criticism*, ed. Seon Givens (New York: Vanguard Press, 1948), pp. 368–389.

"Bios and Mythos: Prolegomena to a Science of Mythology," in *Psychoanalysis and Culture: Essays in Honor of Géza Róheim*, eds. George B. Wilbur and Warner Muensterberger (New York: International Universities Press, 1951), pp. 329–343. Reprinted, minus subtitle, in Campbell, *The Flight of the Wild Gander*, ch. 2. Reprinted, in slightly abridged form, in *Myth and Literature: Contemporary Theory and Practice*, ed. John B. Vickery (Lincoln: University of Nebraska Press, 1966), pp. 15–23. Reprinted in paperback reprint of *Myth and Literature* (Lincoln: University of Nebraska Press Bison Books, 1969), pp. 15–23.

Review of C.G. Jung and C. Kerényi, *Essays on a Science of Mythology*, *Review of Religion*, 16 (March 1952), pp. 169–173.

"Editor's Introduction" to *The Portable Arabian Nights*, ed. Campbell, Viking Portable Library (New York: Viking Press, 1952), pp. 1–35.

"Heinrich Zimmer (1890–1943)," *Partisan Review*, 20 (July 1953), pp. 444–451.

"The Symbol without Meaning," *Eranos-Jahrbücher*, 26 (1957), pp. 415–476. Reprinted in partially revised form in Campbell, *The Flight of the Wild Gander*, ch. 5.

"Hinduism," in *Basic Beliefs: The Religious Philosophies of Mankind*, ed. Johnson E. Fairchild (New York: Sheridan House, 1959), pp. 54–72.

"The Historical Development of Mythology," *Daedalus*, 88 (Spring 1959), pp. 232–254. Reprinted in *Myth and Mythmaking*, ed. Henry A. Murray (New York: George Braziller, 1960), ch. 1. Reprinted in paperback reprint of *Myth and Mythmaking* (Boston: Beacon Press, 1968), ch. 1. Parts III and IV are equivalent to the "Introduction" to *The Masks of God: Primitive Mythology*, pp. 21–29; parts I and II are largely a summary of *The Masks of God: Oriental Mythology* and *Occidental Mythology*.

"Renewal Myths and Rites of the Primitive Hunters and Planters," *Eranos-Jahrbücher*, 28 (1959), pp. 407–458. Reprinted in revised form as "Mythogenesis" in Campbell, *The Flight of the Wild Gander*, ch. 4.

"Primitive Man as Metaphysician," in *Culture in History: Essays in Honor of Paul Radin*, ed. Stanley Diamond (New York: Columbia University Press, 1960), pp. 380–392. Reprinted in *Primitive Views of the World*, ed. Stanley Diamond (New York: Columbia University Press, 1964), pp. 20–32. Reprinted in Campbell, *The Flight of the Wild Gander*, ch. 3.

"Oriental Philosophy and Occidental Psychoanalysis," in *Proceedings of the IXth International Congress for the History of Religions*, Tokyo and Kyoto, August 27–September 9, 1958 (Tokyo: Maruzen, 1960), pp. 492–496.

"Introduction" to Helen Diner, *Mothers and Amazons: The First Feminine History of Culture*, ed. and tr. John Philip Lundin (New York: Julian Press, 1965), pp. v–x.

"Introduction" to *Myth, Religion, and Mother Right: Selected Writings of J.J. Bachofen*, tr. Ralph Manheim, preface by George Boas, Bollingen Series LXXXIV

(Princeton, NJ: Princeton University Press, 1967), pp. xxv–lvii.

"The Secularization of the Sacred," in *The Religious Situation*, vol. 1 (1968), ed. Donald R. Cutler (Boston: Beacon Press, 1968), ch. 17. Reprinted in Campbell, *The Flight of the Wild Gander*, ch. 6.

"Mythological Themes in Creative Literature and Art," in *Myths, Dreams, and Religion*, ed. Campbell (New York: Dutton, 1970), pp. 138–175.

"Contransmagnificandjewbangtantiality," *Studies in the Literary Imagination*, 3 (October 1970), pp. 3–18.

"Editor's Introduction" to *The Portable Jung*, ed. Campbell, tr. R. F. C. Hull, Viking Portable Library (New York: Viking Press, 1971), pp. vii–xxxii.

"Introduction" to *Echoes of the Wordless: Colloquy in Honor of Stanley Romain Hopper*, ed. Daniel C. Noel, Religion and the Arts Series, vol. 2 (Missoula, MT: American Academy of Religion/Society for Biblical Literature, 1973), pp. 1–6.

"On Mythic Shapes of Things to Come—Circular and Linear," *Horizon*, 16 (Summer 1974), pp. 35–37.

"Seven Levels of Consciousness," *Psychology Today*, 9 (December 1975), pp. 77–78.

"Erotic Irony and Mythic Forms in the Art of Thomas Mann," *Boston University Journal*, 24 (1976), pp. 10–27.

"Myths from West to East," in Alexander Eliot, *Myths*, with contributions by Mircea Eliade and Campbell (New York: McGraw-Hill Book Company, 1976), pp. 30–57.

"Foreword" to Rato Khyongla Nawang Losang, *My Life and Lives: The Story of a Tibetan Incarnation* (New York: Dutton, 1977), pp. vi–viii.

"The Occult in Myth and Literature," in *Literature and the Occult: Essays in Comparative Literature*, ed. Luanne Frank, UTA Publications in Literature (Arlington: University of Texas at Arlington, 1977), pp. 3–18.

"Introduction" to *Bulfinch's Mythology: The Greek and*

Roman Fables Illustrated, compiled by Bryan Holme (New York: Viking Press, 1979), pp. 6–9.

"Foreword" and "Symbolism of the Marseilles Deck," in Campbell and Richard Roberts, *Tarot Revelations* (San Francisco: Alchemy Books, 1979), pp. 3–7 and 9–25. Second ed.: San Anselmo, CA: Vernal Equinox Books, 1982. Pp. 3–7 and 9–25.

"The Interpretation of Symbolic Forms," in *The Binding of Prometheus: Perspectives on Myth and the Literary Process*, Collected Papers of the Bucknell University Program on Myth and Literature and the Bucknell Susquehanna Colloquium on Myth in Literature, March 21–22, 1974, eds. Marjorie W. McCune, Tucker Orbison, and Philip M. Withim (Lewisburg, PA: Bucknell University Press, 1980), pp. 35–59.

"Joseph Campbell on the Great Goddess," *Parabola*, 5 (November 1980), pp. 74–85.

"Masks of Oriental Gods: Symbolism of Kundalini Yoga," in *Literature of Belief: Sacred Scripture and Religious Experience*, ed. Neal E. Lambert, Religious Studies Monograph Series, vol. 5 (Salt Lake City, UT: Brigham Young University Press, 1981), ch. 6. Largely reprinted from Campbell, *The Mythic Image*, ch. 4.

"Indian Reflections in the Castle of the Grail," in *The Celtic Consciousness*, ed. Robert O'Driscoll (New York: George Braziller, 1982), pp. 3–30.

"Foreword" to Heinrich Zimmer, *Artistic Form and Yoga in the Sacred Images of India*, trs. and eds. Gerald Chapple and James B. Lawson in collaboration with J. Michael McKnight (Princeton, NJ: Princeton University Press, 1984), pp. xv–xvi.

" 'Our Mythology Has Been Wiped Out' By Rapid Change," *U.S. News and World Report*, 96 (April 16, 1984), p. 72.

INTERVIEWS

Auchincloss, Douglas. "On Waking Up: An Interview with Joseph Campbell." *Parabola*, 7 (Winter 1982), pp. 79–84.

Barbato, Joseph. "Reconstructing a 'Life History' of the World's Myths." *Chronicle of Higher Education*, 28 (March 21, 1984), pp. 5–7.

Bosveld, Jane. "Thus Spake Zoroaster: An Interview with Joseph Campbell." *Omni*, 11 (December 1988), pp. 143–144.

Bruckner, D.J.R. "Joseph Campbell: 70 Years of Making Connections." *New York Times Book Review* (December 18, 1983), pp. 25–27.

Goodrich, Chris. "Joseph Campbell." *Publishers Weekly*, 228 (August 23, 1985), pp. 74–75.

Hecht, Susan, and Louise Foltz. "An Interview with Joseph Campbell." *Stonecloud*, 6 (1976), pp. 45–59.

Keen, Sam. "Man and Myth: A Conversation with Joseph Campbell." *Psychology Today*, 5 (July 1971), pp. 35–39, 86–95. Reprinted in Keen, *Voices and Visions* (New York: Harper & Row, 1974), pp. 67–86.

Kennedy, Eugene. "Earthrise: The Dawning of a New Spiritual Awareness." *New York Times Magazine* (April 15, 1979), pp. 14–15, 51–56.

Kisly, Lorraine. "Living Myths: A Conversation with Joseph Campbell." *Parabola*, 1 (Spring 1976), pp. 70–81.

Leroux, Charles. "Grasping Myths to Extend the Reach of Man." *Chicago Tribune* (January 19, 1984), section 5, pp. 1, 3.

McKnight, Michael. "Elders and Guides: A Conversation with Joseph Campbell (On H.R. Zimmer)." *Parabola*, 5 (February 1980), pp. 57–65.

Moyers, Bill. "The Power of Myth: An Interview with Joseph Campbell." *New Age Journal*, 5 (July/August 1988), pp. 56–60, 80–83.

Newlove, Donald. "The Professor with a Thousand Faces." *Esquire*, 88 (September 1977), pp. 99–103, 132–136.

About Campbell

ARTICLES AND OTHER DISCUSSIONS

Arnold, Bruce. "The Celtic Enigma." *Dublin Magazine* (Autumn/Winter 1968), pp. 85–89. On Campbell: pp. 85, 87.

Beattie, Paul H., "A Perspective on Mythology." *Religious Humanism*, 17 (Autumn 1983), pp. 173–181. On Campbell: p. 179.

Chase, Richard. *Democratic Vista*. Garden City, NY: Doubleday Anchor Books, 1958. On Campbell: pp. 74–86.

———."Myth as Literature." *English Institute Essays 1947*. New York: Columbia University Press, 1948. Pp. 3–22. On Campbell: p. 7.

Clarke, Gerald. "The Need for New Myths." Essay. *Time*, 99 (January 17, 1972), pp. 50–51.

Clift, Jean Dalby, and Wallace B. Clift. *The Hero Journey in Dreams*. New York: Crossroad, 1988. On Campbell: pp. 13–20, 22–23, 28, 35, 45, 126.

Cole, K.C. "Master of the Myth." *Newsweek*, 112 (November 14, 1988), pp. 60–63.

D'Arcy, M.C. "God and Mythology." *Heythrop Journal*, 1 (April 1960), 91–104. On Campbell: pp. 95–104.

De Laszlo, Violet. "The Goal in Jungian Psychotherapy." Spring (1952), pp. 59–75. On Campbell: pp. 68–69.

Dorson, Richard M. "Mythology and Folklore." *Annual Review of Anthropology*, 2 (1973), pp. 107–126. On Campbell: pp. 107–108.

Doty, William G. *Mythography*. Tuscaloosa: University

of Alabama Press, 1986. On Campbell: pp. 52–55, 108–110, 121, 124–125, 176–178.

Dundes, Alan. *Interpreting Folklore.* Bloomington: Indiana University Press, 1960. On Campbell: pp. 224–225, 231–232.

Gill, Brendan. "The Faces of Joseph Campbell." *New York Review of Books,* 36 (September 28, 1989), pp. 16–19.

Henderson, Joseph L. *Thresholds of Initiation.* Middletown, CT: Wesleyan University Press, 1967. On Campbell: pp. 55, 153, 176–177, 226, 229.

Hyman, Stanley Edgar. "Myth, Ritual, and Nonsense." *Kenyon Review,* 11 (Summer 1949), pp. 455–475. On Campbell: pp. 455–456, 470–475.

Jewett, Robert, and John Shelton Lawrence. *The American Monomyth.* Garden City, NY: Doubleday Anchor Books, 1977. On Campbell: pp. xix–xx, 249.

Kerrigan, William. "The Raw, The Cooked and the Half-Baked." *Virginia Quarterly Review,* 51 (Autumn 1975), pp. 646–656.

Klavan, Andrew. "Joseph Campbell, Myth Master." *Village Voice* (May 24, 1988), pp. 60–64.

Leeming, David Adams. *Mythology.* Second ed. New York: Harper & Row, 1981. Partly applies Campbell's heroic pattern in altered form.

Long, Charles H. "Religion and Mythology: A Critical Review of Some Recent Discussions." *History of Religions,* 1 (Winter 1962), pp. 322–331. On Campbell: 325–331.

———. "The Dreams of Professor Campbell: Joseph Campbell's *The Mythic Image.*" *Religious Studies Review,* 6 (October 1980), pp. 261–271.

McGuire, William. *Bollingen.* Bollingen Series. Princeton, NJ: Princeton University Press, 1982. On Campbell: pp. xvii, 41, 65–66, 121, 135, 139, 141–144, 158, 177–179, 235, 291.

———. "Joseph Campbell (1904–1987)." *Quadrant,* 1 (Spring 1988), pp. 5–8.

Miller, David L. *"Homo Religiosus and the Death of God." Journal of Bible and Religion*, 34 (October 1966), pp. 305–315. On Campbell: pp. 306–309.

Noel, Daniel C. "An Analytical and Technological Culture Revels in the 'Power of Myth'." *Chronicle of Higher Education*, 35 (February 15, 1989), section B, p. 2.

Perry, John Weir. "The Messianic Hero." *Journal of Analytical Psychology*, 17 (July 1972), pp. 184–198. On Campbell: p. 185.

Sandler, Florence, and Darrell Reeck. "The Masks of Joseph Campbell." *Religion*, 11 (January 1981), pp. 1–20.

Segal, Robert A. "Joseph Campbell's Theory of Myth: An Essay Review of His *Oeuvre." Journal of the American Academy of Religion*, Supplement, 44 (March 1978), pp. 98–114.

———. "Joseph Campbell's Theory of Myth." *San Francisco Jung Institute Library Journal*, 7 (December 1987), pp. 5–12.

Sharpe, Eric J. *Comparative Religion*. First ed. New York: Scribner's, 1975. On Campbell: pp. 212–213.

Sundel, Alfred. "Joseph Campbell's Quest for the Grail." *Sewanee Review*, 78 (January–March 1970), pp. 211–216.

Watts, Alan. *In My Own Way*. New York: Vintage Books, 1973. On Campbell: pp. 263–267.

Zemljanova, L. "The Struggle between the Reactionary and the Progressive Forces in Contemporary American Folkloristics." *Journal of the Folklore Institute*, 1 (1964), pp. 130–144. On Campbell: p. 132.

APPLICATIONS

Hansen, Terry L. "Myth-Adventure in Leigh Brackett's 'Enchantress of Venus'." *Extrapolation*, 23 (Spring 1982), pp. 77–82.

James, William C. "The Canoe Trip as Religious

Quest." *Studies in Religion,* 10 (Spring 1981), pp. 151–166.

Kaempchen, Martin. "Stages of Development in a Holy Life." *Journal of Dharma,* 8 (April–June 1983), pp. 127–146.

Meigs, Carl. *"Beowulf,* Mythology and Ritual: A Common–reader Exploration." *Xavier University Studies,* 3 (June 1964), pp. 89–102.

Prats, A.J. "The Individual, the World, and the Life of Myth in *Fellini Satyricon." South Atlantic Bulletin,* 44 (1979), pp. 45–68.

Tomasulo, Frank P. "Mr. Jones Goes to Washington: Myth and Religion in *Raiders of the Lost Ark." Quarterly Review of Film Studies,* 7 (Fall 1982), pp. 331–340.

Williams, Anne. "Browning's 'Childe Roland,' Apprentice for Night." *Victorian Poetry,* 21 (Spring 1983), pp. 27–42.

Winchell, Mark Royden. "Bellow's Hero with a Thousand Faces: The Use of Folk Myth in *Henderson the Rain King." Mississippi Folk Register,* 14 (1981), pp. 115–126.

INDEX